ABOU

Elizabeth O'Roark spent many years as a medical writer before publishing her first novel in 2013. She holds two bachelor's degrees from the University of Texas, and a master's degree from Notre Dame. She lives in Washington, D.C. with her three children. Join her book group, Elizabeth O'Roark Books, on Facebook for updates, book talk and lots of complaints about her children.

ALSO BY ELIZABETH O'ROARK

THE SUMMER I DESTROYED YOU

ELIZABETH O'ROARK

PIATKUS

PIATKUS

First published in Great Britain in 2024 by Piatkus

1 3 5 7 9 10 8 6 4 2

A CIP catalogue record for this book
is available from the British Library.

ISBN: 978-0-349-44079-8

Printed and bound in Great Britain by Clays Ltd, Elcograf S.p.A.

Papers used by Piatkus are from well-managed forests
and other responsible sources.

Piatkus
An imprint of
Little, Brown Book Group
Carmelite House
50 Victoria Embankment
London EC4Y 0DZ

An Hachette UK Company
www.hachette.co.uk

www.littlebrown.co.uk

NOTE FROM THE AUTHOR

Emerson's struggles with weight and body image are the product of her own disordered thinking and do not reflect the author's personal views in any way.

Sometimes people (and characters) must admit to hating parts of themselves before they can challenge the thoughts that got them there.

THE SUMMER I
DESTROYED YOU

1

EMMY

I have a theory: the person you were in high school is the person you are for life.

That's why the most popular girl in school still thinks she's cute decades after anything cute about her has withered up and died, and why Silicon Valley billionaires still feel like geeks, no matter how many models they screw.

Donovan Arling was never a geek. He's been a beautiful specimen his entire life and can't forget it for a minute. Even now, while he fucks me, it's not my naked frame beneath him he's staring at lovingly—it's his reflection in the mirror he can't look away from.

Then again, *I'm* down here thinking about what an asshole he is, so maybe neither of us has our head in the right place.

"I love your arms," I murmur, running my hands over his triceps. It's not a lie—he really does have amazing arms—but mostly I just need him to finish so he gets the hell out of my apartment.

"Yeah?" he grunts, a tiny note of desperation in his voice.

"They're so defined," I moan. "Those triceps."

"Oh fuck," he says, and now his voice is all full-blown panic, a guy who knows the end is nigh whether he wants it to be or not. "Oh fuck, oh fuck, oh fuck."

He's busy now, with all the coming and whatnot, so I'm able to roll my eyes at a leisurely pace, knowing even as I do it that I'm being wildly hypocritical.

How many guys have I slept with solely to reassure myself I'm pretty? Many. But Donovan has always been beautiful, so it's not like he's got some kind of vacancy to fill—whereas mine appears bottomless.

If you were ever *the fat girl*, you will always be her inside your own head.

Donovan collapses on top of me. "Fuck, that was hot."

"Cool," I reply. "Now you need to get out of my apartment. I've got to pack."

He flips onto his back, pushing his hair away from his face with a lazy hand. "Is that any way to treat the guy who made you come four times this morning?"

He didn't make me come four times. I haven't come four times total during all the weeks we've slept together.

"Sorry. *Please* get out of my apartment."

He sits up, scowling. "Do you always have to be such a bitch?"

"No, I don't *have* to be." I yawn, waiting to grab my phone until I've heard the door slam behind him. I'd intended to check on my flight.

I forget it entirely when a text from Liam Doherty catches my eye.

He's the point of contact for one of my projects in Elliott Springs. And though I normally avoid friendliness with employees and vendors, it's hard with him. No matter how awful I am, he winds up making me laugh. There is no amount of bitchiness on my end that dissuades him.

I scroll back through yesterday's messages, fighting a smile.

> I'll be in the theater day after tomorrow. I want the ceiling tiles in by the time I get there.

LIAM

> That's a full day's work and I'm currently at the nursing home with my dying grandma.

> That sounds made up.

> I told you about this not five hours ago. It's like you don't hear me anymore.

> I'm doing my best not to hear you. And unless she's loaded, making me happy is the wiser financial decision.

And his reply, which I'm only seeing now:

LIAM

> I guess Nana might have another day, despite what the doctors have told us. I'll just remind her not to walk toward the light.

It's dangerous, allowing myself to be amused. It's dangerous that I've allowed him to amuse me for months now. I should have shut it down. When he expressed concern about me leaving the office late one night or when he said *I think you need someone to take care of you, Em*...I should have reminded him what this was.

A professional relationship, one that's nearly over.

Instead, I read and reread those messages as if they're exactly what they are: the closest thing to love notes I've ever received. And now he's going to meet me and I'll have to put an end to it. But I sort of wish I didn't have to.

I put the phone away, hop in the shower, and descend to the

lobby ninety minutes later, pulling three suitcases with my carry-on slung over my shoulder. I walk fast past Giorgio, the doorman—I loathe unearned friendliness and idle chitchat, and he has an insufferable fondness for both. There was never a conversation about the weather or my destination that Giorgio couldn't drag out five minutes beyond its time of death.

"Rushing off somewhere exciting, Miss Hughes?" he asks, grabbing one of the suitcases.

"Elliott Springs, California." My tight smile is a warning that says *don't ask more questions*. It's a warning he never fucking heeds.

He holds the door. "Can't say I've heard of it."

"No one has." I move briskly toward the waiting town car. "That's why I left."

"Well, you'll be missing some nice weather here," he continues as the driver takes my luggage. "Seventies all week. But it's good to get back to your hometown."

"It is," I reply with my first real smile of the morning. "Especially when you're there to destroy it."

Giorgio's jaw is still open as I climb into the car.

IT TAKES A SIX-HOUR FLIGHT, an hour waiting for the *correct* rental car, and a ninety-minute drive to reach Elliott Springs, a postcard-perfect Northern California village, equidistant to San Jose and Santa Cruz but not especially convenient to either.

Elliott Springs is known for its cobblestone streets, 1800s architecture, and small-town values, which are all things I don't care about. But there's a resort opening on the mountain to the right of the town and two major companies relocating to the left—and I care very much about *that*.

Soon, Elliott Springs will be flooded with wealthy new residents and even wealthier tourists. And will they want to shop at

Cuddlebug Lady's Fashions and Candles? They will not. Will they want to get their hair done at Cuts-n-Stuff after a plate full of Hamburger Alfredo or whatever the hell the local diner calls an entrée? Doubtful. They'll want wine bars, decent food, and hundred-dollar yoga pants. I love wine bars and expensive yoga pants too, but what I like best is the thrill of destroying Elliott Springs.

As I drive through town, I pause for a moment in front of Lucas Hall. Once upon a time, the area's biggest events were held inside its walls. There were wild parties there during Prohibition, fundraisers for the troops during both World Wars, debutante balls during the fifties, and every school event for a century.

The entire town's history is wrapped up in this decaying old building, and my history too. I remember the way they tripped me on the way up to the stage and tore my dress; I remember Bradley Grimm saying, "I feel the building shake when she walks," as I crossed the portico for my diploma. What a nice moment of levity they brought to our high school graduation, here in this building they all treasure so very much. I'm certain they're still laughing about it, and that they laugh even harder about the worse moments, the ones so painful I can barely stand to remember them even now.

But once this building is an apartment complex and I've driven all their businesses into the ground, I bet they'll find those memories about as funny as I do.

I turn down Main Street, heading for the bridge. My boss calls just as I hit it, as if he's tracking my location, which I would not put past him.

"Is everything set?" Charles barks.

"Yes," I reply crisply. It's deeply annoying that he's even asking the question. "The architect's drawings were completed weeks ago, and I'll talk to the mayor before the meeting."

"We're indulging you here," he warns, "but we still expect

results. Once The Hedgerow opens this summer, it might be too late to fly under the radar."

"Yes, I realize that, *Charles*," I say between my teeth. *I'm the one who told you about it, remember?*

I don't fault Charles for being unfriendly—it's hard to cut down the weak branches if you've gotten personally attached to those branches. I do, however, fault him for the fact that he likes to take credit for my work. It's one of many reasons he'll be a branch *I* cut away once I'm in charge. I've had a designer mapping out my tastefully feminine renovation of his office for months.

"Do whatever you have to do," he says before he hangs up.

What he's really saying is *sink to any level necessary to achieve our goals*, an unnecessary reminder since I always sink to any level necessary. But he also means *be fearless*, and as I pull up in front of my mother's home, the place where I endured the worst years of my life, I'm feeling a lot less fearless than usual.

Nothing has changed in the two years since I was here last —the gate is still broken, shutters hang askew, the angel figurines I gave my mother as a child sit on the front porch collecting dust while the ones my brother gave her will sit on glass classes inside like the treasured heirlooms they are.

She won't be pleased to see me. Her voice will drip with disdain as she tells me my expensive purse is tacky, when she says it looks like I've gained weight and that she wishes Jeff was the one here to take care of her instead of me.

And I'm going to suck it up and take it, the way I always have.

The timing of my mother's knee surgery worked to my advantage—I'm trying to arouse as little suspicion as possible about Inspired Building's plans, and this allows me to claim I'm here only as a loving daughter as opposed to some big-city interloper trying to destroy Elliott Springs' small-town charm. I wonder if it could possibly be worth it, though, as I approach the house in the sun's dying light.

The door is unlocked. I enter and drop my suitcases in the foyer, careful not to jostle the glass display shelves, then walk to the back of the house.

"You're finally here," my mother says, the folds around her mouth sagging as she pauses the TV. Her gaze drifts over me, head to toe. "And all dressed up for the occasion, apparently."

"It's lovely to see you too, Mom." I don't bother to explain why I'm in a suit—nothing I say will impress my mother, though I doubt that will stop me from trying repeatedly during the months ahead. No matter how old I get, there will always be this five-year-old inside me who desperately hopes she can make Mommy love her. And the harder I want it, the more she hates me instead.

She nods toward what remains of the back deck while her new screen porch is being built. "Let Snowflake in."

"You got a dog?" I ask. "You hate dogs."

"I don't hate dogs," she argues, though it's what she said, verbatim, throughout my childhood. "He was Jordan's, but he got too big for their place."

This doesn't surprise me in the least. Jordan, my brother's fiancée, is exactly the type to get a dog she could fit in a designer handbag and abandon it once he wasn't willing or able to be carried around quietly. My mother had better warn Jordan that babies won't fit in purses forever either.

I open the door and Snowflake bounds inside, jumping on me with muddy paws. I walk into the kitchen to wipe the mud off, glancing at my watch. I suppose I'll be expected to cook, though God knows what I'll even make—my repertoire in the kitchen is mostly limited to peanut butter and jelly, or things that only require a microwave, and I even manage to destroy those. "It's nearly dinnertime. Are you hungry?"

My mother is holding the remote up, ready to resume her show. It's been two years, but we've apparently exhausted the conversation.

"I don't need dinner," she replies. "And it wouldn't kill you to skip a meal or two either."

My hands grip the counter. I cannot believe she's *already* starting this shit with me. I've lost sixty pounds since I moved away after high school, yet we're right back where we were: my mother smugly proud of her restraint while reminding me I suck at it.

Any time I got a snack growing up, any time I wanted seconds, she'd frown, disgusted with me. *"You can't possibly need that,"* she'd say, and that was all it would take to turn my actual hunger into something darker and emptier, something I could *never* fill with food.

"I'm a size two," I say between my teeth. "Are you seriously trying to imply that I should lose *more* weight?"

She sighs. "Still as easily offended as ever, I see. I'm only saying that as you get older, it's going to get harder to keep that weight off, and we both know it's always been a struggle for you."

I squeeze my eyes shut. I could argue that it was only an issue under *her* roof, but we'd both know that was a lie. I maintain my weight through a less-than-healthy combination of rigorous exercise and calorie counting, two things my mother has never had to resort to, and when I slip up, it feels as if I've fallen into a well and will never, ever be able to scramble back up its slick walls.

I'll eat dinner in defiance tonight, forcing down every bite, and it still won't be enough. I'll want to eat everything that isn't nailed down because she's reminded me I shouldn't want any of it.

I've been home for an hour and she's already begun to win.

THE ROOM that used to be mine is now essentially a storage area, with boxes of my mother's old clothes stacked nearly to the ceiling. I have to create a pile against the wall simply to form a path to the bed. The closet is full of her out-of-season clothes so there's nowhere to put mine. I know mobility has been an issue since she hurt her knee. But I also know she wouldn't have cleaned this room out for me regardless.

I shower and climb onto the bed, kicking the musty coverlet to the floor. I miss New York in a way I never dreamed I'd miss anything. I want my lovely, clean apartment with its floor-to-ceiling windows and utter emptiness. You could roll a marble from the front door to the back wall without ever hitting a goddamn thing.

I pick up my phone. It's absolutely pathetic how often I check my texts now, looking for his name.

> I'm coming by the store tomorrow around 2PM and that ceiling had better be in. How's your grandma, by the way?

LIAM

You don't care about my grandma.

> That's because I don't think you actually have a grandmother. I'm pretty sure you've used her death before.

Everyone has a grandmother. That's how reproduction works.

> Yes, but there's a limit to the number of times you can use a grandmother's death to avoid work.

I have step-grandmothers. I'll use it forever.

I laugh, though I should not. I want to text him back, but

I'm definitely not doing that either. Liam, in person, won't be who he's been by text. He won't be someone who likes me despite all the evidence he should not, someone I can actually trust.

I'm going to miss him once it all falls apart. I really am.

2

LIAM

I began the morning by getting reamed out by a homeowner about delays that were entirely her fault. When that was done, I learned that one of my roofers put a nail through his hand and another of my guys had punctured a drainage pipe, which we'll now be replacing on our own dime.

But even all of that isn't responsible for my foul mood at present—a foul mood my sister Bridget will definitely call me on.

She comes to the door and watches as I walk the path to her house. "Can't even tell you broke it," she says, glancing at my leg.

I grimace. "*I* can tell I broke it." The cast has been off for weeks, but when I'm climbing up a ladder, my right leg is still weaker than my left. Surfing is impossible—I can barely do a pop up. And my checking account sure as *shit* can tell I broke it.

I head toward the leaking toilet she called about, which is the exact kind of thing her worthless husband should be taking care of. I've stopped bothering to ask where he is. Scott either takes more golf trips than any human alive or she's covering for him.

"Got the invite to Caleb's wedding," she says, following me into the bathroom and hopping onto the sink. "Who'd have thought you'd be the last one to settle down?"

I drop my bag onto the floor. "Yeah. No one."

"You're too picky," says Bridget. "You really should have given Missy a chance. Sometimes one date isn't enough to—"

"Hey, Bridge?" I ask, turning to glance up at her from the bathroom floor. "Can we not do this today?"

The familiar conversation entitled *Perfectly Nice Girls You Shot Down* has never been a favorite of mine, especially when I agree with her. A little more than a year ago, my closest friends were all either headed for divorce or confirmed bachelors, and now all three of them are happily taken and that just leaves me—the only one of us who has been out there dating the entire time. I've been out with a hundred girls who were cute and nice and did nothing objectionable aside from boring me. Acknowledging that I'm the problem, and I clearly am, doesn't change the fact that I don't want to tie myself for life to a woman who's got me yawning an hour into our first date.

"Fine. I've got someone else you ought to meet. This single mom whose kid comes into our practice. She's so friendly."

"A single mom?" I shake my head. "No thanks. That's twice as many people to disappoint."

"Three times as many, actually," she counters. "She's also got a second grader. But Liam, you *like* kids. You were great with Daisy. Maybe that's the piece that's missing."

It says everything about my sister's marriage that she thinks *kids* can fill the empty space in a relationship. I'm pretty sure if she and Scott had had one together, she'd see how flawed her logic actually is.

"I'm tired, Bridget," I grunt. "Let it go."

Her head tilts. "What's up with you today? You're in a mood."

I knew she'd fucking ask.

"I met with the bank," I say, holding my hand out for the wrench. I don't feel like discussing it, but I'll have to tell her eventually. "They're not going to give me the loan, which means my investors are out too."

Her mouth falls open. "I thought you said it was a slam dunk."

"That's what *they* said back before I broke my damn leg. I don't have as much saved up anymore. I am 'no longer a good credit risk.'"

My crew did their best, but we fell behind while I was laid up. Why'd I have to climb that roof? It's like I was one guy when I went up there and another entirely when I landed. Or maybe the change had already happened, and it just took a hard fall to make me realize it.

Everyone's been treating me like a beaten dog since then. Everyone but Emerson Hughes, that is. She has no fucks to give about my feelings or anyone else's. If it's possible to develop a crush sight unseen with a woman who's almost invariably cold to you, I'm pretty sure I'm halfway there. I'm also pretty sure that if you're infatuated with someone who hasn't shown a hint of interest in you, you need a shit-ton of therapy.

Which I now can't afford.

I just feel something there. In her mean-but-funny responses and the way she refuses to lower her standards but is always reasonable when we hit a delay. I've never worked harder in my life to peel back someone's armor, but the small glimpses I've gotten of her were worth it. Like the fact that she cries during that holiday ad where a little kid brings a present to the lonely old guy upstairs. Or that she's surrounded by some of the most amazing restaurants in the world, but the best meal she ever had was a box of donuts she and her dad split when she was small. I like it all. I like it more than I should. She just seems to have something the Perfectly Nice Girls do not, and tomorrow I find out if it was all in my head.

Until I do, I've got no time for Bridget's single mom or anyone else.

It's after five when I get back to Main Street, nearly closing time for most of the places in Elliott Springs. Even though I'm in a hurry, my gaze is drawn toward the end of the street.

She's beautiful, standing there in the afternoon light. I'd dare anyone to say otherwise. Simply looking at her is enough to make me really understand what it means to want something. To want it desperately.

Some people—perhaps even most—would say she's too much work. But what I see is her strength. She's been through some shit, but she still stands proud. And she's stunning, sure, but it's her tenacity that makes her so much more than that.

I can't believe the morons on the city council want to turn her into a parking garage.

Lucas Hall was built in the 1800s by a group of rich landowners, undoubtedly off the backs of cheap immigrant labor. Whatever her origins, she is what remains of our town's illustrious beginnings, and I want to make sure she still remains long after the rest of our history's been replaced.

Before the bank turned me down for the loan, I had big plans, plans that would preserve Lucas Hall while bringing in the tourists everyone seems to want. Now, I don't know what the hell I'm going to present when the town holds its first hearing the week after next. I just know I've got to do something to stop the way outsiders are destroying our town.

Reluctantly, I turn and jog across the street to Pearsons' Hardware, ignoring the twinge in my leg, nodding to Jim as I head back toward the plumbing section.

I'm only a few feet inside the store when I notice the shelves are practically empty.

"Hey, Jim?" I turn his way as he comes out from behind the register. "Where the hell is everything? There's nothing back here."

He winces. "You haven't heard, I guess? We're closing up shop."

It's so unexpected that I stop in place, hoping I've misheard him. Pearsons' is an institution. I came here as a kid. My *dad* came here as a kid. "Closing up? *Why?*"

He raises a shoulder. "Got a decent offer so I took it. I'd planned to retire in the next decade anyway...It would be hard to turn down the money just for a few more years here."

I narrowly stop myself from objecting. Obviously, if he wanted to pass this place on to his sons, he would have. If he cared about his family's legacy, the town's legacy, he'd have done something else. Increasingly, it feels like I'm the only one who cares about preserving anything at all. "Who bought it?"

He shakes his head. "Some corporation. MT Enterprises? I think it's gonna be one of those spin places. They bought Cuts-n-Stuff too."

I say goodnight to Jim and walk back outside, my gaze moving from one end of the street to the other in shock.

Right before that roof gave way and I broke my leg, I felt this chill at the base of my spine. Life sneaks up on you, and that chill is the warning that comes too late. You feel it as a roof sags and you realize how easily all your plans could be fucked up. You feel it when you land two floors below and realize it could be days before anyone knows you're missing.

Or when you discover, once the ink is dry and it can't be undone, that some asshole has already bought up your whole goddamn town.

3

EMMY

I'm woken by the slamming of doors outside, a ladder being raised. I shower and go downstairs in shorts and a T-shirt, hair wet, my glasses still on, in need of coffee. Both my mother and Snowflake are awake and only one of them is happy to see me.

"Let her out back," my mother says from her perch in front of the TV as Snowflake bounds toward me. "She needs to pee. And tell them to knock it off outside. I've got a headache."

My hand, threading through Snowflake's fur, stills. My mother managed to get out of bed, make herself coffee, and do her hair, but she couldn't bother to let this poor dog pee after a night inside?

I don't know why I'm surprised. If I'd needed her permission to pee, I'd probably still be waiting too.

I open the door and the dog rushes out to the corners of the yard, past a group of men who stand at the perimeter of the future screen porch. They're facing away from me, but I'm drawn immediately to the one in the center: he's wearing the hell out of those Levi's and, better yet, he's big enough to obliterate me—I like an element of danger in bed.

This is intensely shallow, of course, but why *shouldn't* I be intensely shallow? I don't need a man to pay my way, ask about my day or, God forbid, expect me to ask about his. I'm interested in roughly three body parts—possibly four if he's ambidextrous—and when I'm asking so little, I deserve to get it in a pretty package.

He's not paying any attention to me, but the guys nudge him, and he turns at last. Under the shadow cast by his hard hat, I can't even see his face, but I know he's hot. I can just make out the shape of his mouth—that full lower lip, the sharpness of his jaw, already shaded with stubble. I swear to God, testosterone is rolling off him and I can feel it from here.

But then he steps forward, pulling off the hat, and it hits me suddenly, with a dark, painful thud deep in my stomach: I know him. I'm not sure *how* I know him, but I know that it's bad. It's like that with me sometimes—I can't recall a memory, only the pain it caused. And he, at some point, caused me pain. Many people in this town did.

And I don't forgive, even if I forget.

"My mom says you're making too much noise," I announce. "She wants you to knock it off."

His gaze sweeps over me from head to foot. "Does your mother want this job done, princess?"

Oh no he didn't.

I spend a fair amount of time on construction sites, and this is the exact kind of bullshit I won't take from any man.

"I'm sure she does," I retort. "But she wants it done in a reasonable manner and not before eight in the morning, little hammer."

"*Little hammer*?" he repeats.

"Oh, sorry. I assumed we were exchanging sexist and demeaning nicknames." My gaze falls to his crotch to make sure he got my meaning—his buddies laugh under their breath. "Perhaps I misunderstood, though I'd be surprised if *mine* was inaccurate."

This is entirely false. He carries himself like a guy packing an entire tool chest down there, but he doesn't need to know that.

I turn to go back in the house with a sigh. I'm already alienating people and the day's just begun.

SURPRISING NO ONE, the guys I hired to renovate the grocery store are nowhere to be found when I arrive downtown midday, though the owner, Gary, has been assuring me for weeks that they get in each day at seven and work 'til dark.

Gary and I do not have a fun, friendly relationship, which would be fine if I didn't suspect Gary was a worthless piece of shit. While Liam's been reporting back to me regularly about where things stand, Gary is intentionally vague. I ask for visuals and he sends me photos of a project that is not mine. I ask for dates, and he says he'll have to get back to me.

That is why I did not warn Gary I was coming. I wanted to see exactly how much of a fuck-up he is, and apparently, it's even worse than I'd thought: I've just unlocked the door to the grocery store and the gleaming hardwood Gary said was done two weeks ago is completely absent.

I do not need this shit—not right now. Not when I've got to get the new stores stocked and staffed, buy up a few more properties, sufficiently kiss the mayor's ass, and attend all the meetings necessary to get our apartment complex built, all while keeping my mother alive following her surgery. I'm in Elliott Springs to kill several birds with one stone, which is, of course, simply a metaphor—none of the birds are supposed to die, no matter how ambivalent I am about the survival of one of them.

I step inside the dark store. It looks little different than it did four months when I came here to buy the space. "Hello, Gary," I say crisply when he answers the phone. "How's the space coming along?"

"Still right on schedule," he says with a heavy sigh.

Poor Gary is tired of my nagging. Poor Gary is about to learn how good he had it when I was *only* nagging.

"Wonderful!" I reply cheerfully, pulling the contract out of my bag. "I've got store fixtures being delivered next week. Is that going to be an issue?"

"Well, I'm not sure about next week. Let me get back to you."

Let me get back to you is Gary's favorite phrase. My presence here is going to rob him of fifty percent of his vocabulary. "And the hardwood? You said that's done?"

"Yep, we're all good there." There's chatter on his end, and he returns to the phone. "Well, I'd better get back to it."

Man, I really want to fire Gary. It's a charge in my blood, that desire, but I don't know for a fact that Liam's much better, and I *do* know for a fact that once I meet Liam in person, this friendliness of his will fade away. That's what tends to happen when people meet me in person. Actually, it tends to happen long before then—Liam's been unusually difficult to offend and I've done my absolute best.

"I'm confused," I reply. "Because you're making it sound as if you're in the store, but *I'm* in the store and it's otherwise vacant. I'm also confused because I don't see any hardwood."

There is a long, awkward moment of silence.

I should add that it's not awkward for *me*. I'm savoring this moment like the burn of a good scotch.

"Oh, right. Hardwood didn't arrive," Gary says. "Should be there tomorrow."

I take a glance at the contract in my hand, though I don't actually need to read it. "I'm not sure how carefully you read the terms of our agreement, Gary, but we reserve the right to assess a ten percent penalty on any stage of construction that does not meet deadline, and an additional ten percent penalty for each week that passes. You were due a check for ninety thousand this week. It'll be eighty-one thousand if the job isn't done by the end of the month."

"I'd basically be working for free at that cost," he sputters.

"Then if I were you, I'd get ahold of some hardwood," I reply as I hang up.

Down the street, there are trucks in front of the theater. I loathe the part of me that's excited about this meeting with Liam and putting it off at the same time, like a twelve-year-old with a crush she already knows is misguided. I loathe the part of me that's made *giddy* by the thought of him.

Just get it over with. Liam is definitely going to disappoint me, and it's time to face the music. Texts are deceptive anyway. For all I know, he's a grandfather of twelve with a hacking smoker's cough. Maybe he's one of those aging hippies who pulls his remaining wisps of hair into a scraggly ponytail and only wears sandals. Maybe he drives a truck with a sexy girl painted on the side or isn't allowed within fifty feet of the local schools because of an incident he says was a *misunderstanding*.

In the end, though, he's none of these things.

He's worse.

4

LIAM

Are you enjoying California's fine weather and chill vibes yet?

EMERSON

I'd need to enjoy "chill vibes" in the first place. I like you a little less for even employing the phrase.

So you're admitting you like me. Progress. Have you ever gone surfing, by the way?

I'd look too good in a bikini. I'd be a distraction to the other surfers.

I laugh as I put my phone away. I'd forgotten, until Emerson and I began texting, that I'm still capable of feeling intrigued by someone. I have no idea what she looks like—for all I know she's a million years old, hideous, and extremely pregnant—but when I text with her, I feel entirely certain that she's none of those things. I'm not sure it would matter at this point anyway even if she was. I just *like* her.

When I really don't have the time to like anyone. We're stretched too thin—part of my desperate attempt to get the company's assets back to where they were, and we seem to get stretched thinner by the hour.

I get through all the morning's jobs before I head to the theater to finally meet Emerson. I park and am just outside when my steps stumble: there's already a woman in the building, talking to the guys. Emerson Hughes has beaten me apparently, and the sight of her from behind—long legs, short skirt, dark brown hair that falls past her shoulders—is enough to give me that charge in my gut, the one that says *hell, yeah.*

She turns when I open the door. Pale blue eyes, mouth like a peony about to burst open, the kind of skin that would feel like rose petals to the touch.

"Ugh," she says. "*You're* Liam?"

It's the voice that puts the dots together.

Emerson Hughes is Sandra Atwell's incredibly hot daughter, the woman who came outside wearing little aside from glasses and disdain this morning. I was under the impression that Emerson was sort of *pretending* to be bitchier than she actually is, but this chick isn't pretending shit. "*You're* Emerson?"

"Yes," she says, nostrils flaring. "And you've installed the wrong ceiling tiles."

The disappointment hits hard. There are women in the world whose prettiness hasn't done them any favors, who've been taught that a tight little body and a face to launch a thousand ships are enough, and she's definitely one of them. I wasted two months dreaming about a woman who is more awful in person than she appeared to be by text, and not in a way I secretly enjoy. Why the fuck did I think there was more to her? Just because she liked eating donuts with her dad? Because there's a commercial capable of making her cry?

"These are the tiles your designer chose," I growl, "so take it up with her, *princess.*"

There's something both creepy and magical in the way her

blue eyes flash silver when I say it. I half expect lightning to shoot from her fingertips and snakes to writhe in her hair.

"Mr. Doherty," she says with an icy smile, "as we established earlier today, calling a grown woman *princess* is blatantly misogynistic. I should also point out that a princess generally has very little power, whereas in this situation, I have nearly all of it. My designer didn't choose the tiles, I did, and this is absolutely *not* what I chose. It needs to be fixed."

"Talk to your designer, sweetheart," I reply. My sister would smack me in the head if she could hear me right now, but I'm not going to put up with this witch undermining me in front of my crew at *two* goddamn jobsites. Mostly, though, I'm just pissed that I've invested so much time, so much thought, into a woman who has turned out to be…her.

Her eyes flash once more. "Call me sweetheart again and believe me, you'll regret it. And you'll be fixing that fucking ceiling, I promise you."

She storms out. She has an ass that won't quit, and I'm already trying to forget I've noticed when JP, standing at the back of the room, lets out a low whistle.

"I bet she's a little wildcat in the sack," he says.

"Haven't thought about it."

He laughs. "Liar."

I decide to ignore him since I was, in fact, lying. That charge in my gut, the one that said *hell, yeah* is still saying it. Thank God my brain is wise enough to say *hell no.*

I pick up my phone and text Bridget.

> Send me that girl's number when you get a chance. The one at your practice.

There are worse things than being bored to death during a date.

Wasting two months daydreaming about Emerson Hughes, for instance.

5

EMMY

I walk back to my car, doing my best to ignore this sinking feeling in my chest.

I knew he'd disappoint me. I knew nothing would come of it. And if I allowed myself to feel much of anything other than irritation, I'd probably be sad that it's over, this little flirtation that was never going to amount to anything.

It was ridiculous to have hoped he'd be different. That he'd be kind and trustworthy, unlike the rest of this town's residents. I still haven't put together who he was—there were only a hundred of us in my graduating class and surely I'd remember a guy who looked like *that*—but he was definitely one of the assholes who made my teenage years hell. It's a distinct feeling inside me when I picture his face, some ancient hurt I can't put a finger on yet.

Regardless of who he is, the modern ceiling tile he put in is entirely wrong—the theater is supposed to have a vintage feel to convince everyone Inspired Building *cares* about Elliott Springs' history before we start tearing down their dumb landmarks—which means it's one more problem amidst a mountain of problems I don't have time for.

Therefore, I need to rope in my assistant.

> The morons we hired to do the theater put in the wrong ceiling. I need the contract. Find out who owns Long Point Construction too.

STELLA

> We can only fire so many people in a single week, Em.

> One of their guys called me "Princess", Stella.

> Ah. I guess I'm just glad you're not making me dig a grave.

I arrive at home, laden with groceries. My mother is heavily immersed in *The Real Housewives of Orange County* and doesn't acknowledge me.

"I was going to do steak and baked potatoes and salad for dinner," I announce. Given my cooking ability, I'm sticking to the basics. "Do you know if the grill has propane?"

"Steak and potatoes?" my mother scoffs. "Are you trying to make me explode?"

"A small filet only has three hundred calories, Mom. A small potato has a hundred."

"I didn't keep this figure eating steak and potatoes. I'll just eat the salad. And if you were smarter, you'd just be eating the salad too."

I swallow down a sharp retort.

Jeff was the lucky one, with a metabolism that must have been twice my own. It was a running joke between him and my mother, the sheer amount of food he could pack away. "You must have a hollow leg," she'd coo, as if his ability to eat was some illusive, adorable quality. "I don't know where you put it."

He could inhale eight tacos in a matter of minutes, but if I reached for a second one, her mouth would twist. She'd observe me, repulsed, always with that coffee cup in hand, her ability to *not* be hungry a source of great pride.

It made any hunger I felt seem sick. Unfeminine and distasteful. "Do you really need that?" she'd ask, and I'd put the taco back. And then I'd watch Jeff eat, and my hunger would turn darker and needier until it was beyond my control.

I hate, so much, how little has changed.

I now don't want the steak or the potato. I will eat them only to show her that her words are meaningless, but the endless hunger that will follow it already gnaws at my bones.

IT'S dark when my phone rings. I fumble for it blindly, uncertain if it's night or early morning.

"Do you want the good news or the bad news?" Stella chirps. I wonder if she's calling this early to punish me for making her work last night. I reach across the bed to open one of the blinds. Outside, it's barely light out. Yes, she definitely did it on purpose.

"Tell me," I reply.

"So, you were right about the tile. It's not what you chose. The bad news is that they ran into some supply issues and Julie, the decorator, okayed the switch."

I groan, reaching for the bottle of water on the nightstand. Julie didn't have the *authority* to make that switch. "And did you get the contact info for the owner?"

"I sent it to you. It's the guy you've been dealing with. Liam."

"*Fuck.*" We hired Long Point Construction because they'd been in business since the seventies. Liam wasn't even alive in the seventies, so I never dreamed he *owned* it.

"You know him?" she asks.

I swallow.

In New York, I'm *Emerson*, the size-two workaholic who

makes work calls from her in-office treadmill every morning and takes shit from no one. As much as I like Stella, I'm not about to ruin it all by telling her I was once the high school punching bag, the girl who took shit from *everyone*. "I know *of* him. I think he's older."

"He can't be too much older. Julie said he's hot."

I didn't realize Julie had met him. Something sours inside me. This is clearly Liam's schtick—he's flirtatious and charming with every female client because it makes his life easier. She probably flew out here on the company's dime, slept with him, and let him call all the shots after that—let him offload some cheap-ass tile he had on hand and cut a thousand other corners. I hate that I fell for as much of it as I did. *Me*.

"Speaking of Julie," I reply, "you can let her know she's off the job. I'm not working with her again."

Stella laughs. "I figured this was coming, but she's under contract. You can't just fire her without cause."

"I have plenty of cause. She changed my plans without asking me and just made me look like an asshole. Plus, we're going to have to eat the cost of the new tile, and *I'm* going to be the one Charles blames. And not for the first time. This is probably her third costly mistake this year."

Julie *does* need to go, but I'm honestly not sure what I'm angrier about: her mistake or the fact that I almost got taken in by Liam too.

Not even *almost*. I *did* get taken in by him. You'd think I'd know better by now.

Apparently, I will never learn.

6

LIAM

It's still early when the back door slides open and the dog bounds out. Ten minutes later, Emerson herself appears —legs for days, lush little mouth in a stuck-up pout, calling for the dog while pretending she can't see us.

The dog continues to run around happily, ignoring her. It's solely because I don't want the harpy out here any longer that I intervene. "Snowflake, come here, girl!" She's a sweet dog, if not particularly bright, nuzzling my leg as I walk her toward the house.

Emerson frowns, her eyes wary. "Thank you," she says, sounding more guarded than grateful.

"Any time, princess," I say, mostly to watch those blue eyes of hers flash silver once more.

They don't disappoint. If we were in Salem circa 1650, she'd definitely be undergoing a trial by water right now.

"Still running with that?" she asks through gritted teeth. "Never stop being you, yard boy. And, by the way, those tiles *were* wrong. Julie fucked up."

This I've already heard about. I got a tearful call from the designer mere minutes ago, though I'm not sure what good she thought *I* could do.

"I heard you fired her over a simple mistake," I reply. "Good to know my initial assessment of you wasn't overly harsh."

Her mouth becomes a flat line. "A simple mistake for *you*, perhaps. I need them torn out and redone, pronto."

"It's going to cost you."

"Oh," she says, eyes wide with feigned surprise, "so I need to *pay* you in exchange for labor? Thanks for explaining the most basic principle of supply and demand."

She turns to follow the dog in, and as soon as the door slams behind her, JP is chuckling once again. I'm glad one of us finds her bullshit amusing.

"Yard boy," he says. "I guess it's better than little hammer. She might even go out with you if you keep it up."

I raise a single brow. "*Go out with me?* I'd rather be alone forever than wake up to that."

"It's starting to look like you're planning to be alone forever anyway," Mac, the soon-to-be-married junior project manager, replies.

There it is again—the assumption that I'm not trying hard enough. That I don't want the same shit everyone else does.

When I'm trying. I've *been* trying.

Sort of. My phone vibrates in my back pocket and yeah, there's a fucked up part of me that wishes it was one of Emerson's demanding, funny, *interesting* texts. I was treading water, waiting to see what would happen when she got to town.

Now we know. So why does it feel like I'm still treading water?

STELLA CALLS with the new ceiling tile selection just as I'm getting home.

"It's nine on the East Coast," I point out. "Shouldn't you be off work?"

"Nine o'clock isn't late when you work for Emmy," she replies. "She's lucky I adore her."

"I'm struggling to believe that any employee of Emerson's actually adores her," I sigh, hanging my keys on the hook by the door.

"Don't let her fool you," Stella says with a smile in her voice. "She *wants* to scare people, but if she loves you, she'll fight to the death on your behalf."

That is exactly the kind of person I imagined Emerson was until I actually met her. Because she was demanding and often unreasonable, but anytime I had a *genuine* issue, she folded like a deck of cards. Hiccups in the schedule, delivery issues...she never gave me a moment of shit.

"Are you sure she just doesn't happen to enjoy a fight?"

She laughs. "Let me tell you how I wound up working for her: my boss hit on me, I told a friend who then told Em, and two days later he was being escorted out by security because they'd found inappropriate materials on his computer."

"That sounds like a lucky coincidence." Or *unlucky*, given she wound up with a boss who's making her work nights.

"You don't know her well if you believe *that* was a coincidence. She paid someone in IT to check the guy's search history. She'll pay for the cleaning lady's kid to get braces and buy a plane ticket for the security guard downstairs to visit his dying mom, but she makes *me* take the credit for it so nobody knows."

"Yet you're telling me," I reply.

"Yeah, and she'd hate that," she says. "But I just get the feeling you need to know."

I wish I didn't. My dislike was simple and uncomplicated five minutes ago.

Now, once again, it's not.

7

EMMY

The problem with only having two living relatives is that you don't feel you can afford to lose them, no matter how badly they treat you. That's why my mother can treat me like crap as I drive her to the pre-surgical checkup and mostly get away with it. Why she can complain about my driving and what I'm wearing and tell me Jeff's car is so much nicer than mine without me pulling over to the side of the road and telling her to walk. Because she's all I've got.

"I'm not sure who you thought you were showing off to, renting a BMW," she adds, though I imagine she already knows the answer: I wanted to impress *her*.

It's fucking pathetic that I hoped for it in the first place. She was never going to be impressed. I could save the earth from an approaching asteroid, cure cancer, and win the Nobel prize, and she would not be impressed. She'd still manage to tell me how Jeff could have done it better.

Just give up, Emmy. I hear it over and over in my head. But what do I have left in the entire world if I do? And what does it say about me if I can't convince the two remaining family members I've got to simply *like* me? Even if half the stuff my mother says is batshit crazy, I can't seem to shake off this sense —one I've had since childhood—that she's wiser than me, that her hatred of me must have some merit.

And Liam seemed to confirm it yesterday. *Good to know my initial assessment of you wasn't overly harsh.* I don't know where he gets off acting like I'm the villain here. He knows he seduced Julie into making an idiotic decision. But it left me feeling, just as my mother does, that there's something awful inside me, something that can't be cured.

After I drop my mother off, I drive back to Elliott Springs and park in front of the town's dismal administrative offices. My steps slow as I near the diner, a place that holds more bad memories than good. This is where Bradley Grimm once held court. On the rare nights when my mom would send me here to pick up dinner, laughter would explode from the back of the room. *"How many burgers do you think she eats at once?"* Bradley would ask her posse. *"God, if I were that fat, I'd have my mouth sewn shut."*

I push the memory out of my head as I force myself toward the booth where the mayor eats lunch every single day with his cronies.

"Mayor Latham," I say with a wide smile as I walk up. "I didn't mean to interrupt. I just saw you sitting here and wanted to say *hi.*"

"Emerson!" he cries, with what appears to be genuine pleasure. "Just the person we were discussing. Fellas, this is Emerson Hughes. She's with the company that's putting in the new storefronts and has some plans for Lucas Hall as well."

He introduces me to his two dining companions, members of the town council who are significantly older than me, thank God—they don't know or care about who I once was. "Nice to meet you both," I reply. "I assume I'll be seeing you all at the Lucas Hall hearing?"

"Indeed you will," the mayor says. "Are you going to give us a little hint about what you're coming forward with?"

I bite down on a smile and let my lashes flutter closed, as if I've got a secret I can hardly stand not to share. "I'm *dying* to give you a hint, but you've got to let me wow you. The architectural renderings are nearly done and all I can say is...I think you're going to love it."

I pick up the check waiting on their table. "Let me get this. You gentlemen have a lovely day."

I already know this was a success—the mayor is eating out of my hand. But when I turn to find Paul Bellamy behind the register, my confidence deserts me. Paul is one of many guys who made my life a living hell in high school, and the sight of him turns me into teenage Emmy all over again—cowering, hoping to escape notice.

Are you fucking kidding me, Em? Are you seriously still scared of this asshole a decade later?

That voice in my head spurs me forward, reminds me that I'm no longer someone who gets stepped on. Ever.

Paul's not so high-and-mighty anymore, standing there with a ketchup-stained apron around his waist, but I'm not one to leave punishment up to karma. If there's something more to take away from him, I will find it and smash it until it can't be put back together.

"Hello, Paul," I say coolly, slapping the check on the counter. "Long time, no see. I'm paying the mayor's bill."

He looks at me with a furrowed brow and no sign of recognition. "Have we met?"

"We went to school together. Emerson Hughes."

"Emmy the—?" He narrowly stops himself, but a mean little grin flashes across his face, which means he doesn't mind that he *started* saying it. Of course he doesn't. The kind of guy who thinks your weight is a hysterically funny joke as a teenager never stops thinking it, and in my experience, that's most guys.

Most *people*. The pro-size movement hasn't changed the fact that overweight women earn less, are less likely to get a promotion, and are characterized as undisciplined and less competent based on photos alone.

When I was heavy, I spent my life apologizing for existing, for taking up space, and I was expected to be even sorrier than I was. Teachers would suggest I not have the cupcake every other kid was having; the lunch lady would suggest I not get fries. I saw judgment on a waiter's face if I ordered anything but a salad, if I wanted a soda instead of water. Disdain for my weight breathed its way into every waking minute of my day, and a decade after I lost every excess pound, people are still laughing about the fact that I had to do it in the first place—like this asshole here.

"No fucking shit," Paul says. "What'd you do, Atkins or something?"

"Clearly, I did a lot more than you did," I reply with a smile, tapping my phone against the payment terminal. "Isn't this the same job you had in high school?"

His amusement dies a quick death, and while it's not quite the psychological beat-down he deserved, that's okay.

I've got more coming.

8

EMMY

I can't be late for the bus.

Other girls can be late. Madison can saunter down the hill whenever the hell she wants and the bus driver will just say, "I'm supposed to leave at seven fifteen, you know."

That's why I'm running right now. Because when you're heavy, the whole world believes you need to be taught a lesson. They call you greedy and lazy no matter what you've done. They claim you don't care enough about yourself and are also deeply selfish at the same time. They're all dying to slam a door in your face to show you how much they despise you for it.

My thighs chafe and my waistband digs hard into my skin, but any indignity is better than having to face my mother, having to wake her up and tell her I need a ride.

I can see my classmates laughing. It's easy enough to imagine what they're saying since I've heard them say some version of it before:

Look at how her stomach jiggles.

She's about to bust out of those jeans.

Make her run all the way to school, Mr. Holladay.

The doors close and the bus drives away—even though I'm

*running, even though Mr. Holladay looked straight at me. I'm not
even surprised. I've become used to the way the whole world seems to
hate me.*

And now I've got to go home to the person who hates me most.

I wake. My heart is still beating hard. It's a memory I'd
entirely forgotten, but here it is, lodged in my chest, sharp as a
new knife.

And there are far sharper knives waiting than the one that's
there now.

IT'S one of those cold summer mornings we get sometimes.
Beneath my bare feet, the floor is icy. I pull on a sweatshirt and
go downstairs to find Snowflake outside, whining, with her face
pressed to the door. My mother's already up, already irritated.
"Let her in," she says.

When I open the door, she bounds inside, rushing franti-
cally from me to her bowl and back to me. "Okay, okay," I
soothe, running my hand through her fur, which is colder than
usual. "How long did you leave her out there?" I demand.

"Not long enough," my mother replies. "She's getting up too
early and it's your fault. You need to stop feeding her before
nine."

I ignore this, crossing the kitchen to fill Snowflake's bowl.
She eats as if she's ravenous, sending food flying in her haste. I
don't know much about animals, but I wonder if this is normal.
Was Snowflake always a messy eater, or has the experience of
hunger made her frantic? If it's the latter, I know the feeling.

My mother watches from the corner of her eye as I make
coffee. She watches as I go to the refrigerator for cream and
reach for a banana.

"That's pure sugar, you know," she says with a small, smug

smile as I start to unpeel it. "You'll be big as a house by the time you leave if you keep that up."

"Thanks for the expert nutritional advice, Mom," I reply, rolling my eyes, but inside, that age-old anxiety begins to spin. She's fucking insane, and I know this, yet some childish part of me actually *worries*, as if she might still know something I don't. And if I don't get out of this house right the fuck now, I'm going to be back where I started. I'm going to be binge eating just to silence her voice in my head.

I slam the coffee and the banana in defiance and go online. There's a tiny yoga studio on Main Street with semi-private classes, which means extra attention from the instructor— something I definitely don't want—but at least I won't run into anyone I knew in school.

I make it just in time for the eight AM class. The cute blonde instructor smiles at me from the front of the room, but I don't trust people who smile at strangers so I merely nod and set up my mat at the very back.

"I'm Chloe," she says. "Why don't you move your mat up here? No one comes at this time of day."

I'd ignore her, but then there'd be this weird tension for the next hour.

"What are you hoping to get out of this class?" she asks as I move forward.

"Just a good workout," I retort. "None of that finding-my-inner-child stuff."

She laughs. "I guess that means no releasing chakras either then?"

I offer her a reluctant smile. "No. I hate that crap. I'm only here to stay thin. And to keep from killing my mom."

"Fair enough," she replies, standing. "Let's keep Mom alive another day. Get your ass off that mat and get to work."

She leads me through a soul-crushing cycle of downward

dogs and warrior poses and not nearly as many easy stretches as my studio in NYC.

My arms are shaking during the downward dog at the end. "Oh my god," I groan. "I'm dying."

"I can talk about chakras," she offers.

I laugh as I roll up my mat. "I'm not that tired."

"Come back the next time you're feeling homicidal."

I give her an unwilling smile, "In that case, I'll be back in an hour."

When I return to the house, Snowflake greets me at the door. It's strange, having anyone—animal or human—excited to see me when I walk in. I wrap my arms around her briefly before I walk to the back to let her out.

"My God," my mother says, looking at my crop top, "I hope you aren't dressing like that for work. It's so unprofessional."

Jesus. I love getting second-guessed by a woman who has never held a job.

My eyes roll. "Of course not. I went to yoga."

"You can't out-exercise a bad diet."

"Exercise is good for a lot of things other than weight," I reply. "And how would you know whether or not it's enough? I've never seen you exercise once."

"That's because *I* don't have to."

Is it wrong to hope your mother gets osteoporosis simply to win an argument? Probably.

Liam is in the backyard with some other guy, sinking posts into cement. His T-shirt clings in all the right places. He has my favorite type of body—the kind that comes from actual work and not hours spent flexing in front of a large mirror at the gym. He steps away from the post, rubbing the back of his neck, looking troubled. When he's not talking to me, he actually seems like a reasonable person.

I walk onto the deck. I picture him pulling off that tool belt he's wearing as he prowls toward me. I picture those jeans falling to mid-thigh as I reach into his boxers.

His loss.

He runs a thumb over his full lower lip.

Definitely his loss.

Even in my head, though, this does not sound convincing.

His gaze catches on me—on the crop top, the bare midriff. There's a flare of something in his eyes, something feral and delicious, before he no doubt remembers what he's looking at and turns back to his work.

"When will my ceiling be done?" I demand.

"I ordered the tiles," he says without looking up. "Store's telling me next week."

I want more. I want him to talk, even if it's simply to lash out. "You know, we already started advertising the Bond movie series beginning in July. You've really put us behind."

"*I* haven't put you behind," he growls, turning in my direction. "*You*, like your mother, changed the plan. Not the only similarity, obviously. You might be hot, but it's pretty clear that the apple doesn't fall far from the tree in terms of your attitude."

I can think of a thousand ugly things I could say to him in response, but my throat is oddly tight. I know I'm like my mother. A lot of people would say I'm worse. But whatever I've become, it's because of people like him—people who want me to stumble and fall for their own amusement. This was the only outcome. A *necessary* outcome.

I guess being back home simply reminds me what a terrible outcome it was.

"The only thing I just heard," I reply, turning to walk inside, pushing sweaty hair out of my face, "is that you think I'm hot."

9

LIAM

It was the Friday before New Year's weekend when I fell through the roof.

My last conscious thought before I landed was *"No one's even going to know I'm missing,"* and I was right. None of my friends noticed because they had their own lives, and the people I'd made tentative plans with didn't blink an eye when I failed to show up because that's who I was—a guy who didn't show up for a sort-of date because I'd had a couple beers after surfing and fallen asleep, who didn't show up at Beck's bar because some girl had invited me over, who didn't show up for brunch with my sister because I was too hungover.

Yes, I knew I wanted more—I wanted to be the center of someone's world, and I wanted her to be the center of mine—but I figured there was no rush. That just like George Clooney and Mick Jagger and every other guy who'd spent his life knee-deep in options, I could simply bide my time, waiting for the woman who'd make me sit up straight.

But during the long three days I spent in and out of consciousness, followed by week after week in traction, I began to wish I hadn't waited quite so passively.

That's why I'm meeting Bridget's friend Holly out tonight, and why I'm already dreading it: because I'm trying not to be passive, but the new way of handling things doesn't seem to be working either.

Holly suggests meeting at Beck's Bar and Grill, which is still owned by my friend Beck, though he's barely here anymore and is in the process of selling it. I'm not sure if it was a random suggestion or if Bridget gave her some kind of inside scoop, but I regret agreeing the second I walk inside. Sure, I'm comfortable in this place, but I'm also reminded of the passing of time. I met my friends here every Tuesday for years, but now they're all too busy with their fiancés and girlfriends and work to while away their time with me. Their lives have moved on, and mine has not.

I wait for her at the bar and get roped into a conversation with the guys to my left, two of whom I know only vaguely. They're younger than me, but I built a nursery for one of them last year and recognize another from the lineup at Long Point.

We talk about surfing, a depressing topic as I haven't surfed once since I broke my leg and then about Beck leaving, which also bums me out.

"Can't believe he's selling the place," says Pete, the guy I did some work for. "But it seems like everyone in Elliott Springs is selling, so I guess he followed the crowd."

Beck isn't *following the crowd*. He's following the girl he's proposing to next weekend. But these idiots can think what they want.

"You know who's behind all of it, too?" Rex, the surfer, asks. "Emmy. Emerson Hughes."

Pete laughs. "No fucking way. Emmy the Semi?"

My gaze jerks toward him. "What's that?"

"She was a year behind us," Pete says. "Let's just say she was...*pleasantly plump*."

They all laugh a little too hard. I'm annoyed, but it's not as if

Emerson hasn't recovered and then some. "*The only thing I heard was that you think I'm hot.*" If I hadn't been pissed at her, I'd have laughed.

"Man," says another guy, "you remember how mean Bradley was to her all the time? The shit they did at homecoming?"

Pete turns to me. "They fucking tortured her for her weight," he says, laughing harder than he already was. "Jesus Christ, it was so mean but so funny."

I stare at them, dumbfounded. Why the fuck are they laughing? Even if Emerson was as awful to all of them as she is to me, she didn't deserve *this*.

I set my beer down hard. "You just had a daughter," I say to Pete, "yet you're laughing about some girl getting tortured for her *weight* like it's the funniest thing you've ever heard. What the fuck is wrong with you?"

"Chill, bro," he says, raising his brow at the other guys. "It was a long time ago."

"Yeah? Well, it's pretty sad that you thought it was funny a long time ago, and it's fucking pathetic that you still do. Grow the fuck up."

I walk out of the bar, texting Holly to suggest the diner instead.

I'm not sure what bothers me more...how many people apparently treated Emerson like garbage, or the fact I've kind of become one of them.

～

HOLLY IS IN A TIGHT, corset-style halter and heels, dressed for a bar, not the diner. I feel bad for changing the plan, and I feel worse about the fact that when I look at her and all the effort she's made, I still prefer the terrible Emerson Hughes as she was today, straight from a workout in a crop top and bike shorts, pushing her sweaty hair out of her face.

Holly talks a lot about her kids and asks me a few questions about my work that don't reflect much genuine interest. I'm into surfing and she's into something called "collaging." I like true crime documentaries while she has a seemingly encyclopedic knowledge of reality dating shows. I'm struggling to find any overlap, and it shouldn't matter anyway. So what if she doesn't surf? So what if she talks about her kids a lot? It's not like I'd want to end up with a woman who *didn't* talk about her kids. But it is entirely predictable, my boredom. That's why I told my sister I wasn't interested in the first place—why I was edging away from this woman before we'd even gotten started.

"It's so hard to date around here," Holly is saying. "I feel like everyone's already married or I've dated them before. I'm tired of looking. I just want someone to grow old with."

"Yeah," I say absently. "I know what you mean." And I do, but there's something a little off-putting about Holly's desperation. It's the opposite of Emerson, from whom I tried repeatedly to get even a hint of interest to no avail.

Shouldn't you be out drinking cosmos and hunting for a man? I'd asked her when she'd texted late on a Friday.

That's an unprofessional question, she'd replied. *And you should realize by now that I don't need to hunt. I just wait for things to get trapped in my web.*

I'd laughed. I'd wanted to ask what she hoped to trap and what she might do with it once it was caught. I liked the fact that if my answer wasn't amusing enough, she'd cut me down to size.

I'm not sure what it says about me that I prefer Emerson's mild abuse to sitting across from a pretty girl who wants to talk about her collages and kids. But as I pay the check, all I want is to see her safely to her car so I can stop faking it.

"You live nearby, right?" Holly asks when we reach her door.

"I'd love to see your place." A year ago, it wouldn't have mattered that I was bored—I'd have taken her home with me. But I've changed since I fell through the roof. Realizing you've got no one looking out for you, that it could be days before anyone notices you are missing, made me crave something more in a way I never did before.

I want to settle down. I'm just unwilling to *settle* to make it happen.

"I've got an early morning," I reply. "But this was fun. Thanks for coming out and sorry I changed the plan."

She steps close and raises her face to me, expecting a good-night kiss.

I don't even want to do that much, but now her eyes are closed so I let my mouth brush hers and step away, waiting until she's in her car before I turn toward my truck and check my texts.

There are messages from JP, from Bridget, from Caleb.

It makes no sense that I wish I had a message from a girl I don't even like.

I deliver my mother to the hospital early the next morning. I suppose a loving daughter would actually wait at the hospital until the surgery was over, but my mother doesn't have one of those.

I oversee the delivery of my office furniture, yell at Gary, and return only when the hospital calls to say she's waking up.

My mother looks me over when I walk in. "Not sure why you're always dressing like you're Anna Wintour these days. You're not even a real estate agent. You don't need those suits."

"Some people are cranky when they come out of anesthesia," the nurse says gently as I cross the room.

I'm pretty sure it's not the anesthesia.

My mother carps about the snacks while the nurse pulls together the discharge papers, and then carps audibly about the nurse's slowness. She snaps at the orderly who pushes her wheelchair to the hospital's exit. "Your job is too easy for you to be so bad at it," she tells him.

It's rather pleasant, not being the subject of her ire, but all good things must come to an end.

"Since you're so smart," my mother says as we hit the highway, "I suppose you've figured out how to get me up the porch stairs?"

Shit.

"Didn't they show you how to do it at physical therapy? Can't you just, I don't know, scoot up on your butt?"

"Of course not," says my mother. "I can't believe you didn't realize this would be a problem."

"What was I supposed to do, Mom? Build you a handicap ramp? Look, I can call Jeff—"

"Jeff lives a half hour away, for God's sake, and he's out of town anyway. That's the whole reason I had to have *you* come."

I don't actually believe that for a minute. I believe Jeff *claimed* to be out of town so he wouldn't have to be around for the surgery, but it's not like he's going to admit he lied if I call asking for help.

My mother sighs. "You'll need to ask one of those boys working in the back to help you."

No. "That's not their job. And—"

"Do you have a better solution?" she demands.

Alas, I don't.

I rack my brain for the remainder of the drive, and when we arrive, I admit I'm going to have to do the unthinkable: ask Liam or his guys for help. Mac and JP are both nice. As long as it's one of them I'm asking for a favor, I'll survive.

I turn off the car, go to the backyard, and it's Liam I encounter first, hammering a two-by-four, his lovely biceps on display.

I've got the worst luck.

"Need something?" he asks.

Ugh.

"My mother just had surgery. She needs some help getting up the stairs."

His grin is unbearably smug. "So *you* need some help getting your mother inside?"

"*I* don't need help," I snap. "*My mother* needs help."

"Sure." He smirks, wiping his hands on his jeans. "I'd be happy to help you." He follows me to the front yard.

"If you can get her out," I grumble, "I'll lift on the other side."

He scoops my mother up as if she's made of air. "I've got her. Just unlock the front door."

"Thank you for doing this," she tells Liam. "Emerson should have made plans but she's never thought of anyone but herself in her entire life."

Liam's shoulders stiffen. He probably agrees with her but says nothing.

I open the door. My mother could walk the rest of the way and is *supposed* to be doing some walking, but I don't want to get into it with her in front of him. "Just down the hall and into the living room," I tell him.

"Before you go out back talking about how heavy I am," my mother says after he's set her on the couch, "just know how much worse it could have been. You wouldn't have been able to carry Emerson a foot when she was in high school, much less all the way from the car."

"*Mom*," I hiss, wincing. It's par for the course with her, but it hits a lot harder with an audience.

He glances between us. I brace for a smirk from him, a mean little laugh, but there's none.

"I would never talk about how heavy anyone is or was," he says, turning for the back door. "*Especially* not if she was my kid."

He walks out. It takes me several seconds to realize that he just put my mother in her place—on my behalf.

He sure doesn't sound like the kind of guy who'd have tormented me back in the day. Is it possible for people to change? Can you forgive them if they have?

I pick up my phone. I consider thanking him. It seems like

an awkward thing to do, but if I coupled it with a complaint about his progress at the theater, it might be okay.

In the end, I do nothing.

But a part of me wishes I had.

FOR THE NEXT FEW DAYS, aside from running Snowflake to the groomer, I'm stuck at home with my mom. When I'm downstairs, I find myself watching for Liam in the backyard. When I let Snowflake out, I'm both cringing at the memory of what my mother said and hoping he strikes up a conversation—but he's usually not there and he ignores me if he is.

I practice my speech for the hearing on Lucas Hall, though I've got every base covered, and make my mother food she complains about, while she otherwise ignores me. She's too busy calling everyone she knows to discuss her surgery anyway and seems to be going out of her way to make it sound like she and Dr. Sossaman, her surgeon, are friends...or *more* than friends.

"Harold said I'd be up and about any day now."

"Harold said I'm still young enough that I'll heal fast."

"Harold said if I wasn't so thin, this would have been much worse."

I go to my room and look through Liam's old texts.

LIAM

I can't believe you wanted me to work on the weekend. You're like the villain in a Hallmark movie.

I'm working. Why shouldn't I expect it of you?

Now you sound like the heroine of a Hallmark movie, the one who will realize the error of her ways.

And you sound like a guy who watches a lot of Hallmark movies. Only one of us should be ashamed right now. Hint: it's not me.

Look at you bantering with me about Hallmark movies. I knew you had a soft side.

I didn't think I was lonely before. I threw myself into work and told myself I was too busy for more, but once I started hearing from him all the time—at night, on the weekend—I felt myself opening, a flower finally exposed to light, and I miss that feeling now.

It makes me wish I'd never come here in the first place so I didn't have to ruin things.

11

LIAM

One of my earliest memories is of walking down the street with my grandmother on the way to Lucas Hall. Every time she bought me an ice cream cone, she'd tell me the story of meeting my grandfather there during the Vietnam War. *Her* parents got married there during World War II. The days she described didn't seem so far away to me, perhaps because the town itself had remained unchanged.

I feel the town's history every time I arrive on Main Street. Generations of Dohertys graduated in Lucas Hall's grand ballroom. My "Athlete of the Year" trophy still sits in its awards room, gathering dust. When the world feels especially crazy, I can stand here and feel as if things are still going to be okay—that even if the world changes, it will never be a place I no longer recognize.

But now they're trying to take that away too.

The meeting about Lucas Hall is held *inside* Lucas Hall, which is sort of like enjoying a delicious glass of your cow's milk while you decide whether or not to slaughter that same cow—and there are plenty of people here who want to slaughter her.

Locals haven't seen the writing on the wall. They really think a bunch of rich tourists are going to put Knits R Us or Smiths Insect Control on the map when it should be clear to them that this is not going to happen. Tiny, home-grown businesses don't thrive when tourists come to town—they get run out by the conglomerates who've finally seen dollar signs. How long is Mountain Brew Coffee going to survive when some coffee chain moves in across the street with the power of a multimillion-dollar ad campaign behind them? Not long.

I've done my best to explain this at previous council discussions, but no one's listening. I'd thought I could restore Lucas Hall myself, turn her into a hotel to satisfy the locals while preserving our history, but the bank has shot that plan to hell. All I can do now is appeal to people's common sense, so I've lost before I've even begun.

The meeting's being called to order when Emerson Hughes swans in, wearing a tiny suit and sky-high heels, shooting a megawatt smile at the mayor as if she's his most honored guest.

What's even more annoying is that he smiles back. I'm not sure what our octogenarian mayor thinks Emerson's offering— money, prestige, blow jobs?—but it's pretty fucking clear he's saying *yes* to it.

"Miss Hughes," he says, rising. "Welcome. I believe you wanted to do a little presentation?"

She blushes like a hopeful beauty pageant contestant, smiling shyly at its most important judge. "*Really?*" she asks. "It's okay?"

"Of course, of course," he says, beckoning her to the smart board. "Hook up your whatsit to the whosit here. I have no idea how these things work."

"There's an agenda," I bark, and Emerson slowly turns to me. Her smile holds. In fact, she looks *pleased* by my outburst.

"I'm sorry," she says, ever so sweetly. "It's…Mr. Doherty, yes? If you'd like to go first, that's just fine. I'm in no rush."

Everyone in the room is looking at me like I'm Scrooge. As if Emerson fucking Hughes just wants to give the town everything inside her generous little heart, and I'm the mean old crank who doesn't know how to love.

"I'm in no rush either," I reply between my teeth. "I'm just pointing out that there's an agenda, and presentations are at the end."

"I'm sorry." She offers the mayor a deeply apologetic smile. "I definitely wasn't trying to jump ahead."

The mayor frowns at me. *This lovely young girl is so wonderful that she's apologizing for my mistake,* that frown says. *A mistake pointed out by that jackass near the front. What's his name again?*

"I'll just take a seat next to Mr. Doherty," she says, repeating my name in case he missed it, "and wait until everyone's ready."

"Pleased with yourself?" I grunt as she slides in beside me. Smug pleasure radiates from her pores.

"Exceedingly," she replies under her breath. As she sits, her skirt rides up, perilously close to her panties. I force my gaze elsewhere.

The secretary reads the minutes from the last meeting, where it seems almost nothing of import occurred. When she's done, the mayor glances my way. "Hopefully that was sufficient, Mr. Doherty?" he asks, before summarizing the purpose of the day's meeting, reminding everyone about the mysterious state inspection of Lucas Hall last winter that revealed some serious safety issues—flaws the town cannot afford to repair.

Interesting, the way the building was *randomly* inspected this past winter, when it wasn't due for inspection. Just, you know, a random goddamn inspection of a building barely anyone knows exists.

"As we cannot afford the repairs, we're now opening the floor to other proposals for the land. I assume you'd like to begin, Mr. Doherty?"

Jesus fucking Christ. I'm here to save the town, Emerson's undoubtedly here to destroy it, yet somehow, *I'm* already the bad guy.

"Ladies first," I snap.

Emerson rises and walks to the front of the room, smiling at the mayor and town council before she turns to offer that same demure smile to the rest of us. She is the epitome of earnest, good intention. Her laptop connects instantly, and an image of the town, circa 1910, flashes on the screen. I suspect she was in the building for hours getting set up and that last-minute entrance was simply for added drama—so that every man she passed got a good look at her ass and every woman could admire her expensive suit and glossy hair.

"Hi. I'm Emerson Hughes with Inspired Building. I see some new faces today, and several familiar ones as well." She stops here to grin at the mayor as if he's her father. Or boyfriend. "I was actually born and raised right here, so I want to make something clear before I begin: Inspired Building does not want to *change* all the things that make Elliott Springs so magical. Our town has a long, proud history. It has the warmth of a tight-knit community. The small-town values everyone in this room cherishes. These things matter to us too. That's why we've been working quietly in the background to preserve Elliott Springs' past while we bring it into a new century."

They're turning a hardware store that's been around since the 1800s into a spin studio. How exactly is that preserving the past?

"Our new grocery store," she says as if I've asked the question aloud, "is going to bring the modern conveniences of an upscale grocer to Elliott Springs while never forgetting where it began." The pictures that flash past show smiling cashiers in old-timey aprons, hand-drawn placards announcing fish of the day and fresh-baked pies, a woman biking with a wicker basket full of flowers.

I'd like to see someone attempt to bike down our *cobblestone* streets.

"Our new bookstore and theater open this summer to become the heart of a thriving intellectual community while offering visitors and residents alike a taste of the town's past." The images on the screen go to a suffragette protest, a woman being helped out of a Model T. I've got no fucking clue what that has to do with a bookstore or a theater, but I appear to be the only one in the room questioning it. These fucking idiots are ready to give her a standing ovation.

"But these businesses can't exist in a vacuum. In order to support the sort of shops and restaurants and experiences that Elliott Springs residents deserve, there needs to be the customer base. That's where the Homes of Lucas Hall comes in."

A new picture appears on screen—an architectural rendering of a massive apartment complex, with a little kid on a tricycle and a smiling couple in front.

It's framed by mountains, on the sunniest day God ever created, and it takes me a second to realize it's set in the same goddamn place where we currently sit.

She wants to tear Lucas Hall down and turn it into a fucking apartment complex.

"Two hundred and fifty luxury apartments in a building featuring a gym, rooftop terrace, twenty-four-hour concierge, and ample underground parking for both the residents and town visitors."

A building like that would ruin the town. It would change everything. The roads would be clogged, the schools over-crowded. It would turn Elliott Springs into the same fucking big-city mess that drove people here in the first place.

She smiles at the crowd. "So what does that mean for all of us, the people who are already here?" she asks.

You live in New York City, Emerson. There's no 'us.'

"It means an average of five hundred new residents—residents who will support a bookstore, an upscale grocery store. Residents who'll need haircuts and baked goods and insect control," she says with a nod toward Dave Smith. "And when we prove to the world that Elliott Springs is thriving, it will bring other businesses here, which means access to the same stores, the same restaurants, the same upscale gyms that you see in San Jose and Santa Cruz."

A hand shoots up. I wasn't aware it was a question-and-answer, but she smiles and points to him like she's the White House Press Secretary and he's her favorite reporter.

"I'm just wondering what it'll do to home values in the area," says this guy I've never laid eyes on before.

She nods. "I'm so glad you asked. The nice thing about bringing in five hundred new residents is that it means we're bringing in hundreds of potential *homeowners*. Young singles who'll be getting married and starting families and looking for more space. Meaning home values will skyrocket."

Beverly Grimm, who owns the grocery store across from the one Emerson's putting in, raises her hand next. Emerson's smile tightens, as if she's fastening it in place by force.

"These businesses you're talking about are going to take customers away from the rest of us," Beverly says. "Your grocery store is competition for me. It's also competition for Lori's bakery and even the drug store."

Emerson's still smiling, but there's a hard glint in her eye. "I know change is unsettling." Her voice is saccharine-sweet. "But with an enlarged consumer base, there's room enough for everyone. I assure you, thriving towns can support two grocery stores. They can support a bakery. But Elliott Springs *does* need to grow for that to happen."

If I hadn't already pissed off the mayor, I'd point out that no one's going to go to Bev's shitty little grocery store if there's a better option and that yuppies want macarons and designer cupcakes, not the day-old gingerbread men sold at Lori's bakery. That we are settling for what the town offers because there aren't other options, but once they're there, no one's going back.

"I'll set my business cards here on the table for anyone who wants to give me a call," Emerson concludes, "and I've got a little office in the back of the grocery store if you want to chat in person. But I really hope we can work together. Let's turn Elliott Springs into the town it was meant to be: a place you're proud to call home."

The applause is thunderous. She smiles her beauty pageant smile as she returns to her seat.

"Knock 'em dead, little hammer," she whispers as I rise.

By the time I've reached the podium, the crowd's rapt interest has vanished entirely. I guess I should have made a fucking presentation. It honestly never occurred to me that anyone would be as persuasive as Emerson just was. I also never thought the majority of the town would be dumb enough to believe her.

I'm the good guy here, but I've got nothing to sell these greedy idiots who simply want a payday.

"Lucas Hall has played a vital role in our town's history," I begin. "My grandfather received the Purple Heart in this very room when he returned from his first tour of Vietnam, and he met my grandmother at the ceremony." If Emerson was presenting this, she'd have had a photo of this moment, no doubt. She'd have created holograms of my deceased grandparents, beaming down on us all as they listened in. "I attended Boy Scout meetings here. My prom and my graduation were held here, and I'm sure that's true for many of the people in this room. So this place matters to me. I'll bet it matters to you. What I'm hoping is that it matters enough to all of us to preserve it in a way that will leave its character unchanged."

I can already tell I've lost them. People are tugging at their collars, glancing at their watches. The guy directly in front of me is playing Candy Crush.

"I've looked at the repairs that are necessary and the mayor is right—under normal circumstances, they'd be pretty expensive. But because I love this town and our history, I'm willing to do the work at cost. I still have to buy the materials and pay my crew, but I'd forgo making any profit above and beyond that." I hold the stapled sheets of paper I'd laid on the podium aloft. "I, uh, have an estimate of the costs here, if anyone wants to take a look."

The room is silent, and it's not because they're riveted.

The only person in the whole goddamn room who's smiling is Emerson. And it's a smile that says, "*I won.*"

As annoyed as I am—and I'm really fucking annoyed—I sort of like to see her smiling for once.

12

EMMY

My period starts in science class. A stabbing, unexpected pain that I won't understand until later, when I see the brown stain on my underwear. I press a hand to my stomach and Paul whispers, loud enough for me to hear, that I probably ate too much.

That's how it is now. There's nothing that can happen to me, nothing I can say or do, that isn't turned into ridicule, that isn't made to be my fault. The weight began as a trickle, but now it's an avalanche. Everything I do to stop it only makes it worse. I'll go without food until I'm desperate for it, until I'm shoving anything I can find in my mouth whether I like it or not, terrified my mother will see me do it. I wake up the next day and the cycle repeats. Nothing helps.

My mother isn't speaking to me when I get home, which happens a lot. Her silence is a snake in the grass, waiting to strike. A slap she'll deliver when I least expect it. All I can do is wait until she decides it's time.

That night, I do my homework, ignoring my growling stomach as I wait. I no longer eat lunch at school, because I can be eating half what

Bradley Grimm does and she'll still suggest it's too much, and I don't dare get a snack when my mom's already mad. The clock moves from five to six, from six to seven, and she continues to watch TV and drink her coffee with disapproval pinching her lips. Now that Jeff's at college, there's no guarantee she'll make dinner. The only thing that's certain is that she'll get mad if I make myself something to eat, and she'll be mad if I ask if she's cooking. I'm always choosing the lesser of two evils. Occasionally I long for a choice that doesn't involve any evil at all.

"Are you making dinner?" I finally ask. My voice is too quiet. She'll dislike that. She'll think it's weak and pathetic. But if I ask boldly, she'll say I'm arrogant. Again, it's the lesser of two evils.

She jumps up so fast that I automatically move to shield my cheek. That hand of hers tends to strike without warning on days like this. "What did you just say to me? Am I your servant now?"

"No. I just wanted to know."

She scrunches her face up to mimic me. "I just wanted to know," she says in a nasal, whiny imitation. "Do I suddenly owe you dinner? You're nearly grown."

"I'm sorry."

"I'm sorry," she mimics again, high-pitched and sniveling.

It's a relief when she goes to her room and slams the door shut behind her. I make a peanut butter and jelly sandwich, but even when the sandwich is gone, there's no relief. Instead, I'm more aware of something nameless inside me, something bottomless and suffocating at the same time.

I gather my babysitting money and walk down the road, past the creek that smells like rotting fish and decay, to Black's, a shitty little convenience store that mostly sells beer and cigarettes.

I buy chips and donuts and Skittles and a large blue slushie to wash it down. I don't make eye contact with the cashier, who's probably already deduced it's all for me. I walk back down to the creek, until I'm certain I'm alone, and then I eat all of it—the chips, the Skittles, the donuts. I eat until my stomach hurts, and I continue to *eat past that. I eat until the very last bite is gone, and I'm sick, but I wish I had more.*

People imagine a girl like me devouring her food with unashamed gusto, licking her fingers and sighing theatrically, but that's not how this is. I barely taste it. All I want from food is the way it makes me absent, the way it allows me to float above myself for the five or ten minutes it takes to inhale it and stop feeling anything at all.

I want to be numb.

And I'd give anything if I could just make that numbness last.

I WAKE EARLY to get ready for a call to Nashville. My mother isn't up yet and it's not as if she'd want me around if she were. Aside from when I go grocery shopping and drive her to appointments, I'm pretty sure she wishes I'd just disappear.

Snowflake trots up to me. "Don't get dirty," I warn as I let her into the backyard. "This suit is Max Mara. You don't want to know how much it cost."

I fill her bowls with water and dog food and then I go to the back deck. It's barely seven thirty, but Liam's already setting up for the day, his jaw unshaved and set hard.

I wish Gary had half his worth ethic, and I wish Liam had Gary's so I wouldn't have to fucking see him all the time. Especially now. Because he put my mom in her place and is offering to work for free on Lucas Hall, and no matter what he ostensibly did to me when I was a teen, he no longer seems to be *that* guy. He seems, in fact, to be the opposite—the exact person I imagined he was back when I was in New York, getting to know him by text.

I can't persuade myself he's my enemy, though after yesterday's absolute trouncing at the hearing, I imagine I'm his.

"Hurry up, Snowflake," I call. "I'm on a schedule."

"Yard's a mud bath," Liam says. "You'd have been better off taking her for a walk."

Ah, there's the one thing that will prevent a man from ignoring you: the chance to offer unsolicited advice.

"I'm wearing four-inch heels," I reply. "They're not really ideal for dog walking."

He shrugs. "Then I hope they're made for being covered in mud, because that's what's next."

I ignore him. Snowflake isn't even my dog. If she comes back muddy, Jordan can get off her lazy ass and drive to Elliott Springs to wash her.

"By the way," he says, "your mom told us to toss everything in the shed before we tear it down, but we found a lockbox. Do you guys want it?"

I freeze. The shed was my father's domain, and we left it untouched when he abandoned us. A part of me is tempted to say *yes* and hire a locksmith to break into it, hoping it will provide some answers, but a man who couldn't bother to tell us goodbye when he ran is unlikely to have gone to the trouble of locking away an apology for us to one day find.

"You can toss it," I tell him. "Snowflake! Come here, girl!"

Snowflake emerges from the woods, covered head to toe in mud.

"Goddammit," I mutter. I refuse to meet Liam's smug gaze. "Can you hand me the hose?"

"I wouldn't do that if I were you," he replies. "Have you ever sprayed a dog down? She'll shake herself dry, all over your suit. Throw me a towel. I'll do it."

I stiffen. Why is he offering to help me? Does he think I'll just hand over Lucas Hall because he rinsed off my dog? Even Liam's not that dumb. And allowing people to do things for me always comes at a price. Even if that price is merely being civil going forward, it's more than I want to pay.

He's already taking Snowflake by the collar and leading her

to the hose, however, so I go inside for a towel. When I emerge, mud and water are flying as Snowflake shakes herself off.

I brace for his inevitable irritation with me. I wait for him to say, "*I told you so.*"

It's not like you were all that clean to start with, I'll reply.

But instead, he laughs. "Throw me the towel," he says, reaching out a hand. He seems to catch it without even looking and then kneels down to dry Snowflake off when I assumed he wanted the towel for himself.

"There's a good girl," he coos, holding her by the collar. "Doesn't that feel better?"

I'm uncharacteristically tongue-tied. I wish he'd tell me I'm a stupid bitch for not listening to him in the first place. At least then I'd know how to respond.

"Thank you," I say, the words quiet and hoarse. "Do you... need a clean shirt?"

His gaze drifts over me. "I'm gonna go out on a limb and say we probably aren't the same size."

"I...my father..." I never speak about my father. Ever. It's too hard, and I don't want anyone's pity. "Most of his clothes are still here."

Suddenly, there's something almost gentle in his face. "That's okay," he says. "But thank you."

He sends Snowflake in my direction and pulls up his shirt to dry his face with the underside. *Classy*. But he's got the abs of a Greek god and there's something intoxicatingly male about the gesture, so I'll let it slide.

I follow Snowflake to the kitchen with the troubling suspicion that I'm right back where I never wanted to be: inclined to trust a guy who will end up hurting me in the end.

～

My mother's follow-up with Dr. Sossaman is late that afternoon. While she's in his office, I walk out to the vending machines. My mouth waters at the sight of stale baked goods and candy that's pure corn syrup. I'm not sure I even want any of it. I just know that I've likely got an entire evening ahead with her judging me for the little I *do* eat, and I want to know for certain that I won't go to bed hungry because of it.

"Don't do it, Emmy," I hiss. "It's a slippery slope."

When I walk back to the waiting room, a nurse says Dr. Sossaman would like to speak to me.

"To *me*?" I repeat. "I'm not the patient."

She nods. "It'll just take a minute."

She leads me back to an office where a guy in his mid-thirties sits with my mom.

"You must be Emmy," he says. "I'm Dr. Sossaman."

I find it irritating when doctors presume they can use my first name while not using their own, but I'm too busy being shocked by how young he is to focus on that right now. My mother made it sound like they were *peers*.

"I've been explaining to your mother that it's important to rest after surgery in order to heal," he says, "and I wanted to make sure you understood."

I glance from him to her. There's something a little pointed in this reminder, and unnecessary as well.

I arch a brow. "Doesn't it go without saying that you need to rest after surgery?"

Dr. Sossaman turns to a nurse hovering near the doorway. "Can you take Miss Atwell to the PT room and get someone to show her the rehab exercises listed in her file again?"

I rise when my mother does, but Dr. Sossaman gives a polite cough to get my attention. "I was hoping we could chat for a moment."

I sit back down.

"I wanted to make sure you understand that your mother

can't be forced to do a lot around the house," he says warily. "She's not healing the way we'd like."

I choke on a laugh. "As far as I can tell, the only thing my mother does consistently is watch a lot of reality TV. But I'm happy to turn it off if that's an issue."

He glances away. "She seems to be under the impression that she's not healing well because she's doing too much. And yes, she does need to be walking around, but within reason."

You've got to be kidding me. "Aside from putting on makeup to come here, I haven't seen her exert any effort whatsoever. She doesn't even open the door for the dog."

"Look," he says, his tone diplomatic, "I realize this is stressful, but it's really worked out well for you both, timing wise, and I think if you looked at this as an opportunity—"

"In what possible way has this worked out well for *me*?" I ask, aghast.

"Well, she needs help, and it sounds as if you're between jobs and need a place to stay, so—"

I laugh out loud, the sound half humor and half explosive anger. I slap my purse on the desk between us. "Do you see this bag, *Doctor* Sossaman? It's Hermès. I bought it a month ago for four grand because I had a half hour in the Tokyo airport and was bored. I'm not 'between jobs,' and I *don't* need a place to stay. I have a very expensive apartment in New York City sitting empty, so I can be here to help my mother. You should perhaps consider not taking everything she says at face value."

His mouth opens, closes, then opens again.

"Right," he says. "Okay then. I just thought I could help."

"You can," I reply as I walk out. "Make her better so I can get back to my life."

It isn't his fault, I know. My mother enjoys living in a fictional world in which I am always the loser she's saddled with, and she enjoys bringing other people into the delusion.

But is there really any hope of winning over someone who would tell a story like that about her own kid? Probably not.

The light drizzle turns torrential during the drive home while I try to work out what I'll say to her. I'm outraged—outraged enough that I could see myself taking off, telling her and Jeff they're on their own. But who will take care of Snowball if I leave? And who will secretly ogle Liam? Those jobs aren't going to take care of themselves.

When we reach the house, Liam's guys are running supplies to their trucks. I guess that means Liam's done for the day, which I find strangely disappointing.

My mother frowns at the rain. "You need to go ask Liam or one of his guys to carry me."

I fight what would undoubtedly be a *malicious* smile. Sandra and I need to probably have a more serious chat about her bullshit, but I know exactly how to punish her in the interim. I believe this is what experts refer to as *natural consequences*.

"Actually, Mom, Dr. Sossaman is concerned about the way you're healing. When I explained how much time you spend sitting around, it became clear to both of us what the real culprit was." I'm not certain it was clear to Dr. Sossaman, but I'm sure it *would* have been if he hadn't been so busy blaming me. "So, no, I'm not asking Liam. I'll help you on the stairs and you can use the walker for the rest."

"But I'll get drenched."

"Then you'd better walk fast," I reply. "Just imagine all the stories you can tell *Harold* about how terrible I am now."

The prospect does seem to cheer her up. She manages to get to the house relatively quickly, and I lend her my shoulder as we climb up the steps, which is the closest to affection either of us has perhaps ever come.

She releases me as if my skin burned her as soon as she's

reached the top step. "Your shampoo smells god-awful," she says, hobbling into the house.

It shouldn't surprise me. She's always found a way to wedge some crushing insult where I least expect it. When I asked if I could wear makeup, she said I should worry about losing some weight first. I came home once with short hair, and she told me I'd gotten rid of my only good feature. I can't recall a single time when she wasn't doing her level best to let me know I was despised.

I walk to the back window and stare out at the desolate backyard, remembering how hard things were here after my father left. I started to expect the worst of people because I got the worst at home, and there's been very little in my life to counter that. Other than Liam.

He was different from everyone else back when he was texting me. He was different this morning, too, washing the dog though I'd been awful to him. Cooing "there's a good girl" in that soft voice. Then again, terrible people are capable of being kind to dogs. Case in point: Snowflake now sleeps on my bedroom floor because I don't have the heart to shut the door on her.

My father was kind like that, or so I thought. He'd appear in my room early in the morning, saying "want to go on a secret mission?", and sometimes it was just driving to Santa Cruz for donuts and jumping into the ocean for an icy swim, but my favorite was when we'd go down to Main Street in the pouring rain, clad in my raincoat and boots, to help place sandbags in front of the stores when the river was flooding.

It made me feel like I belonged somewhere. It left me certain the world held more good than bad.

I'd almost forgotten there was a time when I didn't hate it here.

13

EMMY

Liam and I no longer correspond directly, but through Stella I learn that I'm supposed to come in and approve the ceiling before they start installing the new seats. I've got breakfast with the mayor first, but that's not the reason I put on the suit I look best in—short skirt, the jacket perfectly fitted. When my mother asks why I'm dressed like an escort as I get ready to leave, I tell her it's because *I'm* still young enough to pull it off.

Nothing like a crack at Sandra's age to get everyone's day off to a good start. And maybe it's time she realized that when she hits, I can hit back.

Over breakfast at a restaurant that isn't the diner—thus avoiding a run-in with Paul Bellamy—the mayor tells me which town council members are not on board with my plan and what they're objecting to. One of them doesn't like the idea of an outside firm owning so much of Elliott Springs because we won't place the town's interests first; another thinks we're going to run the existing stores out of business. They are correct on both counts.

The mayor is not especially subtle about what he wants—

population growth, a park in his name, or perhaps new administrative offices for the town. He also suggests that he'd ask for something else from me if he was ten years younger, and I smile as if I'm entertaining the idea while thinking that if he were ten years younger, he'd still be forty years too old for me.

I call Stella from the car. "I need a parcel of land somewhere in Elliott Springs that we can snatch up for a park, and a blueprint for the park. Oh, and come up with a name for it that has Joe Latham in the title."

I slide into a spot near the theater and climb out of the car. "And the purchase of the land has to be contingent on the town council's agreement to let us build the Homes of Lucas Hall. I'm not building the mayor his fucking park just because he's a nice guy. Also, he's not a nice guy. I'm pretty sure he hit on me today and he was born before women had the vote."

"That would make him well over a hundred years old, and since the last gift you had me get him was a pair of Beats, I doubt that's true."

"Even centenarians like—"

"Smile, sweetheart," says a guy sitting on the hood of a truck outside the theater.

Stella laughs. "Oh, boy."

"I need to go," I tell her as I end the call and turn toward him. "What was that?"

"Smile," he repeats, brushing something off his construction vest. "You're a pretty girl; it's a sunny day. Wouldn't kill you to smile."

I look around us—at all the people with their heads down, staring at their phones as they walk by. At this fucking asshole telling me to smile, though he himself isn't smiling.

I'm supposed to smile because young women, especially pretty women, are considered adornment, and *powerless* adornment at that. Because guys like this fucking asshole right here want to remind you that you're a pretty face, here for their amusement. That you should rearrange your fucking mood and temperament if a man's requested you do so, even if you were in the middle of a work call and he's sitting there like an asshole doing absolutely nothing.

"Hey, you want to make five hundred dollars real quick?" I ask.

He sets down his sandwich next to his hard hat and wipes his mouth on his sleeve. He's wary, but not so wary that he's going to turn down five hundred dollars. "I mean, it depends on what you need me to do. And I gotta be back at work in ten minutes."

"Nothing illegal and it'll take two seconds," I tell him with my sweetest smile. "Though out of curiosity, what *won't* you do?"

His grin turns positively feral. His eyes dart to my crotch, as if that's the area in need of his help. *Yeah, buddy, you wish.* "If it's not illegal and takes two seconds, I'll do anything you want."

"Excellent," I reply with a smile. "All I want is for you to say 'smile, sweetheart' to someone walking down the street." I nod toward the bear of a man walking our way—the one with biceps twice the size of my thighs and what appears to be a Harley-Davidson tattoo on his neck. "*Him.* And you can't tell him I made you ask. If he asks you to repeat yourself, you stand by your guns. You tell him he's pretty—you can even go with 'attractive' if that's more comfortable—and that it wouldn't kill him to smile. Deal?"

His face shutters. He picks up his sandwich again. "Nah."

"Oh? Why not? Is it because telling someone else to smile is a way to assert dominance? Is it because it's inherently disrespectful to tell a *complete stranger* how they should feel or project themselves in the world and that guy might kick your ass?"

"Fuck you, whore," he mutters.

I laugh as a door opens behind me. "Funny that I'm the one

you're calling *whore*, but you're the one who was willing to do *anything* for five hundred bucks."

Liam is suddenly standing between us, narrowing his eyes at me. "Is there a problem here?"

"Oh, he's one of yours?" I demand. "Then I can guarantee this will fall on deaf ears, but I'll repeat what I just said to him. Telling a woman who's walking past to smile isn't a *friendly* gesture. It's a demeaning one. I'm not an ornamental object. I'm not here to make any man's life more aesthetically pleasing or cheerful."

Liam's scowl grows. I fully expect him to turn on me, the way a thousand other men would, and ask why I'm making a big deal of nothing. Instead, he rounds on the guy. "You told her to *smile*?"

"I was just being—"

"Don't defend it," Liam says, his voice hard. "She's right. You wouldn't say that to me, so you've got no business saying it to her."

I struggle not to let my jaw fall to the floor. The guy who calls me *princess* is suddenly a feminist?

"But the more troubling piece," Liam continues, "is what I heard *her* say as I was walking out. Did you call her a whore?"

The guy rolls his eyes. "She was being a bitch. I just—"

"Get your shit," Liam says calmly, "and don't let me catch you around any of my jobs again."

I don't know who's more surprised—me or the guy who just lost his job. I'm not above firing people—I do it all the time—but this wasn't the outcome I was looking for.

Liam turns to me. "You ready to come inside?"

I nod, waiting until he's opened the door to say anything. "You didn't need to fire him."

"Don't tell me how to run my business and I won't tell you how to run yours," he replies. "There's your new ceiling. Is it what you wanted?"

I glance from the ceiling to him and away. The ceiling is perfect. His response was perfect. He doesn't let men treat women like garbage. He doesn't let me treat *him* like garbage either.

As loath as I am to admit it, Liam Doherty isn't the villain I wanted to believe he was. Only one of us seems to be doing anything shady at all, and it's certainly not Saint Liam, who wants to preserve Lucas Hall for free.

"Yes," I say quietly. "It's exactly what I wanted."

He opens up a schedule on his phone. "We're due to have the seats installed by the end of the week. I'll let you know when they're done."

I wish I could find something to bitch about to make this exchange feel the way it's supposed to, and I can't find a goddamn thing. "Thanks," I tell him, my voice softer and more uncertain than normal as I turn to walk out of the store.

Why does it all feel so incomplete? Why am I sad that the job is nearly over? I should be *thrilled*.

I pull out my phone when I reach my car. I haven't texted him once since I discovered who he was, and I'm weirdly anxious to do so now. But that doesn't stop me.

> Can you give me a quote on a build-out for the bookstore? Stella will send you the specs.

YARD BOY

> Not sure I want to help with your dastardly plan to take over the city, but I'll look it over. We could use a bookstore.

> Dastardly plan? I just want to make Elliott Springs a spectacular place to live.

My mistake. I thought you and your cronies were buying up all the buildings really cheap to run everyone out of business. Then you bring in big-name stores and charge them twice as much.

Four times as much, but yes, that about sums it up.

Elliott Springs is changing whether you like it or not. If it's not me doing it, it'll just be someone else.

I suspect you could stop it if you wanted to.

Except I don't want to. The people in this town treated me like shit for half my life. I owe them nothing.

Destroying other people isn't going to make you feel any better.

That suggests to me that you've never destroyed an enemy before. It's actually quite fulfilling.

I wonder if that made him laugh. I hate that I care.

14

LIAM

When I got out of the hospital on crutches, I had more offers of assistance from girls I'd known or dated than I ever could have imagined. Women offered to cook, to clean, to do my laundry. I even got more interesting offers, of the "you don't have to return the favor" variety. I knew I should be saying *yes* to at least some of these—I was a changed man, after all, ready to settle down—but there was this bone-deep boredom that kept me silent.

I was finally ready to do the *right* thing—the thing my family had been on me about for years—but it felt like a sort of death.

In February, I limped into Beck's bar. "Liam," said a girl I knew from high school, "you're breaking my heart, honey. I'm coming over this weekend to cook for you."

I didn't want her in my home, mostly because I didn't want to be stuck trying to get her *out* of my home, but wasn't this what I was supposed to want? A woman who'd notice if I was missing for three days? Someone I could care about too?

I was about to answer when I got a text.

UNKNOWN NUMBER

> This is Emerson Hughes with Inspired Building. I understand you're my point of contact for the theater we're restoring on Main Street. Hopefully you aren't as slow to complete work as you are to pick up a phone.

I was unamused. I knew some stuff had fallen through the cracks—Bridget thought she'd forwarded my calls to JP, but she'd actually sent them to a random voicemail. My teeth ground as I forced myself to type a civil reply.

> Sorry if you've had a hard time reaching someone. I've been in traction for a few weeks with a broken leg, among other things. I'm just getting up to speed.

> That sounds made up. If you're going to tell me wild stories, get better at lying first.

Inexplicably, I'd laughed. After weeks of everyone treating me as if I were pitiable, Emerson Hughes' utter lack of sympathy was sort of refreshing.

> I'll work on it.

> Work on it AFTER you're done with my theater.

I'm not sure what I thought was going to come of it, but during the months we texted, it really felt like the start of something.

Have I not given up on the idea of her? I guess if I had, I wouldn't still be scrolling through our old texts. I guess I wouldn't be sitting in my house alone, laughing over the one she sent tonight.

That suggests to me that you've never destroyed an enemy before. It's actually quite fulfilling.

Yep, I definitely haven't given up.

15

EMMY

Snowflake needs to pee.

Most days begin this way now that she's sleeping in my room. I'd have expected to find it more irritating than I do, but she's a good girl, shifting restlessly as she waits for me to rise. It's not her fault I'm a light sleeper.

It's at least an hour until the guys are here to work in back. I pull a cardigan over my pajamas and take her downstairs. She bounds out the door happily and I follow, standing on the porch. The air is soft this morning, like early spring rather than summer, and I'm in a weirdly good mood, though I don't know why. I feel the way I used to as a kid—light as air, full of hope, as if the world contains too many good things to be squeezed into my day.

Which it doesn't. At all. I know this.

Snowflake pees and then runs around the yard. "I'm not going back in the woods after you, so don't even think about it," I call.

She listens this time but waits, looking toward me expectantly.

I have no idea what she wants, but I've got a few minutes.

The grass is damp beneath my bare feet as I venture into the yard.

I grab a stick. "Um, fetch?"

I toss it. It's a small thrill when she bounds away and brings it back to me, proud as a toddler producing her first stick-figure drawing. I throw it again, going farther. It's a lot more satisfying than I'd have thought, making someone or something happy.

"Good girl," I say, squatting low to sink my hands into her fur. She licks my face, which is absolutely vile given other things she's licked. "That's sweet, Snowflake, but no thank you. I've seen where you put that tongue."

She does it again and I laugh. "We'll work on it. You're a good girl anyway."

"I thought you were allergic to the yard," says a soft voice. "And possibly the dog."

My head jerks up. Liam is approaching from the side of the house, two massive beams of wood over one shoulder.

"I'm not allergic to anything except for strangers on my property at the crack of dawn." I rise stiffly, pulling my cardigan close over my silk cami and sleep shorts. "Why are you here so early?"

He shrugs. "I'm getting stuff set up here since I'll be downtown all day. Got this really demanding client. She wants me to install a bunch of seats in a theater and potentially build her a bookstore."

"She sounds amazing."

He gives me a reluctant half smile, a flash of teeth. "She's okay."

My heart gives an odd, hard thump. We aren't enemies anymore, and I guess I already knew that. But there's something in that *she's okay*—weak vote of approval though it is— that makes me feel as if I've won the lottery.

And it makes me wish we were friends. It makes me wish I *deserved* to be his friend.

"Come on, Snowflake," I say, turning toward the house. "Let's let yard boy do his work."

I don't look back, but I get the feeling he's smiling. It's only as I walk in the door that I realize I am too.

"THE HARDWOOD IS UNEVEN," I tell Gary.

"It's fine," he says.

I take a deep inhale, trying to control my rage. "Here's how this works, Gary: you, the contractor, aren't the one who gets to decide it's *fine*. If I, the client, want to decide it's fine, that's on me, but I, the client, have *not* decided it's fine because it's fucking appalling, so you need to fix it, pronto."

He throws out his hands. "The floor is level! It just looks like it's not because we've only done half, and we need to add shoe molding along the back wall. The fixtures are coming in soon so there's no time to tear this out and redo it, which would be crazy anyway because it's fine. You'll see."

"I *won't* see," I reply. "And if you put down the rest of that hardwood and it can't be salvaged when I tear it out, I promise I'll be suing you for the full three hundred grand it cost."

I turn away, already texting Stella.

> See what we need legally in order to fire Gary and how much we can get back of what we've already paid. And see if you can find another company to do the job.

STELLA

> I swear ninety percent of my job is helping you fire people.

> And yet you have no qualms about being a smart-ass with me, which is fascinating.

> In order for you to fire me, you'd first need to make ME hire my replacement. We both know that wouldn't work out well for you.

> Whatever. Just make sure I can fire Gary.

When I get home with groceries in the afternoon, my mother watches me unpack. "You'd better not be sneaking food in your room," she says with narrowed eyes. I set a can of tomato sauce on the counter with a heavy thud.

Am I angry over the accusation or am I ashamed because she's right? I *am* keeping food in my room. Just protein bars so that I know I have something to eat if things get bad. So that on those nights when she's judging me, I won't go to bed starving.

"I'm twenty-eight," I reply. "What leads you to think I need to sneak food anywhere?"

Her gaze drops to my ass. I've never been one of those flat-assed girls, no matter how badly I've wanted to be. "You're definitely eating *something*. Have you even weighed yourself since you got home?"

I grip the counter while my stomach tightens, fighting the panic in my chest. Am I gaining weight? Shit. I don't think I've gained anything, but the mere possibility of it is enough to make my skirt feel too tight.

I march out of the room without a word, changing into yoga clothes and driving straight back downtown. Chloe's the only one in the yoga studio. My shoulders drop in relief.

I'm not in the mood for other participants, and I like the way her constant chatter distracts me—she's relatively new to Elliott Springs, having only moved here recently with her boyfriend, but she's surprisingly knowledgeable about the town's residents. She's friendly with everyone it seems—Jeannie, who owns the diner; the old guy who owns the garden center; the teenage girl protesting the destruction of Shaw Lake.

I enjoy getting Chloe's detailed rundown of who has slept with whom, who's fighting, and who's broke. Today, though, it's not quite enough to deplete my anger at Gary and my mom.

"You're still in a bad mood," she comments toward the end of the session, going into downward dog.

I follow suit. "My mother had surgery. It's been trying."

She falls out of position and turns to me. "Oh, I'm so sorry."

"I'm not in a bad mood because I'm worried about her," I reply. "I'm in a bad mood because she told her doctor that I'm some freeloader when the only reason I'm at her house is to take care of her. Oh, and today she implied I'd gained weight."

"Man, your mom really is a cunt and a half, isn't she?" she asks, which makes me laugh so hard that I fall out of downward dog entirely, collapsing to my knees.

"You're a yoga teacher," I gasp, wiping away tears. "Aren't you supposed to be all *namaste* and '*make peace with the pain*?'"

She grins. "There's a reason they only assign me to the classes no one shows up for. Speaking of which, I want a burger. You want a burger?"

Suddenly, I do. I really, really do.

Even as I tell her no, I wish I could agree. I wish I could afford to make someone here my friend.

16

EMMY

I moved from Elliott Springs to LA the day after I graduated high school.

For the next three months, until I left for college, I lived in a group house with seven other girls while waiting tables, and the only meal I got each day was the one I was comped at the end of my shift. Without my mother there to comment and judge, the weight seemed to fall off effortlessly, yet I made no friends in the group house or at work, though perhaps I was simply intimidated by the fact that Perry, the queen bee of our house, reminded me so much of Bradley Grimm.

She was thin and lovely and assured, and she looked at me with thinly veiled disdain every time I walked in the room. "Well, you know she's eating *somewhere* if it isn't here," I heard her say to the others one night, and every last one of them laughed, even the girls I'd thought were sort of nice.

Those words, that laughter—it landed like a slap in the face. I hated all of them in that moment, but I hated myself the most: why the fuck had I ever thought things would be different? I shouldn't have hoped for a minute I'd wind up making friends. People were assholes in Elliott Springs and everywhere else as well.

I celebrated my thirty-pound weight loss at the summer's end by sleeping with Perry's boyfriend, and I left a note announcing this development on the house chalkboard as I was moving out. And it felt good. Triumph was a thousand times better than fucking friendship.

I crave those small triumphs now. And the person I crave them from the most is currently walking straight toward me on Main Street.

Bradley Grimm was my best friend from the first day of kindergarten until she turned on me five years later. We'd *loved* the fact that we were born only two weeks apart, that we were both tall for our age and had blue eyes. For a long time, we'd collected those similarities as evidence of something, though I'm not sure what. She was blonde. My hair was dark. We still told strangers we were twins and they believed us. Our friendship had been the biggest, most important thing in my tiny life. It had felt indestructible.

Which made the way she stabbed me in the back later on that much worse.

I was hoping the years would have reversed our situations, but they have not. She isn't struggling with her weight, she isn't desperate to stop eating while a loved one's acerbic commentary drives her to eat even more.

She's not suffering at all, as far as I can tell. And she probably wouldn't suffer anyway—you've got to have internalized a million nasty comments before you hear them in your own head, and only one of us has.

But I don't need to have achieved a complete reversal just yet. I only need Bradley to realize she didn't win, and as we approach each other on an otherwise empty sidewalk, the differences between us are significant enough that even she must see it.

My keratin-treated hair is glossy, while hers is in a messy ponytail. My immaculately tailored suit makes the out-of-date jeans and Grimm's Convenience T-shirt she's wearing look especially unkempt, and though we are the same height, my Saint Laurent pumps leave me towering over her.

"Well, hello, Bradley," I coo, my smile positively malignant. "What an unexpected pleasure."

Her eyes narrow. She attempts to match my mean-girl smile but can't quite get there. "Off to Lucas Hall?" she asks. "Maybe your *boyfriend* finally made it."

I was expecting bullshit from her, braced for it, and yet I'm still a little stunned she'd take it this far and that she *still* has no shame. What did I ever do to this bitch to warrant her hatred?

I shake my head with a feigned sympathetic smile. "Still relying on something you did a decade ago to feel okay about yourself? Maybe if you spent a little more time focused on your own life instead of mine, you wouldn't be stuck wearing the free T-shirts you get from your mom. Have a great day."

I start to move past her, and she snatches at my sleeve. "You're not going to get away with this," she snarls. "I know you're trying to ruin us and I promise, if we go under, I'll find a way to make you pay for it."

I jerk my arm back and force a laugh though I'm boiling inside. "Trying to ruin you? I don't have to ruin you. Look at where you've ended up. Seems to me you've ruined everything all on your own."

"On my *own*?" she calls as I walk away. "Pretty sure if I'd grown up with half of your money, I'd be doing just fine right now. Keep right on taking what isn't yours, you greedy bitch. I can't wait to see it catch up with you."

I keep moving, but I'm weighed down in a way I wasn't before. Even when I've destroyed her business, it's not going to be enough.

What happens if this plan of mine, the one that's kept me

warm for years, doesn't give me any of the things I'd thought it would?

~

I FLY into Austin for the opening of Damien Ellis's new restaurant, in part to force Jeff to go take care of our mom for a few days—he hasn't visited even once—but mostly because I need Damien Ellis to notice me.

Though Ellis is the kind of guy everyone wants to date, I'm not after him for his incredible investment portfolio and perfectly groomed scruff. I'm after him for his ability to buy out Inspired Building and put me in charge. I want Charles fired, of course, but I've got no doubt the company would fare far better under me than it does my boss, whose only successes have come at my hands.

My dress is red, meant to attract attention. Even if Ellis never meets me, he will definitely say, "*Who was the woman in the red dress?*" at some point, and that's more than enough to make this trip worthwhile. The next time he hears my name, as the person who swooped up Elliott Springs while he wasn't looking, he'll sit up and take notice.

I get a martini at the bar. I hate martinis, but I don't want to be seen drinking something girly when I catch his eye. From there I float around the room, smiling and socializing, two things I don't do in real life. I ask people how they know Damien as if *I* know Damien, and when I tell them I'm Emerson Hughes with Inspired Building, they act as if they know who I am because I've *behaved* as if they should. They tell me what a great guy Damien is, which I doubt, and how impressed they are with the restaurant, though it's like every other steakhouse that's come up in the past four years. I stay until the moment I've been waiting for: the one where I look across the room and Damien Ellis is already looking at me. I give him a half smile and raise my glass. He raises his back and leans over to ask something of the guy beside him, watching me the entire time. He's asking about me, and any minute now, someone will say, "Oh, that's Emerson Hughes with Inspired Building—don't you know her?"

I drain that martini—warm now and absolutely vile—and walk outside to the waiting car.

Everything went perfectly, but as is common when things have gone perfectly, a sort of emptiness descends in my gut. I always expect it to feel like *more* and it never does.

I return to my hotel room, and flop on the bed—physically drained, as if the pretense was a costume of immense weight. I kick off my shoes and stare at the ceiling, wishing my relief felt good rather than hollow.

This is normally the moment when I'd distract myself with work, but the thought of it drains me even more than I already was. I pick up my phone, scrolling past messages from Jeff and Charles and Stella and...

Liam. Liam has texted. I shoot upright, quietly thrilled. I can't open the message fast enough.

YARD BOY

> Is there any chance you can meet me to walk through the bookstore tomorrow?

> I'm in Austin until Monday. And I thought you didn't work on Saturdays.

> I don't, but I want to make sure that I'm still your favorite Construction Boy, or whatever it is you call me.

> Yard Boy, and I don't think I ever said you were my favorite in the first place.

> You texted me for months. It was implied.

> You were texting ME.

> Yeah, there was something implied there too.

I'm smiling as I put the phone down. It no longer feels hollow, being in this hotel room alone.

IT's RAINING when my flight lands in San Francisco, and the drizzle is a downpour by the time I reach my mother's house. Snowflake bounds for me the moment I walk through the door, running in excited circles. An unwilling smile tugs at my mouth. I'm sort of happy to see her too.

"You're back," my mother says, her unhappiness clear. She turns up the television, as if the sound of my quiet steps across the room makes it impossible to hear one reality TV mom accuse another of bad parenting.

I let Snowflake out and stand in the frame of the door as she runs to the bushes at the yard's edge.

Liam and a few of his guys are securing a tarp over the frame of the screen porch. Liam yells something to one of them —it's raining too hard to hear what he's saying—and manages to catch a rope with one hand while holding the tarp with the other. I'm not sure I know a man anywhere who'd look as comfortable as Liam does now, balancing his entire weight on two posts. And I can't imagine why being able to balance precariously in a rainstorm is suddenly such a desirable quality.

He looks me over, eyes catching for a moment on my soaked shirt and moving away just as quickly. He pulls a rope through the grommet of the tarp and ties it down. I'd always thought I was more of a Damien Ellis kind of girl, but no...I'm pretty sure there's nothing hotter than a man standing in lashing rain, all lean muscle and determination, trying to make sure shit's kept dry.

Snowflake returns and I reluctantly close the door to dry her off before I go upstairs to shower. When I emerge, there's a text from Liam waiting.

YARD BOY

> This rain is supposed to keep up and the roads are going to flood. Please stay put tomorrow. That little car of yours isn't made for the kind of flooding we get here.

I think of a hundred ways I can reply, ways that criticize his work ethic, or the misogyny of suggesting that I, a female, need his guidance.

Instead, though, I just smile and scroll through our old texts. I thought what made me so happy those last few months in New York was the imminent vanquishing of my enemies.

Now I'm starting to wonder if it had a little to do with Liam as well.

17

EMMY

"Want to go on a secret mission?" my father asks.

The rain outside is thunderous and he's got his jacket on, so I know we're going to Main Street to help with the sandbags. I scramble from the bed and he grins, telling me he'll wait downstairs.

We'll begin, I know, with Bradley's mom's store, though Bradley never comes out to help.

"Bradley's mom says kids just get in the way," I tell my dad once I've gotten in the car.

He smooths his hand over my head with a small smile. "Moms are wrong sometimes. Your mom is wrong about a lot of stuff, and Bradley's mom is wrong about this. We're going out there to protect the stores, but we're also doing it to remind people that a community is a family, and we have each other's backs when the chips are down. Kids and adults alike."

I startle awake in the dark room. I'm sure it's the rain that made me dream about my father and the sandbags, but it felt more like a premonition or a warning from beyond the grave.

That supposes, however, that my father is dead—something

I don't know—or that he'd care enough to warn me in the first place. Given the way he left, it seems unlikely.

I look at the clock. It's just after four in the morning, but if it's rained like this all night, the lake is already flooding, which means the theater—and all the lovely hardwood waiting to be installed in the grocery store—will be flooded too. Even if it wasn't my father reaching out from another realm, I'm taking it as a sign.

I dive into my closet, fishing out leggings and a sweatshirt, which are the closest things I have to flood attire. I manage to get over the bridge to Main Street, where the water is running a foot high down the road before my car sputters and starts to stall. I gun the engine and make it to higher ground, then park in the historic section and run back down the hill. Water is lapping at the storefronts in the darkness, a vulture ready to swoop.

Fuck.

I've arrived way too late. Why the hell didn't I come down here yesterday? Why didn't I listen when Liam suggested it might flood?

"You brought this whole situation on yourself," I say to myself, but my tirade comes to a sudden end.

There, in front of the grocery store's front door, are sandbags, neatly stacked. And there, a little farther down, are Liam and his guys, saving the rest of the places on the street.

He's here to save everyone, but he started with me.

A warning ache swells in my throat. "I swear to God, if you start crying," I hiss at my reflection in the grocery window, "I will never forgive you."

I walk down to Liam. I'm already so wet that I've given up trying to remain beneath the store awnings.

"Why the fuck are you here?" he growls. "I *told* you to stay put."

So much for feeling moved to tears. Now I feel moved to punch.

"I came to check on the store," I reply, "and no man tells me to *stay put*, FYI."

He runs two hands through his hair. "And you drove here in that tiny car?"

"Sorry," I reply tartly. "My monster truck is in the shop."

"Well, I hope you get it back soon, because that BMW's likely to be totaled when this is all said and done."

I throw up my hands. I was going to offer to help, but since he's being such a dick, I won't. "Fine. I'll drive home."

"You *can't* drive home," he says, glancing toward the lake in the distance. "All that water you came through on the way here? Well, that was at a lower elevation than we are here and it'll be flooded by now. Try driving into it and you're gonna get swept off the road at best. Just go in your shop. When I get done here, I'll give you a ride."

Fuck. He's right about the drive home. But I'm not waiting inside like the princess he thinks I am.

I grab a sandbag from the back of the flatbed truck and sling it up against the door of the bank. It's far heavier than I remember them being, and I wonder how the hell I even lifted these things as a kid, but Liam's hauled at least fifteen of them on my behalf. I owe him that many in return.

"Do you ever fucking do as you're told?" Liam shouts.

"Do you realize that I'm a grown woman who's not under your command?" I reply, grabbing another sandbag.

It doesn't take long to grow accustomed to the weight, to the motion, and there's nothing else to do while I wait anyway, so I continue on after I've thrown the fifteen sandbags I owe him. Other people have come out too, to assist stores that are not their own. Why are they all helping? What could compel this many people to get their asses out of bed before sunrise on behalf of strangers? And how can they be so good to each other when they were all so awful to me?

My heart sinks because *I'm* the common denominator. There's always been something inside me that my mother was unable to like. And there was something that made my dad feel okay about abandoning me, and made the kids at school feel okay about the bullying.

It makes me want to give up, the way I've given up before, but a tiny part of me looks at Liam and wants to give this one more shot.

I want to see if just a little of this care they all feel for each other could possibly rub off on me. If I could care, if they could care about me in turn.

We work for hours, until every single store on the street is protected. My arms hurt so badly I can no longer lift them to push the hair out of my face. I won't be able to do Chloe's yoga class for at least a week.

"Come on," says Liam. "I live about two blocks from here. You can get some dry clothes while JP borrows my truck and then I'll take you home."

I should probably ask why JP needs his truck, why JP can't take me home on the way or why JP can't wait until I'm delivered, but I'm too fucking tired.

He leads me uphill in the driving rain, toward the town's historic section. We walk as fast as we can, but we're too exhausted and soaked to move all that quickly. "It's just ahead," he shouts, placing a hand on my back to steer me down a side street. There's something sweetly possessive in the gesture. I wish I could hate it.

A moment later we arrive at a restored cottage with a little white picket fence that looks like something out of a movie set in the 1950s.

"You *live* here?" I blurt.

He looks at me over his shoulder. "No, Em. I just thought we'd break into this stranger's home to get dry."

I smile. "It's just not what I pictured."

"I'm not sure I want to know what you pictured," he says, opening the door and flicking on the light.

Inside the cottage is warm and dry and perfect. Completely restored, with fresh paint and built-in shelves.

"Come in," he says, shutting the door behind me.

He pulls his jacket off. The T-shirt and jeans beneath it are soaked, clinging to his very, *very* defined chest.

"I don't want to drip on your floors."

He kicks off his boots with a quiet laugh. "I'm a single guy who works in construction. They've seen worse."

He walks into another room and emerges after a moment with several towels and dry clothes. Our eyes catch as he hands them to me. In bare feet, he's a foot taller than me and...very close. Suddenly, I'm considering a lot of ways we could pass the time waiting for his truck.

"Use the guest room," he says, nodding over his shoulder. "There's a bathroom in there, too, if you want to shower."

Apparently, I'm the only one of us considering how we should pass the time.

He turns to go into what I presume is his bedroom while I head to the guest room to change. There was definitely a female around here at some point. Most single guys don't keep Dior lipstick and La Roche moisturizer in the guest room medicine cabinet.

Are they his girlfriend's? My former designer's? I don't know why I care. I don't know why there's a pang in my chest at finding them here.

I turn on the water, strip off my damp clothes, and shiver with pleasure as I step into the hot shower. I help myself to the expensive shampoo and conditioner that definitely isn't Liam's either.

Once I'm dry, I pull on the sweatshirt, which is five times too big, and skip the shorts, which would barely fit a child.

I don't love the fact that Liam has clearly dated someone half my weight, but I do sort of like the idea of being nearly naked in Liam's home.

And then I walk into the living room...where Liam is pretty much naked too.

18

LIAM

E merson's gaze sweeps over me as she emerges from the guest room. "I guess I won't explain why I'm not wearing the children's shorts you gave me since you're wearing less."

So she's not wearing much of anything, or anything at all, under that sweatshirt. Against my better instincts, I imagine how easy it would be to drop my towel, to close the distance between us. To shove that sweatshirt over her hips, lift her onto the table...

Fuck my life. This is not the time for thoughts like that.

"I just realized I left my phone out here," I reply. "I was worried JP might call."

She slides her fingers along the hem of the sweatshirt. "It's interesting that you explain why you're wandering around in no clothes but not why you have children's shorts in your home."

I laugh as I reach for my phone. "They were my niece's. I found them in the laundry room. I'll be out in a sec."

I'm trying not to act like a teenage boy who's somehow gotten the hottest girl in school alone, though it's how I feel.

Mostly because, like that hypothetical teenage boy, I have no idea what to do with Emerson now that she's here.

In an ideal world, I'd take her over my knee for driving downtown in the first place. I flinch. *Let's avoid thinking about Emerson's bare ass in your face for the next hour or so. You can think about it at your leisure once she's gone.*

She impressed me today. She worked her tail off on behalf of people she thinks the worst of, people who seem to have hurt her in the past. It's dangerous to start letting myself think there's something good inside her, something more than she wants the world to see.

I seem to be thinking it anyway.

When I get back to the living room, she's setting her pile of wet clothes by the front door.

Even from here I can spy a pair of red lace panties in that pile. Yep. Nothing on under the sweatshirt. *Outstanding.* "You can throw that stuff in the dryer if you want," I say gruffly. "It's in the kitchen."

She nods, bending over to retrieve her clothes, and I'm looking before I can stop myself. The sweatshirt rides up high enough that I glimpse the curve of her ass before she tugs it down.

Fuck, fuck, fuck. I walk into the kitchen and stab the button on the coffeemaker almost violently.

Think of something else.

Grandma's funeral. The tsunami in Thailand. My other grandma's funeral.

She passes me to throw her stuff in the dryer. I hand her the first cup of coffee as she emerges. "I assume you take it black."

"Why would you assume that?" There's something soft, almost sweet about her face in the kitchen's dim golden light. The lush curves of her bare mouth beg to be kissed.

Tsunami. Grandma.

"Because you don't seem to let yourself enjoy a lot of

things," I reply. Her face dims a little, so I'm compelled to clarify. "I'd just assume you think of coffee as, I don't know, a device to encourage greater efficiency at work."

She takes the mug from my hand, suddenly somber. "I'm not a robot. I enjoy things."

"Then you'd like some milk and sugar for that, I assume?"

She hesitates. I suspect she wants to say *yes* just to prove me wrong. "Just a little milk, please."

I turn to the refrigerator and she moves away, walking across to the living room, looking at my pictures. Since the day she walked into the theater with her high heels and her perma-scowl, I've fantasized about her. I've pictured her bent over the tailgate of my truck or on the table in the back of the theater with her heels still on, one of those short skirts she wears bunched around her waist.

I'm pretty sure the fantasy will now involve her in my living room with her hair wet, wearing nothing but a damn sweatshirt.

"So what's the deal?" she asks. "Are you taking me home?"

"Yeah. JP said he'll be here within the hour. Are you hungry?"

She pauses, as if the question is a trick. With what I've heard about her life in high school, I guess I know why. "I'm okay."

"Bullshit," I reply, opening the refrigerator and grabbing the chicken. "You got down to Main Street just after four this morning and it's nearly lunch. You like stir-fry?"

"Yeah, though I'm not sure it's a good idea to accept food made by my competition."

"If I decide to kill you off, I've got enough sense to do it in a way that can't be traced. But you can come over here and watch me if you're still suspicious."

She takes a seat at the counter while I chop the chicken. "Do you need help?"

"Do you know how to make stir-fry?"

"I know how to *order* stir-fry. And I'm capable of taking direction."

I throw the chicken in the pan and return to the freezer for rice. "Somehow I doubt that," I say, and she laughs. The chicken begins to fizzle and pop in the oil, Emerson's still smiling and I wish I could capture this moment somehow, the coziness of it. "So I suppose living in the city you just order in all your meals?"

"I wouldn't have time to cook even if I cared to," she says just as her phone rings with an incoming video call.

The name on the screen says Donovan Arling, and even though she rejects the call and turns the phone face down on the counter, that name registers like a hard pinch, though I don't even know why he's calling her yet.

"Donovan Arling?" I ask. "As in the Olympic swimmer, Donovan Arling?"

She grins. "Names don't mean much. You're in my phone as Yard Boy."

"So, who's in your phone as Olympic swimmer Donovan Arling?"

Her mouth twitches. "Olympic swimmer Donovan Arling. He's a friend."

I already know exactly what sort of *friend* he is, and I'm jealous as hell though I've got no right to be.

"How do you have a relationship with anyone if you're working so much?"

She rolls her eyes. "I don't bother with relationships. The last thing I need is someone crying about how much I work or insisting that I skip an important trip because he feels neglected."

So she's simply *fucking* Arling. That doesn't make me feel any better.

"Maybe you could choose someone who doesn't cry about shit in the first place," I grumble.

She laughs to herself. "No offense, but you all cry eventually. I'll pass."

There's certainty in her voice. Perhaps this is a conversation we should have had a few months ago, before I started reading and rereading her messages, before I started going to bed each night thinking about what I'd text her next.

I've been enthralled with this girl for months without really knowing anything of substance about her. But the truth is that she's not what I'm looking for—and she's apparently not looking for me either.

A change of subject is necessary. *Focus, Liam.*

"How'd you even know there'd be sandbags available this morning?"

Her arms cross over her chest, as if she's protecting herself from me or the question. "My dad and I used to come down and help with the sandbags when I was little. I honestly have no idea how I lifted them."

I turn to look at her. "I used to come with my dad too. I don't remember you."

She raises a brow. "Were you still a *kid* when I was a kid?"

"Maybe I'm not aging as well as I'd thought. I'm probably four years older than you at most. I doubt it's even that much."

Her arms squeeze tighter. "I don't remember you from high school."

There's something wary in her voice. I think of Pete at the bar, laughing about her weight. Is she always bracing for someone to still be an asshole, all these years later? I'd have thought it was ridiculous if I hadn't witnessed those guys in action.

"I went to Prep," I say softly, when what I want to say is *I know what happened, and I'm so fucking sorry, and I swear to God I wouldn't have let them treat you the way they did if I'd been there.*

She smiles. Her relief is palpable. "Oooh, fancy. I wouldn't have pegged you for a little rich boy."

I carry the bowls to the table and slide one her way. "I wasn't. I went on a baseball scholarship."

Her head tilts. "Ah, a big-time athlete. That explains the overconfidence. Did you play in college too?"

"I blew out my shoulder sophomore year and left when they took away the scholarship. I could have gotten loans, I guess, but my older sister was having a hard time, so I came back to help her."

"If I could offer you some unsolicited advice," she says, "you should start helping people less."

I laugh despite myself. "That's exactly the kind of advice I'd expect you to give."

She smiles. "At least I'm consistent."

We finish our lunch. She helps me load the dishwasher and I guide her out to the living room, the sweatshirt riding high up her legs as she yawns and takes a seat on the couch.

I briefly imagine taking the seat beside her and rule it out, then consider it again.

When she first came into the house today, I was hungry and soaking wet and wanted nothing more than to get myself dry and fed. Now that all that's dealt with, I've got only one desire left in the fucking world.

I don't think I've ever wanted to see someone spread wide on my couch more than I do Emerson Hughes. But it's also pretty clear that nothing is going to come of this, and that I shouldn't *try* to make something come of this. She's the kind of woman you could sleep with but never entirely possess and I think it would make me insane—the not-possessing part.

I take the chair across from her instead.

"My arms are so sore I can't lift them high enough to cover my mouth when I yawn," she says, laughing.

"It'll be worse tomorrow. You might need to take a few days off from terrorizing the contractors of Elliott Springs."

"But that's my favorite part of the job, and Gary is in particular need of some terrorizing."

"What's going on?"

"The floor is slanted. He's trying to claim it's some kind of optical illusion that will be corrected once the fixtures are in, but once they're in, it'll be too late to correct the floor if he's wrong."

Nothing she's saying surprises me. Gary Teller wasn't even *in* construction until about three years ago. He decided his ability to use a drill made him a construction expert, when his only real skill is getting his name out there to people seeking contractors. I've made a lot of money cleaning up his messes since he got started, if nothing else.

"You want me to take a look?" I ask.

Her gaze grows wary. I'm not sure what people are like where she lives, but she seems to think there's going to be a price to pay for any kindness shown to her. "Why are you being nice to me?"

The question irks me. "Why? You think this is all because I'm trying to get in your pants instead of just being a decent human being?"

She shrugs. "It crossed my mind."

"If I was trying to get in your pants," I reply, rising, "believe me, you'd know. I'm going to call JP and see where he is."

I'm not sure if I'm irritated because she was wrong or if I'm irritated because she's, in some small way, right. I'd have done the shit I did today for almost anyone. The difference is that I *wanted* to do it for her. I wanted to save her fucking stores; I wanted to get her in dry clothes and get her fed. I wanted JP to take his sweet time with my truck.

I'm not going to act on it, but yeah, there's a significant part of me that would like to get in her pants, were she wearing any.

Which, goddammit, she is not.

"You almost back?" I ask JP gruffly.

"Thought I'd give you some more time with your new girl-friend," he replies.

I roll my eyes. "Funny. Hurry up."

He tells me he's heading over. I turn to give Emmy an ETA and discover that she is sound asleep, sitting upright. Long lashes brush her cheeks, her full mouth relaxed and soft, free of its habitual scowl. Her body slowly drifts sideways until she is flat across the couch with the sweatshirt riding up once again. I cover her with a blanket for my own sake as much as hers, and then I text JP and tell him there's no rush.

I don't know why the fuck I like the fact that she's asleep on my couch as much as I do. After years of wondering how the hell to get women out of my place, I've finally found one I wish would stay.

And it's the one who can't wait to get the hell out.

19

EMMY

I wake from an extremely hot dream—Liam fixing things in the grocery store, demanding I remove a piece of clothing for each—to discover I'm lying on Liam's couch, and he's in the chair across from me with his legs spread wide, his head tilted backward, sound asleep.

I'm still turned on from the dream and even the way he *sleeps* is straight out of the alpha male handbook. I can think of a few interesting ways to wake him up, but I already asked if he was trying to get in my pants—his opening to ask *'is getting in your pants an option?'* or to sexily remind me I wasn't *wearing* pants—and instead he got *mad*. His failure to take advantage of the situation was deeply frustrating.

So I guess I'll wake him the normal way—by being a bitch about it.

"Liam," I bark. His eyes flutter open and he raises his head. He looks so adorably confused that I don't have the heart to continue yelling. "I need to get home. If my mom dies, it'll be on my head."

He gives me a sleepy smile. "Most people would have just said they don't want their mother to die."

"I was attempting to make it sound believable."

He laughs as he glances out the window.

"The truck's in my driveway. Get your stuff out of the dryer and we'll go."

I go back to the bathroom and change clothes. Now that I finally get to leave, I'm struck hard by a sudden desire to remain. I move slowly, looking at every object in the guest room.

There's a photo on the dresser that I didn't notice earlier: Liam in a high school football uniform, with his arm around a little girl. That version of him, younger and bright-eyed, reminds me of something, but I can't put my finger on it. Maybe it's whatever bullshit he did when I was in high school, that thing I can't remember, but I guess it no longer matters. Even if he was a jerk in high school, it's pretty clear he has a good side too, and that his good side now far outshines my own.

He's waiting by the front door when I emerge. He looks good, standing there. He's comfortable in his body. The arm that's raised while he holds up his phone to read something is perfectly defined and not because he's flexing like Donovan always does.

It makes it that much more annoying that he isn't trying to sleep with me. And why *isn't* he? He was flirty by text when I was still in New York—did he expect me to look better? Has my personality ruined things? Or was it just what I initially suspected—that he flirts with every female he works with in order to ease his way, and he's eased his way with *me* enough?

"You should tell Julie she left her lipstick here," I say, and though I regret how jealous it sounds almost immediately, I already know I'm likely to make it worse.

He frowns as he looks up from his phone. "Julie?"

"My former designer." *Ick.* There it is again, that note of bitterness the words shouldn't hold. "The one you seduced into changing the tile."

His eyes narrow. "I've never even *met* Julie. Is that what you thought? That the tile thing was some kind of trick on my part?"

His voice is more than a little astonished, with a hint of outrage. For the first time, I wonder if I've made some wild leaps in coming to that conclusion. Maybe I was simply hurt that the guy who'd flirted with me so relentlessly had turned out to be someone who didn't even appear to like me much. Believing he was an opportunist meant I didn't have to examine my own flaws.

"It occurred to me," I say quietly.

"Is that why you fired her?" he asks.

"No. She still made a huge, expensive mistake. Several mistakes." Though it's possible my decision was *influenced* by it a little.

He fishes his keys out of his pocket and opens the door. "I'm not sure what you heard about me, but...I didn't sleep with Julie. And I wouldn't have, even if I'd met her. That's not who I am anymore."

He nods toward the truck, and even as I run for it through the pouring rain, I'm wondering what he meant by *that's not who I am anymore*. Does it mean he *used* to be some kind of lothario and no longer is? Did he find God and decide he was going to save his special gift for marriage?

I sort of doubt it—he's too feral, too relentlessly physical. But if it's true, then I'm deeply envious of the future recipient of all that pent-up sexual energy once he finally lets it out.

Which begs the question: when is he going to let it out? And with whom?

"What did you mean when you said that's not who you are anymore?" I demand as he climbs in.

He frowns as he looks over his shoulder to reverse. "I meant that I used to make the most of being a young, single guy," he says, "and I enjoyed it for a long time, but it got old. I want more now. I don't do one-night stands or short-term."

"You want a wife," I say flatly.

"I fell through a roof over the holidays last winter and broke sixteen bones." He swallows. "It took three days for anyone to realize I was missing because my friends all have their own lives now and no one was surprised when I failed to show up for shit. I don't want work to be the only part of my life in which I'm consistent and reliable. I want to be able to count on someone, and I want someone to count on me."

I wince at the idea of him there, alone.

And there's a small wound, right at the place where my heart would be if I had one. Some pathetic part of me still wants the things he does—to count on someone, to be able to *lean* every once in a while—no matter how hard I try to shut the urge down.

Also a bummer? That there's apparently no chance of turning my final weeks in Elliott Springs into *banging the hot contractor* weeks.

"You'd better clear out all the Dior lipstick and expensive conditioner from your home before you find her then," I say quietly.

"It's my niece's."

I roll my eyes. "This is as bad as your endlessly dying grandmas. Is your niece the little kid who owns those shorts you gave me or an adult wearing a twenty-five-dollar lipstick, because I doubt she's both?"

He gives me a half smile. "Both. I helped take care of her a lot when she was little because my sister was single. And then she basically moved in here for the last few years of high school because she hates my sister's husband."

The evidence of Liam's good side is growing disproportionately. It would have been enough that he scolded my mom for talking about my weight. It would have been enough that he was kind to Snowflake and is willing to restore Lucas Hall at cost. But he also doesn't sleep around, didn't fuck Julie into agreeing to crappy tiles, woke before dawn to save stores from flooding, kept *me* from getting washed off the road, and helped raise his niece.

There's an uncomfortable twinge in my chest. It's possible that the only villain in this car is me.

"You know the problem with your Lucas Hall plan?" I ask.

"That my competitor has billions of dollars and can offer to build the mayor a park while I cannot?"

I'm not sure how he knows about the park—I'd have thought the mayor would keep that quiet. "Well, none of that works in your favor," I reply, "but the real issue is that you're not giving people what they want. Lucas Hall just sitting there doesn't benefit anyone. It doesn't raise property values; it doesn't bring in tourists. It maintains the status quo and humans are wired to hate the status quo. We'd never evolve if we didn't."

"I know," he replies, crossing over the bridge, where water is rushing freely. Thank God he stopped me from driving home. "I had a different plan but it didn't work out."

I cock my head. "What was your plan? No, wait—let me guess. Lucas Hall as some lame museum about the town?"

He narrows his eyes at me. "It wasn't going to *entirely* be a museum."

I laugh, delighted with myself. "I knew it."

"I was going to make it a hotel," he says. "A hotel that featured some of the history of the town in the lobby and hallways. We'd keep the ballroom and offer it freely for all the traditional events the town holds."

My laughter fades. It's a really good idea. It would have brought in money without ruining the town's character. "Why didn't you do it?"

"I couldn't secure the kind of loan I needed. I thought I had it, but when I fell last winter, my investors backed out and the bank said I was no longer a good risk."

I'm trying to convince myself he'd have failed before he's finished the sentence. "A plan like that takes a long time to pull together—"

"I started working on it two years ago," he says quietly, cutting me off. "I thought I'd have longer."

Two years. He put two years into this, and that little phone call I placed to the Santa Clara Office of Building Inspection last winter ruined it all.

Yes, I'm definitely the villain of his story, and he, as of yet, has no clue. I'd at least offer him a "*sorry I ruined all your hopes and dreams*" blow job, but he's apparently not interested in receiving one from me.

He pulls into my mother's driveway and I hesitate before I reach for the door.

"You asked once what I do for fun," I say quietly. "I guess this was pretty fun."

He holds my gaze for a half second and then he smiles. "You're saying it was the best morning of your life, then, and the best meal you've ever had?"

I climb out of his truck. "Slow down, yard boy. It was stir-fry."

His stir-fry wasn't great.

But yeah, it was a pretty good morning. Maybe even one of the best.

MY MOTHER IS on the phone talking about *Harold* when I walk in, clearly irritated by the noise as I start on dinner and talk to Snowflake.

She eats in front of the TV and I eat at the counter before retreating to my room and falling into an exhausted sleep.

All my dreams are about home. About Elliott Springs, when it was still a good place, and Elliott Springs, when it became hell on earth.

I dream about helping my father carry sandbags, about being tripped as I walked onstage.

I dream about Halloween and being back in my little ten-year-old body, which had begun growing squishier and fuller the spring before, when my dad left.

"I'm doing you a favor, fatty," Landon Briggs says as he steals my candy. "Maybe if you lose some weight, your dad will come home."

Landon runs, but in the same moment, across the street, an older boy takes off like a shot, chasing him down. He tackles Landon and marches him back to me.

"Give her the candy," the boy says, glancing from Landon to me. I wonder if he's now thinking what my mother said aloud as I left—that candy is the last thing I need. "Give her your candy too, asshole," he adds.

He wasn't thinking it, then. And I don't want Landon's candy, but I wish I lived in a world where more boys like this one existed, a world where someone was willing to take my side.

I sit up in bed.

Liam. Liam was the kid who defended me.

And he was never the villain—not even at the start.

20

EMMY

My makeup is done and I'm in the middle of getting dressed when someone rings the doorbell.

I pull on my robe and run down the stairs with Snowflake at my heels. Liam stands there, looking even bigger and broader than he did the day before. Maybe it's something about the way he fills the entire doorframe. Maybe it's just that I'm currently wearing panties, a bra, and a pretty sheer robe.

His eyes run over me, his nostrils flaring before he quickly looks away. "Sorry," he says. "You're normally ready by now. I was just letting you know I can drive you down to your car when you want to get to work."

"Oh," I reply, suddenly short of words. "You...don't have to do that."

"Were you planning to hitchhike?"

I roll my eyes. "No. I..."

I was assuming I'd call a car, having forgotten the nearest Uber or Lyft is a solid thirty minutes away. "A ride would be great. I'm almost ready."

I quickly throw on a pencil skirt and blouse and then he

leads me to his truck. "How does anyone climb into this thing?" I ask.

"You just put your foot on the floorboard and hoist yourself up. You did it yesterday."

I huff in frustration. "I wasn't wearing a skirt yesterday. I mean, how the hell do you date in this thing? Do you only go out with Amazons?"

"Maybe I just don't date women who whine about everything," he replies, and before I've even formed a comeback, his hands are around my waist and I'm lifted into the air.

"I don't whine about everything," I mutter as he deposits me in my seat. "And you shouldn't lift someone without even asking first. I'm not a *pet*."

He laughs to himself. "You and I must have different definitions of whining."

He climbs into the driver's seat and glances at me as he looks over his shoulder to reverse. "I assume your mom survived yesterday without you?"

"She was so busy talking about her doctor, the dreamy Harold Sossaman, that I'm not sure if she noticed I was gone. The guy is barely older than me, and she talks about him like their engagement is imminent."

He grins. "On the bright side, if she marries a doctor, you won't have to worry about her survival."

"I thought we'd established yesterday that I'm *already* not worried about her survival. Though I probably should stop saying that aloud in case something does happen to her."

"I've been documenting it," he replies. "So I think you're screwed."

I laugh, surprised to discover we've already reached the bridge. The ride went weirdly fast.

"You can just drop me off at the store," I tell him. "Thanks for the ride. I guess I owe you cookies or something."

He gives me a crooked smile. "From what you've implied

about your cooking ability, plus your thoughts on poisoning competitors, let's just call it even."

I open the truck door and carefully place one heel on the running board. Before I can even lower the other one, he's come around to my side of the car and is wrapping his hands around my waist.

For a moment we are standing face-to-face, too close. My gaze meets his, and my breath holds. I don't know precisely what I want to happen right now, but I know I want it to be *something*.

He sighs. It gusts against my forehead as he releases me.

"Thanks again," I say, stepping away, needing distance. My pulse is racing, and I am not a pulse-racing kind of girl. I want to close my eyes and focus on the memory of that lush lower lip of his. I want to pull him down close enough to sink my teeth into it.

I move toward the store, but he keeps walking with me. "I think I can handle walking away on my own."

"I'm looking at your floor, smart-ass."

He'd be a lot more likable if he wasn't right all the damn time.

I enter and he follows me inside, flipping on the lights and scanning the room with a growing frown. "How much are you paying Gary for this bullshit?" he asks.

"Putting in the floors?" I ask. "About six hundred total. Three hundred and fifty grand for the floors."

"Total footage?"

"Twenty thousand square feet. And before you say anything, yes, I know he's robbing me blind. But I'm on a deadline, and he's the only one who said he could get it done."

"He installed the subfloor wrong," says Liam. "Which means you're stuck with an uneven floor unless you tear all this shit out and start again."

"I don't have time to start again," I growl. "The fixtures are arriving soon."

He rubs a hand over his face, and his shoulders sag. "I'll do it. Get your money back from Gary. If he gives you any shit, talk to me."

"But..."

"Do you have a better option?" he asks.

Well, no. But working in a small space with Liam Doherty feels like a recipe for disaster.

I sigh heavily. "Do you have time to look at the plans? They're back in the office."

He nods. "Yeah, if we can do it over breakfast. Grab the plans, and we'll go down to the diner."

I stiffen.

Paul Bellamy could be there. He could call me "Emmy the Semi" or mention one of the other banner moments of my adolescence—the disastrous homecoming dance, the time they tripped me walking onstage to receive an award and my dress tore in half. *They're* the assholes, yet I'm still the one who feels ashamed, as if I deserved everything they did.

"I hate the diner," I tell him.

He raises a brow. "When was the last time you ate at the diner?"

"High school."

He laughs. "Yeah, I thought as much. I'm sure it's not your fancy New York City bullshit, but you'll live. Come on."

I'm not one to allow myself to be forced into anything by a man, but I find myself shrugging in agreement—perhaps because there's something that feels safe about being by Liam's side. I don't think anyone would say a fucking word with him next to me. No one would call me some mean name from my childhood. No guy would say, "Smile, sweetheart," and if they did, he'd make sure they never did it again.

As soon as we start to walk, he scoots me to the inside of the sidewalk, as if I'm a child who might step into the street. As we continue on, I sense him hovering, watching out for me.

I should resent this. I'm not sure why I don't.

He opens the door to the diner, and it hits me that this man has been taking care of me in small ways and large ones since I was ten, though I doubt he's even aware of it.

I pause in the doorway and glance up him. "I remembered something last night. You defended me when I was younger. This kid was stealing my candy on Halloween and you made him give it back."

He stills, frowning. "I vaguely remember that. I'm sorry I didn't do more."

"Do more?" I ask incredulously as he grabs two menus and leads me to a table. "You not only recovered my candy, you made the kid give me *his* candy too."

He slides into the seat across from mine. "Not then. Later." He glances up only for a moment before his gaze returns to his menu. "I had no idea they all continued to give you such a hard time. I'd have put a stop to it if I'd known."

My face grows hot. I wonder how much he's heard. If he has a full grasp now of how fucking pathetic I was. Maybe that's why he's no longer interested in me the way he seemed to be before we met.

"That's okay," I reply. "If you'd stopped it, I'd have had no enemies to vanquish now and where would be the fun in that?"

He gives me a faint smile and sets his menu off to the side. "So, do you keep a written list of these enemies? Is the kid who stole your Halloween candy when you were ten on there?"

I tap my head. "The list is all up here. And yes, the kid who stole my candy is on there, but he moved to Seattle to become a musician and lives with seven other guys. I can't crush his dreams until he has something I can take away from him."

He bites down on a grin. "How unexpectedly reasonable. What are you getting?"

"Just coffee. I don't eat breakfast." I hate how much I sound like Sandra Atwell right now.

"Come on. Stop acting like you're too good for the place."

"I'm not...ugh...fine," I say, snatching up a menu. "I suppose an egg-white omelet is too exotic for Elliott Springs?"

"Live a little. An extra gram of fat or two won't kill you. Get the eggs benedict. You'll love it."

I do love eggs benedict. I love it on the patio of La Grande Boucherie and served with a mimosa, after I've earned it with a long run. I'm guessing the diner's mayo-based hollandaise won't live up to the memory, but I like these little moments with Liam, when it feels as if I could become someone else entirely —the kind of girl who goes out to breakfast with a guy she likes, who wears his sweatshirt and feels safe enough to fall asleep on his couch.

The kind who orders the eggs benedict and doesn't calculate how many miles she'll have to run to burn it off.

I order the eggs benedict and so does he, and when it arrives...the first bite is ecstasy. "Oh my God," I groan. "It's so good."

His eyes flicker, ever so briefly, to my mouth. "I thought you'd like it."

"Is this what you order every day?"

"No," he says with a grin. "I get the egg-white omelet."

After we've eaten, I lay out the blueprints, and he examines them carefully. "I can rip out what he's done so far and have the subfloor fixed by Friday. I'll place an order for new hardwood tomorrow and we'll have it in by Tuesday. JP is checking on the cost right now."

I blink. For the first time in months someone is actually exceeding my expectations. Who'd have thought it would be yard boy, of all people?

He insists on getting the check though I probably make his annual salary in a week. I run down the narrow hallway to the bathroom while he takes the bill to the register, and I'm thinking I've survived a meal at the diner unscathed when Paul Bellamy steps in my path,

"Brave of you to come back in," he says. "You never know who's making your food or who might have spit in it."

My stomach rolls, but I'm not about to let him see I'm worried. "How sad that threatening to spit in my food is the only power you've got, Paul." *And you won't even have that once Inspired Building closes this place down.*

He storms away and Liam's hand lands on the small of my back. "What just happened?"

I startle, turning toward him. "Just one of the guys from high school continuing to be a dick to me."

"What did he say?" Liam hisses.

I wave a hand at it. "It was nothing. He implied he might have spat in my food. But we had words the last time I was in here so, as I'm sure you can imagine, I wasn't entirely innocent in the whole thing."

His jaw grinds. "That's still fucking unacceptable."

An older woman behind the counter says something to Paul and then walks over to us. "Hey, Liam," she says, "is there a problem?"

Before I can answer, Liam does.

"Jeannie, this is Emerson. Paul just implied he might have spat in her food. He's completely out of control."

The woman looks from Liam to me, and her eyes fill. "My son..." she whispers, "he's got issues. Anger issues. His wife left him—took their daughter. He can't even figure out where she is now. I think he's drinking again. But I'm so sorry he just said that."

Ugh. I can't believe I'm about to defend Paul Bellamy. "It's okay. We went to school together and he wasn't especially nice to me, so I said something shitty the last time I was in here."

She shakes her head. "I'm sorry about high school too. We had our share of misfortunes then as well."

I want to argue that Paul couldn't possibly have had misfortunes to rival my own, but what do I know? I spent a lot of time feeling sorry for myself, thinking losing my dad and being bullied were the greatest pains you could suffer. But there are probably a whole lot of people who'd trade my pain for theirs.

I guess some of the people who once hurt me might be among them.

"The second you hold your child in your arms, it's like your heart is outside of you," she tells me. "Out in the open, ready to be crushed. And children will. Even if they make you happier than you ever dreamed you could be, at some point they will break your heart."

To her, he's still the same gentle, round-faced little boy she once sang to sleep. Paul was lucky to have someone like that. And as badly as I want to hurt him, I'm not sure I want to hurt her in the process.

Getting to know the residents of Elliott Springs, as it turns out, makes *destroying* them less fun than I'd hoped.

MY MOTHER'S physical therapy appointments are so brief that there's no point in leaving. I sit in the waiting room preparing for this afternoon's call with Charles, knowing he'll attempt to find one thing I haven't done simply so he can remind me to do it.

Several texts arrive from Donovan. I ignore them, the way I've been ignoring his calls. He has convinced himself that this fling of ours *meant* something, and though I suspect his dumb crush has very little to do with me, when I picture Liam's dimpled grin, I feel just the tiniest sympathy for Donovan. I think I might have a dumb crush of my own.

"Emerson," says a voice.

I look up and find Dr. Sossaman poking his head around the corner. "Do you have a minute?" he asks.

Great. What has she complained about now? If this keeps up, I'm going to start wearing a body camera to prove my innocence. But if this keeps up, I *shouldn't* wear a camera of any sort because I'm probably going to commit a crime.

"Sure," I say warily, following him to his office.

"Your mother just went down the hall to PT and I wanted to clear the air," he says, sitting behind his desk. "I feel like we got off on the wrong foot last time."

"You mean when you implied that I was abusing my mom? Oh, and that I'm an unemployed freeloader?"

"I wasn't trying to imply either of those things," he argues.

"Weren't you?" I ask. "Because it sure seemed like it when you scolded me about letting her do too much and suggested the situation was to my benefit."

"I'm sorry," he sighs, pinching the bridge of his nose. I almost feel bad for him. *Almost.* "I was just going off what she told me. She said that you didn't appear to work much and that she was ashamed of what you did when you *were* working."

I laugh ruefully. "So you thought I was a sex worker, apparently. To be perfectly clear, I'm in property development. My mom just thinks that the only acceptable jobs are doctor, lawyer, and whatever my brother does."

"I'm glad I made the cut," he says with a sheepish grin. "If it's any consolation, my mom thinks the only acceptable type of doctor is a neurosurgeon, so I'm in the same boat."

"Yeah, but does she go around implying to her friends that you're a prostitute instead?"

He leans back in his chair. "Well, no. Possibly because no one would believe I'd make a successful male prostitute."

I laugh. He's sort of cool after all. "This is the weirdest conversation I've ever had with a doctor," I tell him as I rise.

"It's the weirdest conversation I've ever had with a patient's daughter," he says, catching my eye. "But it was a good weird."

It's only when I think about the conversation much later that I realize my mother's beloved *Harold* was flirting with me.

Man, that would chap my mom's ass if she knew.

21

LIAM

I see a lot more of Emmy now that I'm in the grocery store. I have no clue what it is she does all day, but there are way too many meetings and phone calls for it to be solely about three stores and Lucas Hall. My guess is that they're buying places under different names just so no one worries they'll hold a monopoly on the town.

"Off saving the world again?" I ask when she walks briskly into the store, tucking her phone in her purse.

She arches one elegant brow. "Yes, it's just a future world that looks nothing like the one you currently reside in. I have no idea why you want to preserve it so much anyway. This town sucks. The most exotic food you can get here is pasta."

"You can get some exotic food without tearing Lucas Hall down, you know."

She rolls her eyes. "Why the hell do you even care? It's a disaster, and it's barely even used."

I nod toward the front door. "Come on. I'll show you why."

She gives me a one-eyed, doubting squint before she walks out to the sidewalk and lets me steer her in the direction of

Lucas Hall, the late afternoon light casting a golden light across its roof.

"You associate Cupertino with Apple, right?" I ask as we walk. "You associate Palo Alto with Stanford and Mountain View with Google and surfing with Santa Cruz. But what do you associate with Elliott Springs?"

"Assholes."

I laugh. *Of course she does.* "Okay, you were supposed to say *nothing.* Because no one even knows it exists, but it's actually this amazing town with this old architecture and really cool history. It should be known." We've reached the steps to Lucas Hall. I start up them and she follows. "So anyway, once upon a time, I thought I was going to put it on the map."

"With...how good you are at remodeling?"

"No." Inside the building's lobby, I open a door to the left and pull her in beside me. "Baseball." I nod at the biggest trophy in the room, which has my name on it.

She grins at me. "Why does the fact that you were an athlete make you suddenly seem hot to me?"

"You already think I'm hot."

Our eyes hold for a moment. She hitches a shoulder. "You're okay."

I laugh again. It's better than the flat-out denial I'd expected. "Anyway, everyone was sure I was going to play pro, and I had this dream of being on ESPN and talking about Elliott Springs...This is dumb, so bear with me. But you know how they do those retrospective things about an athlete? Well, I thought that we'd get all this coverage and suddenly everyone would realize what an amazing town this is. That while shit goes wrong all over the world, we've maintained our way of life, and it's working."

I shove my hands in my back pockets, waiting for her derision. I can't even blame her—none of those small-town values I want to preserve did much for her when she lived here.

"But you don't want more people in town," she argues. "You're always bitching about what I'm doing."

"I didn't want Elliott Springs to turn into some big generic city full of apartment complexes and chain stores. I wanted it to be an example of what a town could be. And I know it was a shitty place for you to grow up and this will fall on deaf ears, but I loved being a kid here. I want the childhood I had for every kid alive, including my own. And I thought I might be the one to make it happen."

I'd suggest that I'm going to find another way, but honestly...once they've torn down Lucas Hall and made all our old stores into juice bars, I think the jig will be up.

"Well, there was no guarantee your kids were going to get your childhood anyway. Maybe they wouldn't be athletes. Now instead of getting bullied, they'll at least have interesting restaurants and expensive yoga pants to remember childhood by."

"You sound like the villain in a Christmas movie."

She grins. "Not the villain. The *hero*. Swooping into town to bring you all designer athleisure. And making myself a fortune in the process."

I lean against the wall, my arms folded. "So that's what it's about for you—the money plus the revenge?"

"They're both powerful motivators, yes." She shrugs after a long moment of hesitation. "There's also this guy, Damien Ellis. He..."

"I might be from Elliott Springs, but I read the paper. I know who Damien Ellis is."

"Well, I'm better at Damien Ellis's job than he is, so when he discovers what I did here, he's going to want to hire me, and I'm going to ask him to buy out my company instead and put me in charge. He'll do anything to have me glued to his side when he sees the end result."

They called Damien Ellis '*the thinking woman's favorite bach-*

elor' in the article I read, and Emerson is a thinking woman. Just how closely does she want to be glued to him? My skin prickles at the thought.

Her eyes lift to mine. My jealousy is making me stupid, I know. But something inside me no longer cares. *I'm going to kiss her. I can't not kiss her, so fuck it. I'll sort it—*

Her phone rings. She holds up the screen, and we both see that it's another fucking FaceTime call from Donovan. I reach over before I can stop myself and decline it.

"Why the hell did you do that?" she demands.

"I don't know."

I don't know why I'm doing much of anything anymore.

22

EMMY

Over the weekend, the painful dreams about my childhood are replaced by delicious dreams of Liam.

Liam looking at me in that way he does sometimes, soft and heated both at once. Or getting irritated when Donovan calls, except this time he ends the call and kisses me while he lifts my skirt around my waist.

I wouldn't *actually* let him push my skirt up in the middle of Lucas Hall, but it's a dream, so I allow it.

He is none of the things I want and his behavior is frequently outrageous—*who the fuck ends someone else's call?*—and I can't stop thinking about him anyway, even while I'm the phone with my asshole boss.

"Walk me through," says Charles.

"I am," I reply between my teeth, holding the camera aloft so he can see the theater.

It's irritating that he's even making me do this. I'm not some untrustworthy fifteen-year-old niece he was forced to hire for the summer.

But I'm consoled by the fact that someone at Damien Ellis's firm just looked me up on LinkedIn, I assume at Ellis's behest. Charles can go ahead and enjoy these last moments of authority—he's going to have none whatsoever once I convince Damien Ellis to buy the company out.

I take Charles through the theater where Liam's guys are putting in the concession stand, but he's not interested in that, since it's just for show, and we'll sell it off once we've got our apartment complex.

Outside, I hold up my camera to the street, pointing out the future location of the new restaurant, the gym, and the smoothie place.

Charles, of course, only sees the things we haven't been able to get ahold of: buildings we don't own, people who don't want to sell.

"Diner's still there, I see," he says, nostrils flaring as if he's smelled something unpleasant.

I'm not sure how he thought I'd get rid of it in *three* weeks. Since the camera's facing away from me, I can roll my eyes at leisure. "They own the building and aren't interested in selling."

"Then make them interested," he says. "Or make their lives hell. Call the health board on them. See who they're employ-ing...I bet there's at least one undocumented worker back in that kitchen. Call the news and say you've found glass in your food. I don't care what you do, but get it done."

I won't try to claim that using such underhanded tactics is beneath me, but when I think of Jeannie, it gives me pause. Yes, the diner is an eyesore. It won't be winning a Michelin star anytime soon.

And yes, Jeannie raised an asshole who deserves to have his legacy torn away from him. But I'm no longer sure I want to be the one to do it.

I finish up with the grocery store. I should have started with it since it's going to end this call on a sour note. "I'm going to sit in on the grocery store manager interviews so we don't run into another Nashville situation," I tell him, and he doesn't care, because he's focused on the fact that Liam and his guys are tearing the floor out.

"What the fuck is going on there?" he demands.

"We had an issue," I reply over the noise. "The contractor we hired put the subfloor in wrong. I got most of our money back and hired someone else."

"You mean the contractor *you* hired," Charles corrects.

It's funny, the way my successes are ours and my failures are mine alone.

"So the question," he continues, "is why you hired him and how much money I lost."

We lost a tiny fraction of what I'm making for us, asshole. You lost a single drop in the ocean of millions that will come in through *my* hard work.

"You lost very little, as I already stated," I reply between my teeth, turning my face to the camera.

Charles's mouth pinches. "And you hired him because..."

"I hired him because I live in *New York*, Charles, and as always, I'm working with the information we have on hand."

"We have a lot of money invested in this, Emerson," he says. "And without that apartment complex, it's entirely lost. Don't think for a moment that it's *my* head that will roll if that happens."

He hangs up, no doubt satisfied that he's put me in my place and threatened me sufficiently for the day.

"Inspired Building cares," Liam says behind me. "*Small-town values. Quietly working in the background to preserve Elliott Springs' past.*"

He's reciting my speech to the town council verbatim.

"We can care and be ruthless assholes at the same time," I

reply, too wearied by the call to even fight with him. Dealing with Charles' bullshit always zaps my energy.

He frowns. "Have you had lunch?"

"I don't eat—"

"I'm going to spend an entire day with you sometime just to see what meals you will admit to eating. Come on. You're cranky and clearly need food."

"I'm not cranky."

His mouth opens, and I hold up a hand.

"I'm no crankier than normal, which I suspect you still believe is *excessively* cranky, but I'm comfortable with it."

He smiles at that. It's the smile that does it.

"Fine, I'll eat," I tell him. "But don't expect miracles. I'll still be cranky."

He's still smiling. "I wouldn't want you any other way."

He steers me north of Main Street to Beck's.

"We're not eating at the diner?" I ask.

He glances at me, his mouth drawing into a flat line. "No, because if Paul Bellamy starts any shit with you, it's going to get ugly, and Jeannie has enough problems."

"It's not like I'm going to hit him if he starts shit," I argue. "It would just be a war of words."

"I wasn't worried about *you* turning it physical," he replies.

I fight a smile as we enter the restaurant. I knew he'd defend me.

He leads me to a deck with a spectacular view of the mountains. "I always assumed this place was a dive," I tell him. "I had no idea there was a deck in back."

His eyes hold mine. "You know, you might find that a lot of things here aren't as bad as you assumed."

So far, you're the only thing here that isn't as bad as I assumed.

"Doubtful," I reply.

The waitress takes our order. They don't even have salads on the menu so I get the fried chicken, at Liam's suggestion, which means I'm going to have to find time to run this afternoon.

"I think you want me back at my high school weight as badly as my mom does," I mutter once the waitress leaves.

His brow furrows. "So she wants you to *gain* weight? That's not the impression I got when I helped her inside that day."

I unroll my silverware and place the napkin in my lap. "She enjoys feeling superior. It's a competition for her."

He frowns. "That's...really fucked up, Em."

I sigh. I know this, and yet here I am, still affected by it. "She enjoys telling me I won't be able to keep the weight off, and she loves the way it makes me panicky and desperate to prove her wrong while also making me desperate to eat *more* at the same time." Silence stretches between us. My eyes fall closed. "I can't believe I just told you that."

"It seems like the kind of thing you'd need to get off your chest eventually," he replies softly. "Has it always been like this with her?"

I bite the inside of my cheek. "When my father was there, it didn't matter so much. He kept her in check."

"You're sure you want me to throw out that lockbox of his, by the way? Lockboxes tend to contain valuables."

I roll my eyes. "I don't want anything of that man's. You can toss it."

He leans back in his seat. "Can I ask what happened to him? You seemed upset that day you mentioned you had his shirts, but now it's like you hate him."

I blow out a breath. He must be the only person in the state who hasn't heard. "He was helping some very bad people in San Francisco launder money and, from what I understand, was either going to have to testify against them and die on the way to the courthouse, or refuse to testify and get killed in jail. So he fled the country when I was ten. They know he made it to Mexico, but there was no sign of him after that."

His face falls. "I'm sorry, Emmy. That sucks."

I shrug. "He couldn't have been much of a parent if he left me with someone like my mom, so it's probably not much of a loss."

Except it was a huge loss at the time. And a punch to the gut when I realized he'd used *me* to plot his escape.

It took all my memories with him and tainted them. Did we go to the wharf in Santa Cruz or take the train through the redwoods because he wanted to spend time with me, or was it all a trick? Was he making drops? Was he holding a silent conversation with some really shady guy right over my head the whole time? I'll never know.

Our lunch arrives. It's extra fried—I will have to go for *two* runs to work it off—but it's still delicious. We're nearly through when a woman walks up to us, glaring at me and Liam.

"Hi, Liam," she says, her voice crisp and angry.

My stomach drops. I know he's not going to be sleeping with me, but that doesn't mean I want to meet the women he's slept with instead.

"Hi, uh...."

"Holly," she snaps. "Jesus Christ. It's bad enough you're already out with someone else, but now you can't even remember my name?" Her head jerks toward me. "Enjoy your date. But assume you'll be ghosted when he's done with you."

He groans aloud as she walks away. "I knew I was going to regret that."

It seems his principles are a lot more flexible than he implied. "I thought you were against one-night stands."

He runs a hand over his face with a weary sigh. "I never

even *slept* with her. I kissed her because she made it incredibly awkward not to, and then I walked away."

I should be calling bullshit on this, because no woman gets that pissy over a kiss, but all I can think is this: if he's telling the truth about boycotting flings, he must be *dying* to get laid by now.

"I'm still not sure why you can't have one-night stands. I mean...you've got to miss it a little?"

"Yeah, I'm starting to." There are a thousand words spoken by that soft growl in his voice, by the way his gaze meets mine. It's a growl that says he *really* misses it, that it's been a while and he's in need of some relief.

And the way he's looking at *me* says he wishes I'd offer it.

"But I think it got in the way of finding something lasting," he adds. "When you fuck a girl in the bathroom an hour after you've met her, it's hard to go back to the part where you learn about who she is."

I'm picturing it before I can stop myself—my back against the bathroom door, him pushing my skirt up, pulling one of my thighs around his hip. My eyes flutter closed for half a second, and I squeeze my legs together.

"There are probably some girls you could still fuck in the bathroom," I tell him, the words a soft purr. "Save the tedious real dates for your future wife."

He bites his lip.

He's considering it. And I'm suddenly so unbelievably ready for him to agree. For him to ask me which girl I'd be, for me to say *meet me in the bathroom and we'll see.*

He shakes his head. "Fucking someone in the bathroom is like getting a bunch of small snacks. You're never quite hungry enough for a meal afterward but never quite satisfied either."

I promise you'd be satisfied.

I barely keep the words in, but I've thrown myself at him enough.

He insists on paying the bill again. He's just handed his credit card to the waitress when my phone rings.

"Donovan again?" he asks, scowling.

I shake my head. "Orthopedist."

I bark an annoyed *hello* into the phone. I'm not sure why the hell the office is calling me anyway, unless my mother has made more allegations of abuse.

"Emerson? It's Dr. Sossaman."

My irritation that he's once again using my first name but not his own is like a sharp poke. "Hi, *Harold*," I say pointedly. "You've called my cell. Were you looking for my mother?"

His laughter is nervous. Embarrassed. "No, actually, I was calling to speak to you. There's an art exhibit in San Jose this weekend. I was wondering if you'd like to attend."

"With you?" I ask gracelessly.

He laughs. "Yes, that's generally how it works when someone asks you out."

My eyes widen. "Sorry," I say after a moment. "I just couldn't make the transition fast enough from you being the doctor who thinks I'm abusing my mother to...this."

"I never thought you were abusing her," he says. "But anyway, back to the exhibit—what do you think?"

Under normal circumstances, Harold wouldn't be my type. He looks like the kind of guy who has very soft hands and calls sex *lovemaking*. But the fact that this will piss my mother off makes him a lot hotter than he'd be otherwise. I give Liam one last glance, wishing he was actually an option instead.

"Sure, that sounds great."

When I hang up, Liam is studying me. "You're on a first-name basis with your mom's doctor?"

My tongue pokes my cheek. I'm smiling ear to ear. "I am now. He just asked me out. My mother is going to *hate* it."

His face remains blank. "Are you going out with him because you like him or because it'll piss your mom off?"

"It's kind of hard for me to tease all those emotions apart," I reply. "The second piece is definitely a major factor, but he's not a bad guy."

A vein I've never noticed before starts to throb in his temple. "And how far are you planning to take this date to get back at your mom?"

"Well, I'll have to marry him obviously. That would bother her the most."

His smile is slight. "I'm going to assume that was a joke."

"Yes, that was a joke. Marriage isn't for me. But I haven't had sex in weeks, so that's a possibility."

His pen sinks right through the receipt he's signing. "Seriously?"

I shrug. I definitely won't fuck him if he mentions *love-making*, that's for sure, but I'm not ruling anything out at the moment. "I mean, it's not like *you're* planning to put out. You've made that pretty clear."

A muscle ticks in his jaw. "I have no memory of making that clear."

For fuck's sake, Liam. You just made it clear about five minutes ago.

"At your house. I asked why you were being nice to me and if it was just because you wanted to get laid, and you acted like it had never even *occurred* to you."

"You were questioning my motivations, princess. I can want you fed and dry and not getting swept off the road in a flood simply because those things matter to me. It doesn't mean I've never thought about bending you over the back of my truck and fucking the snide smile off your face."

Gulp. "You know I could fire you for saying that."

"I could countersue for sexual harassment. You just admitted to propositioning me."

I reach for my purse. "That's ridiculous. Why would I sexually harass you when I've got my mother's pretend boyfriend to meet my needs?"

His teeth grind audibly. That muscle in his jaw ticks again.

I'm not sure what I like more: the fact that this whole thing is eventually going to infuriate my mom, or the fact that it's *already* infuriating Liam.

23

LIAM

"You're making that face," says Bridget.

I sigh. "What face?"

"The face you make when you're pissed but you won't admit it."

I nod toward the door and she opens it so I can carry the nightstand out. "I have no idea what you're talking about."

"Yes, that's what you always say when you're pissed and you won't admit it."

I love my sister, but she has a way of needling me like no one else. You'd think on a day when I've driven all the way out here to help her, she'd give this shit a rest. "Maybe I'm pissed because you're accusing me of feeling something I don't feel and refusing to take no for an answer?"

She shakes her head. "Nah. You looked like that before I said anything."

Yeah, I was thinking about Emerson, but I wasn't pissed. I was just...vaguely frustrated. I mean, why the fuck is she actually going out with this guy? Sandra's a shrew who, as far as I can tell, has never been decent to her daughter, so why does Emerson give two shits about her opinion? And Emerson is so busy insisting that Elliott Springs is terrible and she hates marriage, and suddenly she's talking about marrying this guy and settling down here?

I guess she was joking, but it frustrates me anyway.

Or maybe I'm just frustrated by the fact that I don't think she was joking about sleeping with him.

"It's a girl," Bridget says. "Oh my God. Is it Holly? Did you go out with her? Are you fighting? Why are you already fighting? Is it her kids? I know. I should have warned you. The younger one is cute, but the second grader's a little bitch."

"Bridget, you realize that you just described a seven-year-old as a *little bitch*, right?"

She shrugs. "I just wanted you to know that I got it. I don't like that kid either. But it's a phase. She'll grow out of it."

"It's not Holly and I haven't met her kids, nor will I meet her kids. She was nice, but we had nothing in common."

"Why do you need to have anything in common with her?" Bridget demands. "Scott and I don't share a single interest."

I raise a brow, my way of pointing out that she's hardly the poster child for marital bliss—I haven't seen her husband in this house since the holidays.

"Fine," Bridget says. "I've got one more girl for you to meet. Mel. She surfs. And her dad's a builder so she'll get what you do."

I sigh, running a hand over my face. Mel does sound like a better fit than Holly, and she'd sure as hell be a better fit than Emerson.

I just wish...I don't even know what I'm wishing for anymore. I just know that I'm not gonna get it.

I finish helping Bridget move the furniture and return to my place, collapsing heavily on the couch. The same couch upon which I was supposed to have manipulated an earnest conversation into sex with Emerson, apparently.

I pull out my phone, though I know I should not.

So apparently, the way to your heart is either by dating your mother or taking advantage of you during a flood.

THE PRINCESS

I have no heart. But those are the best ways into my pants. Not that you would care, as you've eschewed all premarital pants-entering.

I didn't say I'd ESCHEWED premarital sex. And a guy named Harold Sossaman wouldn't know what to do with your pants, much less what's inside them.

He's a doctor.

An orthopedist.

I'm sure there were female cadavers in med school.

What are you implying he did to the cadavers?

I just meant he was familiar with the parts. But your eagerness to discuss necrophilia with a relative stranger is a red flag. Maybe I'm glad you refused to fuck me in the bathroom at Beck's.

1. You're not a stranger. 2. You're the one who brought up necrophilia, so that's not on me. 3. I don't recall you OFFERING to let me fuck you in the bathroom.

Well, I was but now I'm saving myself for Harold Sossaman. I appreciated what you said about meals versus snacks, however. I might even wait until we've gone through the whole stupid art exhibit before I let him have his way with me.

I'm even more frustrated than I was when I started texting her.

No, actually, Bridget was right...
I'm not frustrated. I'm pissed.

24

EMMY

Harold texts with details. He suggests we meet at his office rather than my mother's house to avoid making her uncomfortable, which is disappointing, as her discomfort was the thing I looked forward to the most.

"You definitely sound like your heart's in the right place," Chloe chides later, adjusting me in tree pose. "Every ounce of excitement I've heard in your voice is related to how mad it's going to make your mom when you use this guy."

"I'm not *using* him," I argue. "I'm giving him a shot. Maybe I'll like him. And it's not like he isn't hoping against hope to use me right back. He's in this to get laid—nothing more."

"And I guess you'll do it just so you can text your mom and rub it in her face?" Chloe asks, going into triangle pose.

"Think how much better every Disney fairy tale would be with that," I reply, following her movements. "Dear Evil Queen, the prince just said I'm prettier and better in bed. Love, Snow White."

"I don't think Prince Charming ever *slept* with the evil queen," Chloe says. "But I hate that you're otherwise correct."

The sun is setting as I walk back down Main Street afterward. Bradley is across the road, glaring at me as she climbs into her beat-up car. I give her the finger and smile as I continue on toward the grocery store, where Liam's truck is now the only vehicle parked in front. I'd normally avoid being seen in my current state, but after an hour of exercise, I'm positively ebullient. I don't care that I've sweated off my makeup, that my hair looks like crap.

I don't even have an excuse to go see him. I'll come up with something.

I push open the door and enter the store, which is growing dim in the dying light, to find him on the floor with a level and a tape measure.

"I can't believe I'm saying this," I announce as I walk in and hop up on the folding table, "but I think you work too hard."

His eyes flicker to my crop top and pants before he returns to his work as if I haven't spoken.

I shouldn't be in here and he is doing exactly what I'd theoretically *want* him to do, but the fact that he's ignoring me is deeply annoying.

"Shouldn't you be on your date?" he finally asks.

Ah, there it is. That's what I wanted from him—a reaction.

"That's not until tomorrow," I reply. "I need a day to get everything waxed anyway."

He hits a button and the tape measure whips shut. He rises and the distance between us seems to shrink a little, though he hasn't moved any closer.

"Are you actually going to sleep with this guy?" he demands. And then he *does* move closer, until we are a few steps apart. I sit up straighter. The air between us is so thick I can't take a full breath.

I don't know if it's tension or anticipation, but I'm already glancing at his belt buckle, already picturing the way his jeans would slide to mid-thigh if I undid it. I bet he'd be hard in seconds, and despite my previous comments about his size, I'm guessing I'd be impressed.

"I'm sure you have some kind of tedious, backward belief that women should wait for marriage while you yourself should not," I reply with a roll of the eyes. "But I don't want to get married, and I'm not going to apologize to you if I want to get laid."

"There's a world of difference between sleeping with a guy to piss off your mom," he says, moving closer still, until my knees are brushing up against his thighs, "and sleeping with someone because you can't stand not to."

He's close enough to push my legs apart and step between them if he wanted to.

He's close enough that he could lean down and press his lips to my neck. His index finger could trace a nipple, skirt along the seam of my yoga pants. I glance down and see a bulge in his jeans that wasn't there a minute ago. I can taste victory on my lips. In this single misguided moment, I want all of it—his hands on me, his mouth on me, his *other* parts on me—more than I want anything else. More than I want Lucas Hall. More than I want revenge. God knows I'd feel otherwise in the morning, but right now...it's this, only this.

"You sure seem like a guy who wishes it was *him* I was about to fuck at an art exhibit."

He places one hand on either side of me, bracing himself against the table, bringing us face-to-face. "I don't need to take you to an art exhibit, princess," he replies. He leans close so his mouth is beside my ear. "We both know I could tell you to get on all fours right now and you'd do it. I could tell you to get on your knees and suck me off. You'd do any-fucking-thing I asked."

The effect is primitive and immediate: my nipples pinch, my core clenches so hard it hurts, and I'm pretty sure I just ruined a pair of panties.

"You have the confidence of a much more financially successful man," I reply, but my voice is weak. I hold still, aside from my hands, which cling to the lip of the table as if they're all that's keeping me from melting into a puddle on the floor. "And if you're so sure of yourself, why aren't you telling me to get on my knees?"

His head lowers. His mouth is so close that I can feel his lips brush mine when he speaks. "Because I refuse to obsess over a girl who's never going to stick around."

He steps away as fast as he moved in, grabbing his keys and walking out the door.

I wait until he's gotten into his truck. And then I scream in frustration.

I DRIVE to Harold's office on Saturday afternoon. The parking lot is empty aside from Harold's BMW, which is the same model as mine. I can't wait to tell my mother Harold drives the car she thought was so *showy*, so much worse than Jeff's.

He climbs from the driver's side as I pull up beside him. He is not quite as cute as I remember. There's nothing wrong with him, but it's possible I was initially so surprised to discover he wasn't *old* that I'd overlooked several things—like the fact that his hair is thinning, and he's kind of skinny, and his shirt is dumb, and mostly that he in no way resembles Liam. I bet this guy has never growled at a woman, has never said *I could tell you to get on your knees and suck me off. You'd do any-fucking-thing I asked.*

None of this will prevent me from going out with him and running straight home to tell my mother, however.

"I hope this is okay?" he asks. "There's really no conflict of interest as your mother's surgery is complete, and she's got no more follow-ups scheduled with me, but I can hand her chart over to another doctor if you're more comfortable with that."

"No, not at all," I say with a forced smile. I hadn't realized until now that my mother wasn't going to have any further appointments with Harold, but that's definitely disappointing. "I'm sure she wouldn't care."

I get in his car, and we head toward San Jose. We talk about the weather, about the art we are going to see, and I decide these two topics bore me about equally. I found him amusing when we spoke before. Now he's an unfortunate combination of anxious and uptight.

"You don't date a lot, do you?" I ask.

He frowns. "Is it that obvious?"

"You seem nervous."

"I'm just getting out of a long-term relationship," he replies. "So I haven't been on a first date in a decade. I feel like I've forgotten what to do."

My stomach sinks. I don't want to be his first date in a decade—I doubt this will be an experience he looks back upon fondly one day. "A decade? That's a long time. What happened?"

I quietly pray that the breakup was his fault.

"We ran into some problems," he says, "and she realized this wasn't what she wanted."

Fuck.

"What kind of problems?" *Please let the problem be that you were cheating on her, Harold. Please let it be that you kept telling her to lose weight.*

His lips purse. "This is probably TMI, but we had some trouble getting pregnant and learned, along the way, that I'm infertile. I'd have been happy to use a sperm donor, but it just changed something for her. Maybe she thought it made me less of a man? I'm really not sure. It's been hard."

Fuck my life. So far Harold is entirely blameless. I hate that for me.

"Our wedding got postponed because of the pandemic, and then she kept postponing. Maybe I should have seen the signs."

Goddammit, Harold. I think you've cut my cruel enjoyment of this whole thing by half.

We arrive at the art exhibit, which is held in some sad, abandoned storefront in downtown San Jose that looks as if it was once a car dealership. The art sucks, and they aren't even passing out champagne—we have to go to a little stand at the back where they sell bottled water instead. If this was a standard Saturday date with Harold, I understand why his fiancée cut bait.

Harold is currently explaining the causes of low sperm motility and assuring me it has nothing to do with organ function. I suppose I could say, "*Let's see how that organ is functioning right now*"—I'm sure there's a bathroom here somewhere—but it would be awkward, given how fucking miserable he is about the whole thing. I decide to hold off.

We get coffee afterward and he tells me about the honeymoon they were going to take—watching wolves migrate through Canada by helicopter—which sounds incredibly expensive and also incredibly lame. I'd have postponed that wedding repeatedly too.

I'm not going to proposition him. The coffee shop is small, and everyone would see us walking into the bathroom. I also think there's a strong possibility that he will cry during sex—he seems like the type. Mostly, I just don't think I can go through with it. I suspect—*thanks, Liam*—I was never actually going to go through with it in the first place.

He drops me off at my car and kisses my cheek without suggesting he'll call, and I should be offended, but instead, I'm swept with relief. It's only in this moment that I realize how deeply I'd *dreaded* this date going further than it did. This might prompt a wiser girl to question whether her need for revenge is more destructive than helpful, but I mostly just feel like I dropped the ball.

When I get home, I make dinner while my mom watches some show where all the realtors are scheming and hot and dressed like expensive escorts. I'd fit in with them perfectly.

Afterward, I'm cleaning up and accidentally let one of the cabinets close too loudly. Closing anything too loudly was enough to get me hit as a kid. Even all these years later, the sound of someone carelessly letting a cabinet slam shut feels like a slap in the face.

And indeed, my mother's head jerks toward me, her eyes narrowed. "Are you being loud on purpose," she asks, "or are you simply that graceless?"

I meet her gaze. This is where I could tell her how I spent my afternoon. This is where I could ruin all her fantasies about Harold. But instead, I keep it to myself. There's power in knowing things she doesn't. And the next time she says, "*You're never going to keep that weight off*" I'll be able to think *you don't know everything, Sandra*, and actually have some proof on my side.

I smile at her. "Cabinet doors occasionally slam, Mom. Feel free to cook the next meal if it bothers you though."

I go upstairs, pulling off my push-up bra as I go. I shimmy out of the tight jeans at the top of the stairs and throw them toward the hamper as I flop onto the bed. So much effort and discomfort and no revenge achieved whatsoever.

Both Liam and Chloe have texted. Because I'm weak, I read Liam's first.

YARD BOY

So, how was your date? Are those wedding bells I hear ringing?

> Do we live in a feudal society where I can be forced to marry? Otherwise, no. Because, as I've made clear. I do not want to marry. I simply wanted to defile the good doctor and rub it in my mother's face afterward, as one does.

> So you're saying you did it.

> I'm saying that it's none of your business. I had needs. You were unwilling to meet them because you want someone who will find you if you fall through a roof.

I wait for him to reply. I'm joking, obviously. Sort of. Though it isn't his business, I *do* have needs he was unwilling to meet, and he *does* want to find someone who will find him if he falls through a roof.

So, I guess I sort of wasn't joking.

And he doesn't reply, which I guess means he didn't find it funny either.

It leaves me feeling restless and unhappy, too much of both those things to possibly fall asleep. So I text Chloe and tell her to meet me at Beck's instead.

25

LIAM

> I need a beer. Who can meet me at Beck's?

HARRISON

Sorry. Out of town.

BECK

Wish I could, but my lovely wife has just informed me that we're watching Love, Actually. Also, I live ninety minutes away.

> Kate wants to watch Love, Actually? Did you marry a different Kate than the one we know?

BECK

Apparently she was joking. We are watching a movie about a female vigilante who traps rapists in a basement and tortures them.

> Okay, that lines up.

CALEB

Fell asleep on the couch. Twins woke us up at 4 today and Lucie's already asleep. Give me fifteen minutes and I'm there.

BECK

> Liam's never getting married if you keep telling him stories like that, dude.

CALEB

> Harrison's getting divorced, and you just married my ex-wife. If that hasn't scared him off, nothing will.

I'm halfway through my first beer when Caleb walks in, unusually disheveled and deeply in need of a shave.

"You look like you're coming off a four-day bender," I tell him.

"I feel like it," he says, pouring himself a beer from my pitcher. "When Sophie wakes up, the whole goddamn house wakes up. She makes sure of it."

Despite all this, though, Caleb radiates contentment. I want that contentment for myself, and I'm highly unlikely to achieve it if I keep pining after Emerson fucking Hughes.

I fucking hate that she slept with him.

You're here to stop thinking about Emmy. So stop thinking about her.

"Still can't believe Kate and Beck eloped," I say. "Is that weird for you?"

He runs a hand through his hair. "It's weird but I've gotten used to it. I'm a little too focused on my own wedding to give it much thought."

I nod. "How are the plans coming along?"

"Getting there. I'm just excited we'll finally meet Harrison's mystery girlfriend."

I know nothing about Harrison's girlfriend, except he's clearly whipped as fucked. He's in LA every weekend, and I don't think she's come up here once. "He RSVP'd for both of them?"

Caleb shrugs. "Not yet, but I assume he'll bring her...I mean, God, he's dated her for like six months, right?"

"Has he even told us her name?"

Caleb frowns. "I'm not sure he did. Anyway, since when are you free on a Saturday night? This is prime time for you."

It's a testament to how little I've seen of my friends this year that he's even asking the question.

"I haven't taken a girl home since last December," I tell him. "I mean, the broken bones were responsible for a lot of that, but...I don't know. It got old. I wasn't willing to make an effort before and now I am."

Caleb waves his hand through the crowded bar. "Then the world is your oyster. If you were ever good at one particular thing, it was making an effort on a Saturday night."

Except that's not what I want. I'm not in the mood to chat someone up, but I think the more precise issue is that what I want is a woman whose eyes flash silver when she's mad, who's prickly at the best of times and often far worse. "My sister sent me the number of some friend of hers she wants to set me up with. The girl surfs, apparently, and her dad is in construction."

"That's perfect for you," Caleb says, "Text her."

He seems relieved, assuming the problem's been solved, but it feels like a mistake the moment I send the text. And why the hell is it Emerson I can't stop thinking about when she's clearly not thinking about me?

Jesus Christ, she pissed me off today. I can't believe she slept with him. I really can't.

"For a guy who just solved all his problems, you sure don't seem any happier," Caleb says just as Emerson walks into the bar with a friend. Of all the fucking bars, she had to choose this one.

"I didn't solve every problem," I say with a sigh, watching her.

Her hair is down and she's in jeans and a very fitted tee. I've seen her in less—*thank you, yoga*—but I don't necessarily like how many other people are seeing her as she is now. I don't like the way the crowd parts for her, the way men continue to watch her after she's walked past. I don't like the fact that in a few weeks, she'll be gone, and there will be no one here to torture me at all.

Caleb laughs, his gaze following mine. "Who's the girl?"

I'm not even sure how to describe her. "What word would you use for a woman who's awful and trying to destroy everything you care about, but who you also are more than a little obsessed with?"

"Nemesis or future wife," he says. "It could go either way."

I turn away from the bar, draining a second beer. "Well, I guess I know which one she is since she doesn't even want a relationship, much less marriage."

Caleb laughs. "Be that as it may, based on the way she's looking at you, it sure seems like she wants *something*."

26

EMMY

D id I know Liam would be here? Of course not. I'm not psychic.

Just because it was his friend's bar and he told me he's here a lot doesn't mean there was any *guarantee* that I'd run into him.

And I don't care that he's here anyway. I have bigger fish to fry, because Chloe just pointed out some idiot named Troy, who's eye-fucking *me* within an inch of his life.

Oh, and he happens to be Bradley's boyfriend.

"Bradley *Grimm*?" I confirm as the bartender delivers our drinks and when Chloe nods, I sigh. I've got an Ivy League education, an investment portfolio any retiree would envy, yet my best means of revenge once again requires offering my vagina to a man I don't even *like*. Not really a step forward for womankind, but we all do what we must. "Well then, you may be leaving here alone, then."

"Okay, wait," Chloe whispers. "So what did Bradley do?"

"It's a long story," I say.

Mostly though, it's just a story I don't want to tell. I was so goddamn pathetic. So desperate for someone to date me or befriend me that I'd have believed anything. And so I *did* believe anything, and I'll never live down the shame of it.

The silver lining is that I'm now prettier than Bradley, wealthier than Bradley, better employed than Bradley. Oh, and I'm about to acquire her boyfriend, so there's that too.

Chloe waves Troy and his friends over and introduces us. "You must be new around here," Troy says, "because I would have noticed a girl who looks like you."

Troy is the kind of attractive that won't age well, and he's obviously a cheater. I wonder if it would hurt Bradley more *not* to interfere, but no—I want to see the look on her face when I tell her. She needs to realize her actions had consequences.

"My mom lives down here," I say. "She had knee surgery, so I came back to help her out for a while."

He leans closer. "Wow, so you're the kind of girl who comes home to take care of her sick mom. What a keeper."

Yes, that's so me.

"Now I just need to convince you to stay," he adds.

I bite down on a smile. "How exactly do you plan to do that?"

"I got all kinds of ways, baby," he purrs.

Ick.

He finds us a table. I sip my beer while Chloe tells us some story about peeing herself during yoga and try very hard to pretend Liam isn't here, isn't sitting across the room like some kind of really hot priest who inspires lust while making you feel guilty about that lust at the same time.

When our first and second beers are done, Chloe goes to the dance floor, Troy goes to the bar to get another round and I go to the bathroom. I reapply my lipstick in the mirror, noting with genuine satisfaction that I don't at all look like a woman certain she's about to make a huge mistake.

And then I step out of the bathroom and Liam waits—all

long-legged ease, broad-shouldered, and so pretty. It just pisses me off.

I walk past him, but his hand wraps gently around my bicep to stop me.

"Why are you throwing yourself at Bradley's boyfriend?" he demands. "Was sleeping with your mom's doctor not enough?"

I roll my eyes. "I didn't sleep with anyone. And I'm not throwing myself at that guy. If you haven't noticed, *he's* doing all the work."

"This is all about Bradley, isn't it? That's why you're putting in the grocery store...just another of your grudges."

It sounds petty as hell when he describes it like that, and it's not petty at all. "Don't you ever tire of trying to be my moral compass? Enjoy your search for a soulmate and stop judging me for the fact that I don't want one."

I pull, but he doesn't let go, instead turning me so my back is to the wall and he is in front of me, his hand on my hip both heavy and light at the same time, crowding me in.

"I wasn't judging you, princess," he says, stepping closer. His mouth drags from my temple to my cheek, warm, light as air. I give a tiny, involuntary gasp. "I just want you to stop giving away something we both know ought to be mine."

I arch toward him involuntarily, wanting more. Trying to breathe in the smell of his soap, wishing I could glue myself to him when I should be walking away.

"I thought you wanted meals, not snacks," I whisper. I'm breathless, my pulse ticking fast in my throat.

"I think you can be both," he says, his lips close enough to brush mine. "And I know that's crazy. But I can't seem to stop thinking it."

"I won't be, Liam," I reply. "I'm definitely leaving, and this isn't what I want."

His hands mold to my waist as he presses against me, as his mouth lands fully on mine—warm, heavy, full of need. His whole body is taut, restrained, but barely so, and I gasp for air as his tongue tangles with mine.

I've been kissed more times than I can count, and this is better than all of them. A mix of contrasts: hard and soft, sweet and dirty, a beginning and an end. This isn't a requisite step in some ten-point plan to get me in bed—it's a kiss just for its own sake.

His nostrils flare as he steps back. "Don't go home with him, Emmy," he warns, and it should annoy me, but that hint of fever and possession in his gaze before he walks away makes my knees weak instead. By the time I recover myself enough to follow, he and his friend are walking out of the bar.

"I was scared you weren't coming back," says Troy when I return to the table and take my seat next to Chloe. He has the same face and the same smile and the same body, and he is no longer who he was before. He was chips and now he's sandpaper, so unpalatable I can't imagine what I saw in him.

But I'll be damned if I'm going to let Liam win. I'm not. He's not ruining this for me, with his bullshit about meals instead of snacks.

"I ran into a friend. Not a friend," I correct. "A colleague."

I smile, but my heart is no longer in it. Chloe's boyfriend texts to say he's home, and as she gathers her things to leave, her eyes dart from me to Troy. "Are you gonna be okay?"

"Yeah," I reply. But I'm still shell-shocked by that kiss. I certainly hadn't expected it, hadn't asked for it...but I've been wanting it. For months, I've wanted it.

I think you could be both.

Fuck.

"Actually," I say, grabbing my purse, "I'll walk out with you."

Troy pleads with me to stay, and I tell him maybe another night. As I walk out of the bar with Chloe, I'm angry at myself for blowing this chance to punish Bradley.

And for the second time in a single day, I'm also sick with relief.

This dress doesn't fit.

I used my babysitting money to buy it in a store that was full of other girls shopping together, or shopping with their moms. Beside me, on the other side of the partition, I could hear a mother fretting over the fit of the dress her daughter was trying on. "You look beautiful, hon, but why don't we go up a size and have it taken in? That's better than wearing a dress that's too tight all night—believe me." And the daughter was inexplicably annoyed. She'd had no clue how lucky she was to have someone who cared enough to put in that much work, who'd come with her to shop, who could offer an opinion that wasn't laced with small barbs.

Me? I didn't even tell my mother I was coming tonight. It was easier than enduring her questions, her derision.

And now I'm standing on the steps of Lucas Hall in a dress that's way too tight because it was the largest size they had, waiting for a boy I really wanted to impress—which seems less likely by the second, with the way I'm sweating.

My phone buzzes in my hand.

> JAMES
>
> I'm so sorry. We're finally off 280. My mom says we should be there in about twenty minutes.

My shoulders sag. God, another twenty minutes? It would be one thing if I could have waited at home, but no...instead, I'm on full display in front of everyone, stuffed into this dress, my feet pinched by these cheap high heels. Everyone who walks past stares as if I've wound up here by accident. Of course they do. They can't believe for a fucking minute that Emmy the Semi could get a date.

> I'm sorry it's been such a long drive. I can't wait to see you!

JAMES

> It's all worth it. I can't believe it's finally happening. I'm so fucking nervous.

> Same. We'll be nervous together.

I WAKE SWEATING, as if I'm still tugging at that tight dress, still waiting, still trying to ignore everyone laughing as they pass.

And then I'm bitterly disappointed in myself.

I had my shot last night, and I didn't take it. All because... what? Because Liam kissed me? Because he asked me not to? It's easy to take the moral high ground when you're not the one with an axe to grind. It's easy when you're not the one who wakes up drenched in sweat from terrible memories.

Would Liam ever truly understand what my life was like back then? That I spent every day being ridiculed and taunted, and then came home to a mother who was even worse?

Of course he wouldn't. He thinks this whole thing with Bradley and the rest of them is just some petty bullshit on my part. He doesn't understand that my past is like a scarlet A I'm forced to wear, and the only way I right the balance is by making sure all of *them* are forced to wear their shame too. One day, when they realize how they've caused their own suffering, none of us will be laughing. But not if I keep letting Liam get his way. Not if I keep letting him stop me from punishing Bradley and taking my mother down a peg.

And maybe it's all a trick. Maybe this has been a long con on his part, one he began late last winter, to convince me not to take Lucas Hall. He's slowly and insidiously bending me into someone I'm not.

I close my eyes, though, and think of that kiss, of the way his lips pressed harder and his hands staked a claim. I press my fingers to my mouth.

I think you can be both, he said. I shouldn't believe a word of it, but it felt real. It felt really, really real.

But I've thought that before, haven't I? And I've always come to regret it.

Liam is not going to ruin this for me. I'm done letting anyone in this town trick me into believing impossible things.

~

HE'S in the backyard early on Monday, getting set up.

I follow Snowflake out to the deck, tugging my sweatshirt down over my sleep shorts.

He drops the plywood he's carrying and his gaze meets mine. There's something in the way he looks at me—something gentle and feral at the same time—that makes me wish I was a different girl.

For a moment, I want to abandon this entire plan.

"I slept with Troy," I announce. "A tiger can't change her spots."

My stomach drops at the flash of pain in his eyes. Some small voice in my head—a child's voice—screams at me to take my lie back.

But instead, I just walk into the house, emptier than I was when I left, with a ridiculous desire to burst into tears when things with Liam were never going to work out anyway.

They really weren't.

27

LIAM

On Monday, we cut out of work early for Mac's bachelor party. As the most whipped groom who has ever lived, he insisted on nothing raucous: no strippers, and no females whatsoever. We've spent the day giving him shit about it—one of the guys gave him a tiara and an "*I'm the bride!*" sash, and he wore them with pride all day long—but the truth is that I suspect I'd be the same way with the right girl.

I bet, with the right girl, I'd look exactly the way Mac does tonight: as if he'd just as soon be home with his fiancée, as if a part of him is eager to put all this behind him.

And that right fucking girl is never going to be Emmy.

That kiss was all I'd thought about from the moment it ended until I saw her on the deck Monday morning. And I'd begun thinking other things too. I'd begun thinking that she felt it, the way it was different with us. That she and I'd had a connection all along, one we didn't have with anyone else.

I still think it. But she's made it pretty fucking clear we won't be exploring it.

It's on the late side Wednesday when she finally walks into

the grocery store. I can tell just by her stride, the precise *clip, clip, clip* of her heels, that she is all business today. Our eyes meet, and she looks at me as if I'm a stranger and walks past to her office.

"It takes me less time to get off on Pornhub than you just spent watching her walk across the room," JP says.

"We've discussed this before, JP. Being able to finish quickly is nothing you want to brag about."

"What's up with you two anyway?" Mac asks. "You act like you hate each other, but it's all lingering glances and romantic tension whenever you're in the same room."

I grin. "Cassie's been making you watch *The Notebook* again, hasn't she?"

"Cassie's never stopped making me watch *The Notebook*. I know that goddamned movie by heart at this point."

"Nothing's up with us," I tell him. Nor will it be. It's done. I'm done with the whole goddamned thing.

I'm wrapping up for the day when she emerges from her office, striding out to the sidewalk as she eviscerates someone on the phone. It's only the two of us in the store when she walks back in. Her gaze falls to the toolbox in my hand, and I somehow sense her displeasure. "Early day for you."

I glance at my watch. "It's after six."

"I wasn't complaining," she says. "You just normally work later."

I grab my keys. "I have plans."

She hops onto the same table where she sat last week to bait me. Just as she did then, her legs cross, her foot swinging playfully. "Oh, *plans*. How exciting. Is it a date?"

She's smiling, but there's a glint to that smile, as if she's hiding a knife behind her back as she asks.

"What was it you said to me the other night?" I ask. "Oh yeah. That's none of your business. But yes, I have a date."

A date I desperately wish I hadn't made.

She leans backward on her palms. "Ah, yes, the hunt for your soulmate. I'm curious about this actually...Do you have other requirements or is it mostly just someone who will notice if you fall through a roof?"

"Well, I'm also looking for a woman who doesn't fuck random men to get back at her mother or a high school enemy, but that goes without saying for most people."

She frowns. "Still judging me, then."

I grab my toolkit. "As I think I mentioned on Saturday, I wasn't judging you."

"It would never have worked out with us," she says softly. I hear a question in her voice, as if she's hoping I'll argue.

I walk out the door. "You made sure of that, didn't you?"

TALKING to Melanie might have come easily a year ago. Now, it's a lot like craving a steak and being forced to choose from a vegan menu. Even the best dish won't suit.

And unfortunately, I came here, I suspect, hoping to find a different version of Emerson—a girl who's sharp, funny, and tough, and who has an ass that won't quit—but a version of her who surfs and wants to settle down, a version of her who wouldn't be quite as hard to win.

And Melanie is not that.

She is chatty, but she isn't amusing. She has lots of opinions, but I suspect she wouldn't stand by a single one of them if pushed. And she's spent the entire dinner trying hard to sell herself, trying to tell me how sought after she is, how well-traveled she is, how generous she is...and the more she sells, the less I'm interested in buying.

The entrees have just arrived, and I'm already wondering how soon I can escape.

"Bridget said you surf?" I ask.

"I like to go down to Costa Rica," she says. "That way I'm contributing to their economy too. So, you know, I visit all the shops and I make sure I tip—that kind of thing. I just think it's important to give back."

"So you don't surf locally?" I ask, politely restraining the urge to suggest that shopping in Costa Rica isn't the same as *contributing*.

"I went down to the wharf once in Santa Cruz," she says.

The wharf is where you *learn* to surf, which tells me Melanie *has* surfed, but does not actually surf. And why the fuck does it matter anyway? When Emerson said, "*I'd look too good in a bikini. I'd be a distraction*," I'd laughed.

Five minutes ago, she was telling me she's thinking about volunteering to play with the dogs at the animal shelter. "*They just break my heart, you know? I want to adopt every single one of them.*"

Before that, she was telling me how she can't drive through San Francisco anymore because all the homelessness makes her cry.

I'm guessing Melanie has never spent several hours unloading sandbags without telling everyone she did it. I bet she's never quietly cuddled a dog she purports to hate without talking about how much it made her want to cry. I bet she's never gotten someone fired to protect a colleague.

And it isn't necessary that she do those things. But with Emerson, I liked the way it felt like I was peeling back layers, getting closer to the sweet spot, while Melanie's outer layers are already too sweet, the sort that makes me think what lies beneath them has probably begun to decay.

Melanie says she can't surf at the wharf anymore because of an ex who's obsessed with her, and then says Bridget told her I used to surf with Luke Taylor before he joined the tour. Before I can even confirm this, she starts telling me how she saw Luke and his wife walking into a restaurant once in Hawaii, which she somehow spins into a fifteen-minute story about her and her friend waiting in the parking lot for Luke and Juliet to finish dinner.

While I'm pretending to listen, my phone vibrates. I wait until she's chugging her wine and asking the waiter for another to glance at it.

> THE PRINCESS
> How's your date?

I wonder if Emmy's down at the bar, doing her level best to ruin someone's night. I swear to God, she's ruining mine without even being in the same section of town.

Stop thinking about Emmy.

"So tell me about your job," says Melanie, who seems to have finally exhausted the topics of charities she cares about, exes who are obsessed with her, and friends of mine she's stalked.

It's too broad a question to reflect any actual interest, and I'm saved from replying by some acquaintance of Melanie's who walks over to the table.

I glance at my phone as they chat and discover another text from Emerson.

> THE PRINCESS
> Is she pretending to be fascinated by your job yet? You should pull out your little hammer. That might interest her.

> It's not all that little. Which I assume you know. I've caught you looking in that direction more than once.

> I can't believe you're texting me about your dick size when you're on a date with someone else.

> You STARTED that conversation.

> Yes, but a gentleman would have refused to participate in it.

She's right. I'm going to stop. I put my phone away just as Melanie's friend leaves, and I spend the rest of the meal listening to Melanie talk about how much she hates cancer.

I sort of thought *everyone* hated cancer.

Melanie goes to the bathroom while I pay the bill. Against my better judgment, I pick up my phone again.

> So, is there a reason you're texting me about my dick on a Wednesday night?

THE PRINCESS

> Maybe it's because I've been wet for hours thinking about how you might put it to use.

> Bullshit. You're just trying to mess up my date.

> Seems to me that you're the one messing it up by texting another woman, but I can provide proof. Hang on.

I wait, my whole body tied in knots, to see what she'll say next. I know she's just trying to bait me, but it's fucking working anyway.

There's nothing I want in the entire world right now more than a glimpse of her proof.

Melanie comes out, and I tuck my phone away before I walk her to her car. "I had such a nice time," she says. "It's cool that we both surf."

"Yeah," I say, and I'm already edging away. "Thanks for coming out."

Her smile starts to fade as she realizes the date didn't go so well after all. I'm being rude, I guess, but I can't bring myself to care. I wave to her and turn toward my truck, already pulling out my vibrating phone.

Emerson's sent a photo—I see a long leg stretched above her desk and suspended from one heel—a thong.

A thong with a tiny wet spot dead in the center.

Fuck.

She's at the office right now in those fucking heels with her panties off.

And I'm tired of being toyed with.

28

EMMY

I've never sent a nude in my life, but this photo could prove pretty embarrassing too. And the bigger question is why I sent it.

Why am I fucking up his date? Liam's a good guy. He deserves some sweet, devoted girlfriend who makes sure he hasn't fallen through a roof at the end of each day. Why does it bother me so much when I have no intention of being sweet or devoted myself, and I work way too many hours to consistently monitor his roof issues?

I don't know. But I've had a pit in my stomach since he said he had a date, and that pit grew immeasurably when he walked out the door this evening as if he'd given up on me. I just wanted to fight with him a little. I wanted to give that string between us a little tug to see if he was still holding the other end.

And he was.

I open up the laptop and begin watching more of the interviews for the grocery manager's position. While I'm not normally involved to this extent, everything in our attempt to win Lucas Hall has to be perfect. I refuse to throw it all off track because some new manager with a snotty attitude is making us look bad.

I've watched the interviews of four lackluster candidates when the front door wooshes open.

I grab scissors and have barely climbed to my feet when Liam enters the office. His eyes are black in the dim light. There's not a hint of a smile on his face.

"Come here, Emerson," he says. "And put down the scissors."

I walk around the desk slowly. "Why are you in my office?"

"You just sent me a picture of your panties hanging off your heel. Why do you think I'm here?"

A shiver runs through me. As many times as I've fantasized about this, I'm also not prepared. I guess maybe I just never thought he'd give in.

"Right," I say dryly. "We've played this game before—the one where you act like you're going to do something and then just walk away."

He closes the distance between us, grabs my hips and spins me toward the desk, pressing his mouth to my ear, his chest to my back. "No, this time I'm going to give you exactly what you want." His hand slides over one breast and my nipple tightens beneath it. "You want me to treat you like a whore, Emerson?"

This is where I'd normally lash out and insist that there's nothing whorish about women wanting exactly what men do. Except...I like it. I don't want him to take it back. I want him to use me until I can't stand straight and walk away without a word.

His palm wraps around my throat. "Admit it."

I swallow. "Yes."

He sets his keys and his wallet on the desk beside me. "Then bend over." His palm presses between my shoulder blades until my face is against the monthly desk calendar and my ass is in the air.

A cool breeze hits my legs as he lifts the skirt around my hips.

"You should have left the panties off," he hisses.

And then he tears them, as if they're made of paper. I should object to that, too, but instead it has me absolutely soaked.

His hand slides between my legs and air hisses between his teeth when he discovers the effect he's already had. As his fingers circle my clit and slip inside me, it's as if my tissues are swelling around him, tightening to grip and keep him right where he is. He very clearly has a lot of experience at this, but it's more than that. It's that I've been craving this, from him and no one else, for a very long time.

His fingers continue to circle and press until my gasps take on a rhythm, until my hands cling to the far edge of the desk to keep me upright. That's when his hands leave, and I hear the tearing of foil.

The head of his cock pushes against my entrance. He's not even inside me and I can feel the fullness of it, the way I will have to stretch to accommodate him. He thrusts inside hard, without warning.

"Fuck," he whispers, perhaps more to himself than me. His palm presses flat to my back as he thrusts again.

I groan aloud, and I don't know if I'm complaining or begging him to continue—because it's both. It's too much, too tight, and unbelievably good at the same time. He moves faster, and I grip the desk for dear life.

I'm so fucking close and we've barely started. "Liam," I warn, my voice low and breathy, swept up as my stomach tightens and a charge moves down my spine.

"Don't you dare come, Emmy," he growls. "Don't you fucking dare."

"I can't, I can't...oh, God." I cry out as I let go, my eyes squeezed shut, clamping down around him until he's all I can feel.

"Goddammit," he says and then he thrusts faster, finishing with a low groan. "Fuck."

My eyes remain closed as he hovers above me, hands pressed to the desk, milking the last of his orgasm.

My thighs bite into the edge of the desk, my legs strained from leaning over the way I am...but I wish we could stay like this for a minute—his harsh breaths on my neck, his chest rising and falling against my back, his hand still gripping my hip. I don't want it to be done, whatever this was.

He pulls out and starts tying off the condom. I push my skirt into place, so wet that moisture drips down my inner thighs as I stand. It bothers me that he isn't meeting my eye. That he's getting dressed again as if I'm not even in the room.

"I didn't sleep with Troy," I say quietly.

He glances up, his hand still on the zipper of his jeans. A muscle in his jaw clenches. "Why'd you tell me you did then?"

I swallow. "Because you had unrealistic expectations of me. You were acting like this was going to turn into something, and it's not. I don't want to be someone's girlfriend. I'm not even staying."

He steps toward me, tucking a finger in the waistband of my skirt to tug me against him. He presses his mouth to mine. "Don't lie to me again."

"I'll lie to whoever I want. You don't own me."

He shakes his head. "Em, I know I don't own you. But you and I have texted daily for months. Asking you not to lie is a pretty minimal request. Now get your stuff and I'll walk you out."

"I'm still working," I argue.

"You can get your shit or I can sit right here until you're done, but it's not safe for you to be walking to your car alone this late."

I release a heavy exhale. "For fuck's sake, Liam. You're *already* acting like I'm your girlfriend."

"I was also going to wait for you back when I was calling you a whore," he replies. Our eyes meet. "You know you loved it, so don't complain about that too."

I fight a smile as I turn to grab my laptop. "It was okay."

"That's high praise from Emerson Hughes," he replies, elbowing me.

We walk out together, and he locks the door before we go to the driver's side of my car. "I'm not going to kiss you," he announces. "That way, you won't accuse me of trying to be your boyfriend."

"Good," I reply.

He bites down on a grin. "We both know you want me to, though."

I roll my eyes as I climb into the car, but I feel a little incomplete as I drive away.

I guess, perhaps, I wanted him to.

29

EMMY

I'm awake early the next morning. I feel bruised in the best possible way—there's an ache between my legs, my lips are swollen to the touch—and I'm also steeped in regret.

Regret that it's already done and can't be repeated, regret that I did it and now things will be awkward as fuck until I leave. For my remaining time in Elliott Springs, there's going to be this weird tension, and anytime I demand something of Liam, he'll have that look on his face—the one that says, "I've seen your vagina."

And I also still have to make it clear we won't be doing it again...more unnecessary awkwardness.

I take Snowflake into the yard when I get up, throwing her a stick in the damp grass. I picture him walking around the corner—clean-shaven, fresh from the shower, T-shirt clinging in all the right places. I can almost smell his soap. I can almost feel his pec beneath my palm as I place my hand on his chest and tell him it's done.

But he doesn't arrive and once there are guys working in the yard, he's not among them. Later, I get to the store and he's not there either.

"Liam had to go down to Santa Cruz to give an estimate," Mac says. "He'll be by later." There's something gentle in his smile that worries me, as if he knows about last night and thinks Liam's letting *me* down easy when it's actually going to be the reverse.

This is all so much more aggravating than it needs to be.

I have a long teleconference with the company bringing in the spin studio, and then meet a designer in person to show her the space. When I return, Liam is there, looking over plans with JP. I wait for him to shoot me some lingering glance, smile at me in a new kind of way, but he doesn't even look up from his drawings.

I go back to the office, itchy and discontent, as if I've had too much caffeine but have no place to burn the energy. I mean, this is excellent news, the fact that he's not making this into a big deal. We can return to our professional relationship with no messiness whatsoever. I slide into my chair, tuck my purse in a drawer and lean back, remembering last night. How firm his lips were and how every single inch of him was hard. How he'd barely touched me before I was ready to explode.

I've nearly convinced myself we could afford to do it twice —I mean, things are *already* so awkward, it would be hard to make them worse—when Liam walks in, filling the entire frame of the door with well over six feet of lean muscle. Mentally, I'm ten steps ahead. I'll tell him to lock the door and that this time I want him on top. I'll tell him I'm on the pill if he doesn't have any condoms. Maybe *I* have condoms? I slide my purse toward me to check.

He sets a hard hat on my desk. "We're working in the room above you," he says. "If you're gonna sit in here today, wear that."

And then he walks right back out the door. As if last night

didn't matter to him at all. And of all the ways I imagined today could have gone, this was not among them.

For the rest of the afternoon, I can hear him upstairs, yukking it up with JP and Mac—not a care in the world. And by the time I get to Chloe's studio, I'm pissed that this day has gone exactly the way I'd hoped it would.

Chloe's eyes widen. "Uh-oh. What happened?"

"What makes you think something happened?" I ask, scowling as I unroll my mat.

"You can either tell me now or I can lead you through the most physically painful yoga class of all time, and you'll tell me at the end. You're a chatterbox once you're exhausted."

Ugh. She's probably right. "I slept with Liam last night."

Her eyes gleam. "Wow. Was it amazing?"

I shrug. "It was okay."

"You're a goddamned liar, Emerson Hughes. There's no way sex with that man was just *okay*."

"Fine, it was good. But nothing's going to come of it. He's my employee..."

"Not really."

"And I'm moving."

"You don't have to move."

Oh yes, Chloe, I absolutely do. For my own sanity, if nothing else. "It's just a bad idea."

"Okay, so what's the problem? He doesn't seem like the type to break into a home and boil a rabbit on your stove. Just tell him you're not interested."

"I would, if he'd even look at me," I sulk, copying her as she gets into warrior pose. "He's barely acknowledged my presence today."

She starts laughing. "Now I get it."

"Now you get *what*?"

"The problem isn't you having to fend Liam off—the problem is that you don't *have* to fend Liam off."

"Well, it's bullshit!" I cry, throwing my hands in the air and falling out of the pose entirely. "You don't just fuck someone you work for the way he did and pretend it meant absolutely nothing."

"So, *you're* saying it meant something."

"Not to me, it didn't. But it should have meant something to him."

She grins. "So just to clarify: the reason you're upset is that the guy you *don't* want to go out with appears to not want to go out with you either."

I roll my eyes. "You're oversimplifying it."

She laughs. "No, I'm not. It really is just unbelievably simple. You *like* him and you wanted to be secure in the knowledge that he likes you while you continue to fend him off."

"I just think it's shitty to imply you like a girl in order to get laid and then ignore her."

She is bent over but grins at me from between her legs. "Quick question, hon: did you at any point last night remind him that it didn't mean anything?"

I bend over. "Possibly," I mutter.

"So he's doing exactly what you asked him to do?"

I groan. "I've had enough of this conversation. Just give me the worst workout ever."

Chloe is laughing as she goes into downward dog.

When I get home, my mother is on the couch watching *Love is Blind*. I run my hands through Snowflake's fur and endure her licking my face while a sparklingly pretty girl onscreen attempts to converse with the dullest man of all time, a man she apparently believes she's in love with though he's still hidden from view—a perfect example of why any semi-intelligent female should write relationships off entirely. Because you otherwise risk becoming someone so desperate for connection, you persuade yourself to love a guy who can't string four consecutive words together without an awkward chuckle.

Love means handing over your power and your sanity, and it never lasts anyway, so what reasonable person would bother?

"You're going to be mighty unhappy when you meet him in real life," my mother says to the TV.

It's possibly the first thing we've ever agreed on.

"She ought to be mighty unhappy already," I reply. "That guy's an idiot."

My mother turns to me, the look on her face withering. "That's your problem right there, Emerson. You think you're too good for everyone."

Pot, meet kettle. The only person alive that my mother doesn't think she's too good for is Jeff, her mini-me.

"I don't think I'm too good for everyone," I reply, "but I'm sure as hell too good for that guy."

My mother smirks. "You'll never be happy. You'd have met someone by now if you were going to, but if it hasn't happened at age twenty-eight, it never will. You're sure not going to get *better looking* over the next decade."

It's a conclusion I'd already come to myself, a conclusion I'd embraced, but hearing it from her mouth makes it sound truer than it did before, and I guess some part of me still hoped it was an outcome I'd evade—that despite my terrible attitude and personality and general unloveableness, some man would see a good thing inside me. And that he'd push his way in.

"Do you have a point?" I ask between my clenched teeth.

"My point is that you'll die alone and miserable, and it's entirely your own fault."

I let the dishes fall into the sink with a crash. "You think you're not dying alone and miserable, *Sandra*?" I ask, my tone as scathing as hers. "You think Dr. Sossaman wants to marry a woman decades older than he is?"

My mother's eyes narrow. "*I* have Jeff and Jordan. I have *friends*."

"Yes," I reply as I walk away, "it's clear how involved Jeff and

Jordan and your friends are. They've really been beating down the door, haven't they?"

I climb the stairs to my room, feeling worse than I did when I came home. Because as bad as she is, I'm the one who just reminded a senior citizen she's unloved. I'm not sure even my mother would sink that low.

I lie flat on the bed and stare at the ceiling, thinking of all the nights my father used to come in and sit beside me, reading me stories that always had a happy ending. I loved knowing that Jo March would eventually become a writer if that was what she wanted. I loved feeling certain Harry Potter would one day put the Dursleys in their place.

I'd thought real life was the same, but now I know better. I watched my grandmother die miserably, mostly alone and in pain, after spending decades with an abusive spouse. I watched my aunt die two months after discovering her husband had knocked someone else up. She never got a second chance at love, and karma never came for her husband—he married his mistress and they went on to have two more kids.

There's not a single reason to think my outcome will be any better. How happily can *The Victimized Teenager Who Comes Back to Take her Revenge on her Small-minded Hometown* end? Maybe I'll experience the joys of vengeance, but what will be left once it's all said and done? What's left when I've ruined Bradley's family business? When I've destroyed Lucas Hall?

As much as I hate what my mother said, what I hate most is that she's probably right.

I'll never be happy. I'll never be loved. I'm going to die alone.

Sometimes I wonder if destroying all the people who ever hurt me will be enough to make up for it.

30

LIAM

Bridget meets me at the grocery store Thursday and patiently waits for me to gather my stuff and lock up. I'm glad she suggested dinner because I need the distraction.

There hasn't been a minute of the day, asleep or awake, without Emmy in my head. Every goddamn second of that night in her office is like a spark, igniting me from the inside out. The slick feel of her, how tight she was when I pushed inside her, the way she said *yes* when I asked if she wanted me to treat her like a whore.

I'd never have said it if I wasn't furious. But God, it was hot when she agreed. It's the first time Emerson has ever given an inch, and what a fucking inch it was.

I wake rock hard every morning and have to actively shut down the memory simply to get through a day of work. I want a repeat more than I've ever wanted anything in my life, and I know she wants one, too, because it was too goddamn good for her *not* to want it. But she has to come to me this time.

I just hope she doesn't make me wait long.

Bridget links her arm through mine and lets her head rest

against my shoulder for a minute as we walk. "I can't believe my baby's really coming home for the rest of the summer! I'm so excited."

"What changed her mind?" I ask. "I thought she had some big internship."

Bridget shrugs in a weird way. I'm not sure if it means she doesn't know or if she simply doesn't want to tell me, and I'm about to grill her when I see Emerson.

That's all it takes for every thought that isn't Emerson-adjacent to vanish.

She's indecently lovely in her yoga attire, flushed and sweating. It reminds me of her face as she came—cheek pressed to the desk, mouth open. My jaw grinds with the effort to *stop* thinking about it.

Her gaze meets mine and her smile fades. She turns toward her car, now looking every bit as miserable as I am.

"You gonna tell me who that was?" Bridget asks with a grin.

"You always do this." I frown, continuing on toward Beck's. "I get within a hundred feet of anyone with a vagina and you're there, trying to make it seem like it meant something. I'm doing a job for her, and I'm doing a job for her mom. You want to go meet her mom, too, so you can see which vagina is the better fit?"

Bridget laughs. "You haven't changed since you were five, Liam. I'd ask you who some cute little girl in your class was and you'd start screaming about how much you hate her."

I shake my head. "Well, if I screamed it this time, it'd be relatively accurate. Because that one in particular is driving me crazy."

"I can see why she'd be driving you crazy. I'm straight and married, and I think *I* want to sleep with that girl."

I turn up the road to the bar. "This conversation would be a lot more interesting if you weren't my sister. But since you are, drop it."

She elbows me. "I'll stop if you admit it."

"I'm not admitting something that isn't true."

I *don't* want to sleep with her. I want to punish her, devour her, make her beg, tear her apart, and put her back together. There wouldn't be a minute of sleeping.

It's late that night, and I'm about to climb into bed when Emmy texts.

THE PRINCESS

So, was that the soulmate? Is she willing to meet your roof surveillance needs?

Why? Are you jealous?

Of course not. I just don't know why you'd call me a whore when you've had multiple sexual partners in one week.

I didn't call you a whore. I asked if you wanted me to treat you like one and you said yes. And, I should add, you fucking loved it.

It was okay.

I wasn't on a date—you saw me with my sister. And you're jealous.

The fact that I hear nothing back from her pretty much confirms I'm right. Now I just need her to realize it.

31

EMMY

I *wasn't* jealous.

Jealousy is an emotion reserved for people who want to possess a thing, and I don't want to possess anyone. I'd simply borrowed his penis for a brief—*regrettably* brief—period of time and thrown it back into the wild.

That wasn't jealousy. It was irritation. He doesn't get to judge me for Troy and Dr. Sossaman and end a call from Donovan as if he owns me, all while he himself is actively seeing other women. Maybe she was his sister, but I didn't know that. I objected to the hypocrisy of it all.

But when I close my eyes and recall seeing him walking down the street with her, I still feel exactly the way I did then: as if I'd been punctured. As if he'd stuck a thousand tiny knives in the center of my chest and all the air was escaping.

Which is not the way one typically reacts to hypocrisy.

Shit.

I go to sleep thinking about him groaning my name and wake remembering how rough and demanding he was. I should hate all of it, but I don't. I love the way sweet, sweet Liam turned aggressive. I love the way he didn't take a minute of my shit, the way he tore my panties and pressed his palm flat to my back.

God, I loved it so much.

He's in the backyard when I walk outside in my sleep shorts and sweatshirt, Snowflake at my feet. I feel exquisitely naked under his gaze.

"Good morning, princess," he says.

I should hate that too, but my mouth curves instead. "Good morning, yard boy."

He meets me at the stairs, his broad hand grasping the rail, one foot casually resting on the bottom step. "Surprised I didn't hear back from you last night. It's not like you to take an accusation of jealousy lying down."

I smile and walk down the steps until I reach the second from the bottom, which puts my mouth a millimeter from his. "Liam, I was *already* lying down. With my legs spread wide, thinking about the way you fucked me in the office. I guess I was too distracted to reply."

And with that, I turn and walk back into the house. He's silent, but I swear to God I heard him gulp.

I MEET with the mayor to show him the plans for the park and am nearly back to the store when I spy Liam across the street, talking to the kind of guy I *would* have said was my ideal before Liam: tall, hot, dark hair, nice suit.

Now, for some reason, I only seem to want Liam in his worn Levi's and boots. I'm sure I'll get over it, but it's highly inconvenient when I need to be distancing myself.

I keep moving toward the store, and Liam jogs across the street to catch me. That he's still thinking about what I said this morning is written all over his face. It's as if no time has elapsed at all, except now I can't simply saunter away without him following me.

I'm not sure I want to saunter away anyhow. I'm pretty sure I'll implode if I don't get a repeat of the other night somehow.

"Who was your hot friend?" I ask, nodding at the guy across the street.

He raises a brow. "Are you trying to make me jealous, Em? Jealous the way *you* were last night?"

Yes.

"Not at all. But I've got a couple more weeks in town, and I have some unmet needs."

We enter the store. I keep walking to my office and he follows, as if this was our plan all along. A shiver moves down my spine.

"I'm not sure what you're doing," I say as I walk into my office. "But I don't have a lot of time."

The door clicks shut behind me.

"Fuck it," he says, and without warning, his hands are on my hips and he's spinning me so that my back is against the closed door.

Yes.

He's already hard when his mouth lands on mine. The rasp of his jaw abrades my skin, one hand squeezing my hip, his fingers digging into my ass, while the other one palms my breast.

"You've got plenty of time," he says against my ear, pinching my nipple hard.

A soft sigh escapes me. "I have a *little* time."

He falls to his knees, pushing the skirt up before he slides a finger between my legs.

"Admit you were jealous last night," he demands.

My eyes fall closed as my hands press flat to the door behind me. "I was...irritated."

"By jealousy."

He leans close, tugging the panties to the side.

And then his tongue sweeps over me.

"Oh. God."

He pushes two fingers inside me, hard and unexpected. My knees wobble and I grab his shoulders to stay upright. "Just admit it, Em," he croons. His hot breath ghosts over my clit, a tease I can barely stand not to give in to.

"You talk too much," I whisper, running my hand through his hair. I feel the gust of his laughter against my core, but nothing beyond it. "Fine. I was jealous."

"Good girl," he whispers.

I should hate that too, but dammit...I don't.

A muscle low in my belly contracts as his fingers glide in and out, keeping time with his tongue. That initial hint of need I felt before is now a heavy ache, as if I'll explode if I don't come, and yet...it's not going to be enough. My breath is coming fast, my hands are tugging at his hair, but this isn't what I want. I don't merely have unmet needs. I have an almost desperate desire to watch *him* come apart with me.

I release him and slide away. His pupils are dilated, his mouth wet with me.

"Come here," I pant, marching toward the desk. I lift my skirt around my waist as I sit atop it. When he's close enough, I tug at his belt and pull his jeans and boxers down. He's rock hard and throbbing against my palm as it wraps around him.

"Fuck yes," he groans, pushing my legs apart as I pull his mouth to mine. I kiss him as if I plan to *devour* him, as if I'd fucking destroy him this way if I could. It is not inaccurate. I'd like to destroy him in a thousand ways, a thousand times over. I want to smash him into a million pieces and bury those pieces all over the world so he can't be put back together, so he can't exert this effect on me anymore.

"Fuck me," I demand, leaning backward.

He grabs a condom from his wallet. Another pair of panties is effortlessly shredded, and then he is shoving inside me hard, knocking the air from my chest. He glances between us at the point where we are joined. "Jesus," he says, seemingly more to himself than me. "I think I could come from the sight of this alone."

"*Don't*," I hiss, as my head falls backward. "Not yet."

But it's not going to take me long. I was close before, and it's so much more when he's inside me, as if I'm filled to the point of pain, yet there is no pain. It's just heat and need and this ever-growing ache.

"I'm going to come," I warn, and his eyes darken. His thumb presses to my clit and I go off like a bomb, wrapping my legs around him as he thrusts hard and buries his mouth against my neck to stifle his own cry.

We remain pressed together, both of us slowly coming back down to earth. His lips graze my neck, moving over my jaw and up to my ear. "Thank you for admitting you were jealous."

"I was horny. I'll say anything when I'm horny. Ask me now."

He laughs and thrusts inside me, still hard. "I'm pretty sure I could convince you to say it again."

Yeah, probably.

He pulls out and ties off the condom. "Let's go to lunch."

"I don't eat lunch."

He rolls his eyes. "Princess, at a certain point, you'll have to acknowledge we aren't just fucking."

I climb to my feet, straightening my skirt. "Look, it's nothing against you. I just don't date."

I'm worried he's about to ask for a heart-to-heart, that he's going to ask why I'm so broken and then try to convince me I can be healed. Instead, he presses his lips to my forehead while fixing my collar.

"Okay, Em," he says. "But you're twenty-eight. Maybe it's time to start."

It scares me how badly I want to agree.

32

LIAM

> Did you land safely? Don't worry. I am not asking as someone who thinks he's your boyfriend. I ask this of all my clients.

S he is in Dallas, to be followed by Nashville and Atlanta. It's strange, how empty this town seems without her. I've lived here my entire life, and sure, it isn't what it once was—my friends are settling down, I haven't been able to surf since last fall—but Elliott Springs has never seemed so dull, so lifeless before. I'd still like to preserve our history, but I can see where maybe we do need to change. Sometimes it takes an influx of new blood to bring things back to life.

THE PRINCESS

> Safe as in "Did you arrive in one piece?" Or safe as in "Did you arrive without incident?" Because there were incidents. They only had the vegetarian meal option and we hit turbulence, so they never refilled my wine.

> It's probably for the best that they couldn't refill your wine. I've seen you when you're drinking. You'd probably ask the pilot to go into the bathroom with you.

> Only if my mom liked him too.

> Or Bradley Grimm.

> Well, yes, obviously.

> Are you ever going to tell me what happened between you guys?

Those three dots circling, disappear, circle again. It takes her a moment to reply.

> **THE PRINCESS**
> I'd rather not.

I sigh. I'd mostly expected this answer. It only frustrates me because I don't know any other way to get past those walls of hers.

> One day, you'll trust me enough to tell me everything.

> **THE PRINCESS**
> That sounds boyfriend-ish. And I leave in a couple weeks, remember? There is no "one day."

She's wrong. I'm stupidly certain of it, certain she will stay or somehow the world will shift on its axis to bring us both to the same place. But how much longer do I even have to make it happen?

∽

MAC'S WEDDING is on Saturday. He and Cassie have been together since they were twelve, but JP's wife still thinks they're rushing into things.

"Twenty-two is so young," says Brenda as we watch Mac and Cassie take their first dance. "They've never even dated anyone else. Seems risky."

I disagree. I think they're lucky in a way few other people are: they found the person they want to spend their lives with without a thousand false starts first. I want what they have, but I'd settle for a lot less. Right now, I'd settle for Emmy admitting she's even *with* me.

After the reception, I go out for a drink with Caleb and—shockingly—Beck, who's in town only for the night.

Giving up the bar and marrying Kate has stripped years from his face. He looks like a guy who has the whole world at his fingertips again and sort of can't believe his luck. It's somewhat awkward that he's achieved this happy ending with *Caleb's* ex-wife, and there was a time when I faulted him for making it so clear how he felt about her, but now I get it.

There are women you can't look away from, or stay away from, no matter how evident it is that you should.

"So Harrison still hasn't introduced you to her?" Beck asks of the LA girlfriend. "You think there's something...wrong with her?"

I laugh. "Like what? Like she's unattractive? Harrison's wound up with the hottest women since he was twelve."

"I don't know," Beck says, shaking his head. "I just don't think things in London went quite the way he claimed they did. You don't give up your whole fucking life to move to another country for your wife, only to come back two months later wrapped up in someone else."

"Speaking of being all wrapped up," Caleb says, turning to me, "what's going on with you and the girl from the other week?"

"What girl?" Beck asks, grinning indulgently as he sets his beer on the bar.

"He's in love," Caleb says with a laugh. "You should have seen him...this girl's flirting with Troy Alexander, and all of a sudden, Liam's on his feet, following her to the bathroom."

Beck chuckles under his breath. "How long was he gone?"

I flip him off. "I had to man the bar after you threw Kate over your shoulder and carried her back to the office last summer. Let's talk about how long *you* were gone."

"Difference is you're discussing my wife, and I'm discussing a girl you haven't even admitted to liking."

"There's nothing going on," I say stonily. I'm not spilling my guts about Emerson when she refuses to even admit we're dating.

"What's up, boys?" asks Paul Bellamy, throwing one arm around me and one arm around Beck.

I push his arm off me. "Nothing."

"I was just trying to find out who Liam has a crush on," Beck says, helpfully.

Paul smirks. "I'll tell you who. Emerson Hughes. Emmy the Semi. She—"

I've got Paul by the back of the neck before he can finish what he was about to say. "You'd better shut your fucking mouth right now," I hiss.

Paul throws up his hands. "Hey, man, I'm not faulting you for it. She's hot now, even if she was a big tub of goo back in high school."

I slam Paul's face into the bar so fast that there isn't even time for Beck and Caleb to intervene.

Girls scream, drinks go flying, and I don't give a shit. We'll see how much he wants to run his mouth once he's spent a night in the hospital because of it.

"Jesus Christ, dude," he cries. "I think you broke my fucking nose."

"You think this is bad, motherfucker?" I demand, still holding his neck. "Say one more word about her, here or anywhere else, and you'll see how bad it can get."

Beck and Caleb grab me before it can go any further. Paul scurries off into the crowd, his nose pouring blood. I feel bad about it, for Jeannie's sake, but she wasn't going to pull him into line, and he had it coming. It's because of people like Paul that Emmy *doesn't eat lunch*, *doesn't date*, is so incessantly guarded. It's because of people like him that she'll never decide to stay.

"Bro," says Caleb, "what the fuck?"

"I'm sick of him talking shit about her," I growl.

Beck laughs quietly. "Yeah, it definitely sounds like there's nothing going on."

33

EMMY

Damien Ellis is clasping my hand between both of his. "The woman in the red dress," he says, leaning close so he can be heard over the noise of the party. "We meet at last."

"Emerson Hughes," I begin, "with—"

"With Inspired Building," he says with a smile. "Believe me, I know. I looked you up after Austin. Very impressive stuff you've done so far. That area south of Charleston seems to be doing well."

"Thank you," I reply with faux modesty because it's not doing *well*—it's amazing. "I'm pleased with how it turned out."

"And what did you think of my restaurant?"

"Very nice," I reply. "I didn't try the food, but the service was impeccable."

"I thought it looked like every fucking steakhouse," he says, and I laugh. "You thought so too."

One of his assistants is pulling him to meet someone, but his hand wraps around my elbow. "I have the penthouse upstairs. A few of us are coming up to have drinks. Join us. We'll talk some more."

It's the precise opening I've been waiting for—my chance to tell him about opportunities Inspired Building has missed, how much more we could do with smarter management. I'm a little unnerved by the idea of going up to his suite—these group things have a way of turning out to be one rich guy and the stupid girl who didn't know they'd be alone. But it's not an opportunity I can pass up.

"I need to talk to a few people here first," I tell him.

He smiles as if I've just agreed to something more. I hate that. There was a time when I'd have said that there were worse things than sleeping with Damien Ellis to get my way. Right now, though, I can't quite think what they'd be.

I circle the room until I'm out of view and pull out my phone, stalling, trying to plot out my next move. Hoping Liam has texted something so obnoxious or so amazing that the decision is made for me. But the only text is from Chloe.

CHLOE

Interesting scoop for you.

> If this is another story about employees having sex at Cuts-n-Stuff, I don't want to know.

It has more to do with employees having sex in the back of the grocery store.

My stomach drops. It's not too hard to picture a worst-case scenario here. Liam and I have had sex in the office twice now. Maybe he told his guys. Maybe we weren't as quiet as I thought.

> What are you talking about?

CHLOE

> Paul Bellamy just talked shit about you and
> Liam smashed his face into the bar. And then
> he said, and I quote, "You think this is bad?
> Say one more word about her, motherfucker,
> and you'll see how bad it can get." His friends
> had to pull him away.

Something warms in the center of my chest. It's pretty easy to imagine what Paul said, and while I hate that Liam heard it, I love that he did something about it. I spent most of my adolescence with no one defending me. Bradley would make some crack about how my desk was creaking too much for her to concentrate and Mr. Green, our bio teacher, would snicker before he scolded her. When I got tripped walking to the podium at that awards ceremony and my dress ripped, my mother blamed me. *"You were about to bust out of it anyway."*

No one ever took my fucking side, and finally someone has. For the first time in eighteen years, I long to be in Elliott Springs, just so I can show him how grateful I am. I suppose I'll have to settle for texting him instead.

> Hey.

YARD BOY

> Wow. A text from you that isn't pretending to
> be about work?

> I can ask you if you got the fixtures in if that
> makes you more comfortable.

> I liked it better the first way. What are you
> doing? Are you at your party?

I look around me. Damien Ellis and his posse are gone. It's my big chance to press for the things I want. I know he's going to hit on me and I'll struggle to escape unscathed, but how many opportunities like this will fall in my lap? I press the button for the elevator to the penthouse.

> I'm leaving now.

YARD BOY

If I promise that I don't think I'm your boyfriend, can I call you?

> It sounds boyfriend-ish. I'd probably bitch at you about the store just so you knew where things stand.

I would expect nothing less.

I press the button for the fourth floor at the last moment, and he calls just as I walk into my room. I put him on speaker while I kick off my heels and walk toward the sink.

"What are you doing?" he asks.

"I'm getting ready to brush my teeth," I reply, squeezing out the toothpaste. "Tired Emmy is not my most exciting persona."

"I'll brush mine too," he replies.

On the other end of the line, I hear the creak of a door hinge. An electric toothbrush turns on. "I always figured if we were going to be doing something at the same time over the phone," I say as I brush, "it would be slightly sexier than this."

"I can make this sexy," he replies. His voice drops an octave. "I bet your mouth is so full right now, isn't it, Em? Are you going to swallow it for me like a good girl?"

I laugh so hard I start to choke and have to spit the toothpaste out. "I'm not sure you're supposed to swallow it."

"It's full of protein," he says as he spits. "Just take my word for it the next time I tell you to swallow."

I could easily make this conversation sexual—well, *more* sexual—but I don't. I shrug off the rest of my clothes and climb into bed, unwilling to end the call just yet. I don't ask him about what happened at the bar and he doesn't mention it. Instead, we talk about a little of everything. About Mac's wedding, about his sister getting pregnant at seventeen, about how weird and vague his friend Harrison's been about some new mystery girlfriend.

He asks me about my dad—and I tell him about our secret missions, how we'd go for donuts or drive down to the wharf in Santa Cruz. How we'd watch *Dr. Who* and when I was terrified of the crying angels, my father helped me craft a plan to combat them if they ever showed up in real life. How for every ugly word he heard my mom saying, he'd find a way to make sure I knew she was wrong.

"He sounds like he was a pretty good dad," Liam says.

"He was," I reply, with a yawn. Those years with him were everything, and I don't know how to reconcile them with the way he ended up leaving me behind. "Well, I guess I'd better get to sleep—"

"I want to take you on a date, Em," he cuts in. "A real date. One you admit is a date before it begins."

The conversation was going so well. I was pleased, but now I'm itchy, *fragile*, and I hate feeling either of those things. "You're ridiculous. Are we going to sit around holding hands and talking about our feelings?"

"No," he says softly. "But if you'd pull your head out of your ass, you'd realize I've already told you about mine."

I LEAVE Dallas for Nashville to check on our project there.

"We're probably taking this whole phone thing too far," I tell Liam when he calls that night, though I'm smiling. "What's even left to discuss?"

"You love it," he replies. "Let's figure out where we'll go on our first real date."

"We're not going on a first date." I sink onto the edge of the bed and kick off my shoes.

"Yeah, we are. We'll discuss it later. Or I'll ask your mom for some pointers."

My eyes fall closed. "Please promise you'll never discuss me with my mom."

"Because she wouldn't approve of you dating a college dropout?" he asks. He phrases it like a joke, but there's something tense in his tone.

Liam's so confident all the time. It never occurred to me until now that he could feel otherwise.

"No, because my mother hates me, and she'll say awful things to you and worse things to me if she knows." I rise and walk to the bathroom, putting him on speaker as I go.

"Why does her opinion even matter anymore? Why haven't you just washed your hands of the whole situation?"

"Because she's the only parent I have."

"That's like saying '*I only have one open sore*.' Sometimes it's better to have zero of a thing than one. I suspect she falls into that category."

"It still feels," I say quietly, soaking a cotton ball with makeup remover, "as if I can do the right thing or say the right thing and I'll finally win her over."

"Em, parents are supposed to be the only people you don't *have* to win over. They're supposed to love you simply for existing. And if you have a parent who still needs to be persuaded about you after all this time, then you don't have the parent you deserve and you never will."

My stomach sinks. He's right, of course. I've known that long before now. I mean, it would require total memory loss for my mother to no longer hate me, and I suspect even then, she'd quickly decide I was the enemy.

"When enough people hate you, Liam, you can be reasonably certain that *you're* the problem."

"Is this about high school?" he asks. "Are you ever going to tell me what happened?"

"No. You wouldn't want to describe your most humiliating moment for me. I don't want to describe mine for you, okay?"

"When I was fifteen, it was my first blow job, and I came all over the girl's hair."

I laugh, throwing the cotton ball in the trash. "That's not even unusual. A lot of guys—"

"It happened when she was pulling my pants down," he says. "And going forward, when we're talking about sex, please don't mention anything you've seen happen with *a lot of guys*. Anyway, that's tied for the number-one spot with this night when I had the flu. I was driving to meet my friends and then I realized I was going to shit my pants. So I turned around to go home, driving like a maniac, and I got pulled over."

"Oh no."

"Yep. They thought I was drunk. They made me get out to take a sobriety test and I shit my pants during it. You know those cops are still laughing. So there you have it. Do you see me differently?"

"I don't want you in my car if you've got the flu," I reply.

He groans. "*Em.*"

"I just don't understand why you need to know."

"Because there's this huge swath of your life you don't want me to mention, but it's driving everything you do in Elliott Springs," he replies. "It's sort of the elephant in the room."

"Literal elephant," I reply as I pad to the bed.

"Don't do that," he warns, suddenly harsh. "Don't use the bullshit people once said about you against yourself."

I'm on the cusp of arguing when I realize he's right. I say the mean shit about myself now to beat other people to the punch when maybe what I should have done all along is not surrounded myself with the assholes who'd have said it in the first place.

Sure, I didn't have a lot of choice as a teenager. But I've got all the choice in the world now.

"Fine," I say warily. "What do you want to know?"

"I don't understand why it happened," he says.

"Why I gained weight?" I ask. "I don't know. I think I was upset about my dad leaving and—"

"No," he corrects, "I meant why *they* were so awful. Because kids are mean, but they're not *that* mean, so consistently and for so long. And you couldn't have been the only overweight kid in your school. So why'd they pick you as the target?"

He's right. And no one was tormented the way I was. "It was Bradley. We were best friends growing up. She just turned on me after my dad left, and they all followed her lead."

"You don't think that's weird?" Liam asks.

"Not especially," I reply. "Little girls are bitches."

"I have a sister. I have a niece who was bullied through middle school too. I know little girls can be bitches. But what you're describing is kind of extreme, even for the worst of them."

He has a point. I assumed it was because of my weight, because that was certainly what was the most upsetting part to my mother. And little girls *are* bitches.

But I guess it *was* still pretty fucking weird.

Liam calls while I'm waiting at the Nashville airport. I tell him he's pushing it but wind up talking to him until I'm already on the plane and they're telling me, *specifically*, to turn off my phone.

I arrive in Atlanta, drop my bags at the hotel, and head out to meet with city officials about a tract of land we'd like to develop. The only difference between dealing with a big city versus a small town is that there are more asses to kiss and more people you've got to buy. It will take me a year or more to successfully get the land zoned for commercial use, and that's what makes Elliott Springs the find of the century: there's no delay. For very little investment, Inspired Building will soon be printing money off the businesses we've brought to town, whereas we'll have invested a lot in Atlanta to get only a moderate return. Charles should have promoted me, and I'm angered anew by the fact that he hasn't, that he's done his best to keep me small so he can keep stealing credit for all my hard work.

God, I can't wait to take his job, to watch him being escorted from the building with all his shit in a file box. It's so close I can almost taste it. So is the destruction of Lucas Hall.

But when Liam calls as I get to my room that night, it hits me deep in the center of my stomach how empty it will be when I've gotten everything I want, but I no longer have his voice in my ear at the end of the day.

34

EMMY

My mother is irritated with me when I get home, and not in the normal way she's always irritated with me. Her shoulders are stiff; her jaw is locked. The sound of me quietly talking to Snowflake as I pour food into her bowl is enough to merit the swift jerk of her head and narrowed eyes. I wonder if she somehow knows I've been sleeping with Liam, and if the accusations about this will leap from her mouth later today or tomorrow, fully formed. Entire paragraphs about how terrible I am, all the evidence she's pulled together to support it. She'd have been a good lawyer if she'd chosen to go that route. She's able to gather seemingly unrelated facts about me into a cohesive indictment with just a little thought, so convincingly that even *I* will believe her.

I drive her to physical therapy, and she yells at me for hitting the brakes too hard and accuses me of driving recklessly when I'm only five miles over the speed limit. After we park, I put my hand on the door to walk in with her and she stops me. "You'll wait in the car if you know what's good for you," she says as she climbs out.

It says everything about her that I'm now an adult, and she

can barely hobble down a hallway, yet she still thinks she can physically threaten me and get away with it. How many times did I hear that phrase as a kid? She hit me in the face so often— simply for the crime of looking at her—that I still have to *force* myself to look strangers in the eye.

Or maybe I'm the one it says something about even more, because she treated me the way she did and I'm still here taking it, aren't I?

I text Jeff after I've dropped her off. He and I speak infrequently—my phone history with him is a long record of one of us saying "happy birthday" and the other saying "thanks," year after year. He'll always be the person who took my mother's side against me. Who'd say, "Look how the car rises when Emmy climbs out" when we went somewhere, seeking Mommy's approval when he was twenty-two fucking years old.

> Tell Sandra to rein it in. I'm not staying here if she continues to behave like this.

JEFF

> She said you have a bad attitude.

I roll my eyes. That was a favorite theme of hers back when I lived at home. She'd make fun of my weight over dinner until I was weeping and tell me to leave the table if I couldn't take a joke. She'd say, "What the hell is your problem?" when I walked in from school and then tell anyone who'd listen that I had a bad attitude, that I was a chore to be around. As if a healthier person wouldn't mind being ridiculed, wouldn't mind being lashed out at as soon as she walked in the door.

Who *wouldn't* have a bad attitude under those circumstances? I know this intellectually and yet I can't stop believing that if I was so uniformly hated—at home, at school—there must have been something wrong with me too.

I will never grow into a person she and my brother respect

or care about. They're all the family I have, but when do you finally accept that, as Liam said, sometimes you're best with zero of a thing?

Writing them off would feel like a failure.

But it might also feel very much like a fresh start.

AFTER I'VE DROPPED my mother at home, I return to town where I meet with a rep from the company we've hired to manage the theater. They are kicking off with a James Bond retrospective—the older movies will cost us almost nothing and it adheres to our retro theme—and while I, personally, find the misogyny in the older movies infuriating, I'm also wondering if Liam might want to go see one with me.

Weak, on my part. I'm certain I'll regret it.

As I walk to the grocery store in the meeting's wake, I'm annoyed at myself for thinking ahead with Liam, annoyed at Liam for making me do it though he's got no idea he did.

He's close to the door when I walk in, and I want to remain annoyed, but I just sort of can't. He didn't shave this morning, and there's not a man in the fucking world who looks as good as Liam when he skips the razor.

"You had lunch yet?" he asks.

"I don't eat lunch. And besides," I say, smirking as I lean close so only he can hear me, "it makes me wet seeing you so hard at work. I couldn't possibly eat in my current state."

I walk back into my office and am taking my stuff out of my bag when he walks in and takes a seat...in my desk chair.

"Come here, Emerson," he demands, patting his lap.

I cross my arms. "You don't actually expect me to sit on your lap behind *my* desk. Anyone could walk in and see that."

"So, it's okay for you to make me hard as hell talking about how wet something made you, but God forbid anyone should see you in my lap."

"It's about respect."

His lips tip up. "I think it's about someone not putting their money where their mouth is."

"I'm happy to put my mouth anywhere you want," I reply, and he groans audibly. "Just not publicly."

"No one's coming back here," he says, patting his lap again as if I haven't spoken.

I glance over my shoulder at the open door and sigh heavily as I cross the room and perch gingerly on his knees. "Fine. And why, exactly, are you insisting on this somewhat demeaning display?"

He tugs me backward, fast and without warning, so that I'm no longer perched on his knees but pressed right against his very hard cock with my skirt riding up. "I figured you deserved to see what that smart little mouth of yours produced, firsthand."

It's like a bolt of lightning, served right between my legs. I can't help but rub against him. Maybe I'm torturing myself, but that's okay if I'm torturing him too. And based on the way he groans again, I definitely am. "It would be so easy for you to slide inside me like this," I whisper, pulling his hand between my thighs and under the seam of my panties. I'm absolutely soaked already, just from the idea of it. "I could pull down your zipper and rise up just enough for you to slide inside me, right here, with that door wide open."

"Christ," he whispers, and he no longer needs my guidance. His fingers are moving on their own now, circling my clit and pushing inside me. "Let me."

I gasp. "Why should I? I can come just like this."

He withdraws his fingers entirely. "Then I'd better make sure I get mine first," he whispers. "Get on your knees, Emmy."

I look behind us at the door, still open wide. Even if I'm

hidden under the desk, it'll be pretty fucking obvious what's going on if Liam's groaning with his head thrown backward.

"I wasn't asking, Emerson," he growls. "Get on your fucking knees."

I can't get to the floor fast enough. He's already yanking his jeans open, reaching into his boxers.

"Suck, princess," he commands.

I glare up at him. "I think I can figure it out from here, *yard boy*."

He starts to laugh, but it's cut off as I pull him into my mouth. As much as I don't want one of his guys to come back here and witness this, I can't help but play with him a little bit. Fisting him but keeping the pressure light. Sucking hard then backing off entirely.

I'm a woman of few talents—really just two talents: ruining my enemies and this—and I'm going to make sure he doesn't forget today.

"Goddammit," he groans. "Stop torturing me."

"Say please, yard boy," I demand, and find myself in the air, lifted with his hands beneath my arms and deposited in his lap again, straddling him this time. He pushes my soaked panties to the side and thrusts, sliding into me in a way that leaves us both gasping.

It's so rude. So thoughtless. And so unbelievably hot, the way he didn't ask, the way he just took. With his hands beneath my ass, he lifts me again and thrusts upward.

"You know, you're supposed to ask me first." It's a struggle to sound annoyed when it feels this good. I'm so wet, and he's so hard, and I'm irritatingly close to coming already. He should have had to work harder at it.

"You like it better when I don't ask, I'm clean and I saw the pills in your purse," he says, his fingers inside my thong, sliding along the crack of my ass. A single finger presses inside and the discomfort of it makes me clench around him, makes the wet slide of his cock a thousand times better. "I bet you'd let me do just about anything I wanted, wouldn't you?" he asks, pressing in farther. He no longer has to lift me. I'm riding him like I'll die if I don't come. "I bet you'd let me fuck this tight little ass, too. I bet you'd beg me to do it."

He thrusts hard then, unexpectedly. His finger goes deeper, and I come apart, gasping his name.

"Oh fuck," he inhales, and then his head falls back as he explodes inside me.

I slump against him. "Holy shit," I breathe. I just let him fuck me and finger me and say the dirtiest shit imaginable with his employees right around the corner. "I can't believe I went along with this."

I start to pull away and he yanks me back, holding me tight against him.

"I texted JP the second you started running your mouth and told them all to go to lunch because we were about to have a fight," he says with a laugh.

I smile against his chest. "Pretty sure of yourself, huh?"

"No, I figured there was a fifty percent chance we actually would end up fighting. And, anyway, I'd never let the guys see you the way you just were."

I pull away from him. "Why's that?"

He pushes a lock of hair behind my ear—his fingertips grazing my cheek, his eyes searching mine. "Because I don't want anyone but me to know what you look like when you come."

He's not my boyfriend. I don't know why we can't just fuck without him saying all this relationship-type stuff. "You—"

He cuts me off with his mouth on mine. "I know," he says. "I don't need to hear you say it. Now let's go to lunch."

"Are we going someplace where it's okay to have cum leaking down your inner thighs? Because that's the current situation."

He laughs. "Clean up. I'll wait. And I got hard again hearing you say that, so I'm going to need a little time myself."

I'd started to lift myself up, but at that, I settle against him once more. And indeed, that lovely bulge of his is growing.

"I don't eat lunch anyway," I tell him as I rock my hips, and with a groan, he pulls my mouth to his.

"I'm going to fuck you one more time," he says, "and after that, the shop is closed until we've been on a date."

I grind against him with a smirk. "Yeah, we'll see about that."

35

LIAM

It's late afternoon and I'm talking to Emmy as I drive down to a job in Santa Cruz. She's been in San Jose all day—something to do with the grocery store.

"Well, if you missed me today and you're ready to go on that date," I tell her, "let me know."

"Come by my office tonight and I'll show you the parts I've missed," she replies. "I'll pay so much attention to those parts it'll blow your mind. Well, *something* will blow anyway."

My dick hardens embarrassingly fast.

Goddamn, I wish I could just agree and stand my ground on another day. I don't know why she's willing to have furtive sex in her office and talk to me on the phone for hours, yet a date is where she draws the line. "Nope."

"Come on, Liam," she groans. "You can't be serious about this bullshit."

"I'm not giving the milk away for free anymore. You've missed *all* of me, whether you want to admit it or not, and we aren't sleeping together until we've gone on a date."

"That's ridiculous," she says. "I'm calling Troy."

"No, you're not. Get ready for dinner by candlelight."

"Get ready to jerk off in the shower alone."

I laugh again but when we hang up, I'm questioning my strategy. I know Emmy likes me. I'd stake my life on the fact that she wants more than a quick fuck on her desk. But I'd also stake my life on the fact that she'll hold out way too goddamn long to prove a point.

I arrive in Santa Cruz and find that absolutely nothing is happening. Every one of my guys is standing out on the sidewalk beside their cars, deep in conversation, which is exactly the kind of shit the homeowner will throw in my face later on. We have even a single delay and he'll be saying, "*Well, if your employees weren't standing around all day, maybe you'd be done.*"

I park the truck and storm toward them. My mouth opens and then falls closed again at the look on JP's face.

A look everyone else seems to share. *Fuck.*

I brace myself for the worst. A nail through the hand, a fall off the roof, the homeowner's incredibly expensive car crushed by falling bricks. "What happened?"

"It's—" JP's voice cracks.

"It's Mac," says one of the younger guys. "He died."

I stare at him, trying to think of anyone we know by that name other than the healthy twenty-two-year-old who I just watched getting married last week.

"*Our* Mac?"

The guys nod. "Snorkeling. One of those face mask things. They think carbon dioxide built up inside it. Cassie thought he was fine, and then she realized he'd been still too long. They couldn't revive him."

I slump against the side of someone's truck.

Six months ago, he was showing us all the ring he was going to propose with. Two weeks ago, he was gamely walking around the store with that sash on.

A week ago, he was trying not to cry as he and Cassie said their vows.

And he had no idea. He saw an entire future ahead for himself, for both of them. You know life is unpredictable, but you never think yours is. You know lives end early, that people get taken away from you, but you always assume you're somehow immune to it.

I help the guys pack up, as quietly stunned as they are, and then I go by Mac's brother's house to pay my respects. It's evening when I get home. I stand in the shower, letting the spray hit my back. Two days ago, Mac still had his whole future ahead of him. He probably showered thinking only of the hours ahead, thinking of dinner with his pretty wife. I can't get over the fact that it all ended for him so quickly, so unpredictably. He thought he'd kiss Cassie ten thousand more times. He thought he'd sleep with her nearly that many. You just never know when you're nearing the end.

I dry off and get dressed. I'm not sure what exactly I'm doing when I get back in my truck and start driving, but I wind up on Main Street, parked in front of the store, dialing Emmy's number.

"Come out to the truck," I say. "Now."

"Ohhh-kay?" she says as if it's still in question.

She walks outside. I catalog everything about her as she locks the door behind her—the long silk skirt that will slide through my fingers like water; her bare arms; the stubborn, luscious set of her upper lip. I've missed her since yesterday. I've missed her all weekend. This town is going to be empty as hell for me once she's left it for good.

There's uncertainty in those pale eyes of hers as she climbs into the passenger seat.

"What's happening right now?" she asks as I reverse out of the space without a word.

"You'll see," I reply gruffly.

"You know it doesn't turn into a date if I haven't agreed to go on it," she says.

I don't reply as I turn onto my street and swerve into my driveway. I go to her side of the truck, wrap my hands around her waist, and set her down. Her feet are barely on the ground before I'm stepping into her, letting my palms glide over the silk covering her ass.

"Well, well, well," she begins. "Looks like somebody didn't mean—"

My fingers tighten. "Can we not?"

She hesitates, her smug grin slowly fading. "Can we not *what*?"

"None of your jokes about how this is meaningless, okay? I know you're leaving. But just this once...I want to feel like something you're not going to forget."

She studies my face and I watch hers, as it goes from surprise to wariness and then something softer. "Okay," she whispers.

I grab her hand and turn toward the house. She comes, but reluctantly. I can feel her skittishness as if it's my own. This is different for us, and she wants no part of it.

When we get inside, I turn toward her. My hand rests on her jaw, and she swallows.

There's something fragile in it, in her. She's smart as hell, and tough, but somewhere in her, there's a girl, too. One who was wounded badly, once upon a time, and is determined not to be wounded again.

My mouth finds hers, my hand moving down to her hip, to the small of her back. She reaches for my belt...always rushing, always wanting to bypass the parts of this that are intimate, that make her feel vulnerable.

I lay my hand over hers to stop her, and she clicks her tongue in disapproval. She'd prefer a quick fuck against the wall, after which she'd demand I return her to her car.

One of many reasons I'm not leaving this up to her.

"Come on." I slide my fingers through hers and pull her

back to the bedroom, then slowly lift her tank and pull it over her head. My palms glide over her shoulders, down to her ribs. I cup a breast in each palm, letting my thumbs skid across those peaked nipples visible beneath the lace.

I almost miss her quiet intake of breath, the barely visible shiver in response.

"Are you going to tell me why you're being like this?" she asks.

"Since when are you eager to talk?" I reply, unzipping her skirt and letting it fall to the floor. That silences her. I figured it would.

She takes a seat on the edge of the bed, in nothing but a bra and panties and those fucking heels, watching as I pull off my shirt. She's incandescent in the dim light, all legs and curves and uncertainty.

I'm still only half undressed, but I'm too impatient to wait another minute. I push her back to the mattress with my lips first on her neck, then tugging at her nipples as I work to get the bra away. My mouth runs over her stomach and presses between her thighs.

She's soaking wet, and as much as I'd like to take my time with this, tonight I'm not. I climb up the bed, pushing the boxers down before thrusting inside her. She gasps in surprise.

"Too much?" I whisper, wincing with pleasure.

"No," she says. "God, that was so hot. I wasn't expecting it." I slide in and out slowly, wanting to savor this. Wanting to pretend we are in some parallel universe where having her in my bed, all flushed and hazy-eyed, isn't a one-off but something that happens every night, and that will continue to happen every night for the rest of my fucking life.

Her nails dig into my ass, silently pleading with me to move, and when I do it, her hips arch to meet mine because it's still not enough.

I'm pretty sure I know what she wants, but it's time she

started using her words. It's time she admits that she likes me. It's time she admits that we aren't simply hooking up, but barring all that, she can, at the very least, tell me she wants me to fuck her harder.

"Tell me, princess," I say against her ear. "I want to hear you ask for what you want."

"Harder," she says.

I laugh. "Sentence form, Miss Hughes."

"Fuck you," she says, arching again, trying to get there on her own.

I pull out, hovering above her, pressing my lips to her damp hairline. "Look at me, Em," I demand. "Tell me what you want."

She swallows, her cheeks flushing prettily. "Fuck me harder," she says.

I pull one thigh over my shoulder and slam inside her.

"Again," she says. Her eyes are closed, long lashes grazing her cheeks, lush mouth ajar.

"Look at me."

I wait until she does before I give her what she wants, and I stop when she looks away, training her to give me what *I* want. She's so closed off, but during sex, there's always a moment when it feels as if I'm looking straight into her soul. I want to be there when she goes over the edge. I want to know it's me and not Donovan fucking Arling or anyone else in her head when it happens.

We are slick with sweat. The blanket is kicked off. I am going to come so fucking hard the minute she lets go. My fingers move to her clit as I rise up, pulling her so high that only her head is still on the bed as I piston in and out.

"Oh, God," she swallows. "I'm close."

"So am I, baby," I whisper. At the sound of that endearment, one I have never used once in my life, she clamps down, crying out. And for a moment, right before she closes her eyes, I see everything inside her laid out like a buffet.

And it's glorious. Under that tough exterior, she's soft as a cloud and fragile as glass. Under that smart fucking mouth and those flashing eyes, she's fiercely loyal and scared and sweet as hell.

I let go, sinking into her with one last thrust, and when I finally come back to earth, she's watching me. Her mouth is swollen, her cheeks flushed, her eyes a summer storm. She's allowing me to have this, this handful of earnest seconds, and she's terrified I'm going to make her regret them.

Her mouth opens and I already know it's to say something that's both mean and funny at once. I press a finger to her lips as I roll to the side. "Don't, okay? Don't ruin it. Please."

She bites her lip, pushing herself up to a seated position, covering her tits with the sheet, as if she's a different person entirely—one I wasn't coming inside twenty seconds ago.

"Now, are you going to tell me what's up?" she asks.

I sigh heavily. "Mac, one of my guys—"

"I know Mac," she says, her voice low and worried. "He's the one who just got married, right?"

I sink into my pillow. "He was snorkeling on his honeymoon. They think too much carbon dioxide built up inside his mask."

"Is he okay?" she asks.

I swallow. "No. He didn't make it."

"God." She covers her eyes with a single hand. "I'm so sorry. He was a really good guy."

"He was."

I pull her back down to me and we remain like that in silence—her head on my shoulder, her hand in mine.

"I'm the last person you should have sought out," she whispers after a long minute. "I'm sure you know some female who's less emotionally stunted than me."

"That's pretty much all females," I reply, and she swats my arm. "But you're the one I want. Even if you insist it's just sex."

Her swallow is audible. "I'm sorry. It's just how I'm built, I guess."

"Bullshit. It's not how you're built. You're scared. That's it."

"I'd normally argue with you but given the circumstances, I won't." She starts to sit up again and that arm I've got around her tightens.

"Stay."

Her gaze drifts between us. "I'm pretty sure I just met your needs."

I tug her close and press my lips to her neck. "You haven't even begun to meet my needs, Em. But the night is long."

36

EMMY

I'd thought we were done, and I'd thought I was satisfied, but the minute he says *you haven't even begun to meet my needs, Em*, in that deliciously growly voice, I feel as if I haven't gotten laid in a decade.

There's no way I'd turn him down even if it didn't have that effect. He's upset about Mac and looking for an outlet. He wants to be worn out, he wants to forget, and I'm happy to help him get there.

I climb on top and pin him down before I slide between his legs and begin to torture him with my mouth. It's only when he's perilously close to coming that I back off entirely, crawling over him, grinding against him until he *begs* for more.

I wrap my hand around his cock, pressing him to my entrance, preparing to tease him again, but he grabs my hips.

"I can't stand it," he says, thrusting into me, and we've barely begun before he's flipped me on my back and taken charge.

If he was anyone else, I'd complain. But I like it with him. I like that he doesn't let me get my way all the time, but he makes sure I get what I need.

The second orgasm hits me and he hisses between his teeth, pushing into me with his head thrown back.

And when he finally comes down to earth, when he falls to the side and pulls me to his chest, I allow myself to stay, briefly. There's something so luxurious about being like this with him—bare and sweaty, the sheets destroyed. I wish it could last.

I wish I didn't have to force myself to leave.

I tap his chest twice, a silent *goodbye*. One large arm wraps around my waist before I can go anywhere. "You aren't attempting to just take off, are you?" he asks.

"I have no idea why guys *always* want to cuddle after."

His hand tightens on my hip. "Just for the record, guys also don't want to hear about *other* guys while they cuddle."

I laugh as I reluctantly allow him to pull me to his side. I guess it's tolerable. He's warm and I'm exhausted, and I can feel myself relaxing. Too much.

"Should go," I mumble against his skin.

His arm tightens. "Stay."

So I do.

A NOISE CRACKS THE AIR, and I sit upright in bed. The room is pitch black and I *was* sound asleep. Now, however, I'm wide awake and full of fury.

"What in the *actual fuck*?" I demand.

"What's wrong?" Liam asks sleepily, blinking up at me in the near-darkness.

Somewhere in the distance, I hear the noise again. *Cock-a-doodle-doo.*

"Who lives in a city and owns a *rooster*?" I snarl. "And why's it up in the middle of the night?"

Liam laughs. "That's Frank. He belongs to the Willoughbys.

And it's not the middle of the night. If Frank's making noise, it's four forty-five."

"If Frank's done this before, I don't know why you haven't snapped his neck. I swear to God if he doesn't stop, I'll go do it myself."

Liam laughs, pulling me back down to him. "Is it weird that it turns me on listening to you talk about killing someone's pet?"

"You've got a problem, but admitting it is half the battle," I reply.

"What's the other half?" he asks.

I let my hand slide down his perfect torso. He's already rock-hard. I move down the bed. "Let me see if I can figure it out," I reply. I tease him until I'm too worked up not to be on the receiving end, and then I crawl over him and slide his cock inside me. I slowly swirl my hips, getting closer and closer to where I need to be. His fingers go to my clit and he hisses a warning between his teeth. "Em, fuck, slow down," he begs, his voice all gravel and need and desperation, and it's the sound of it that finally sends me over the edge.

He lets go the moment I cry out, and I allow myself to collapse on top of him and let his hand smooth over my spine. I'd like to stay like this forever—with him inside me, with his hand on my back, with his lips pressed to my ear—but I can't afford to fall asleep again.

"I have to go," I sigh. "I don't want my mom to know I didn't sleep there."

"You're twenty-eight."

I climb from the bed. "Yes, I am. So I've had twenty-eight years to know how badly this will go if she realizes I didn't come home."

He bites his lower lip, watching as I search the floor for my clothes. "You're the last person I'd expect to care about her mother's opinion."

I wish it were true. I wish I could stop trying to change her mind about me.

He takes me back to my car, pulling his truck into the space alongside it. "I'll see you later, I guess," I tell him, grabbing my purse and reaching for the door.

"Em," he says, and then his hand wraps around my neck as he pulls me toward him. "We're not just fuck buddies, so stop treating me like one."

He kisses me, hard and soft at once, thorough yet not enough, silencing any objections before I can voice them.

"I'll pick you up at seven tonight," he adds.

"What?"

He raises a brow. A brow that says *we're not just fuck buddies and we're going on a goddamn date, and don't you dare even pretend to argue with me because we both know you want to go.*

"Whatever," I say as I climb from the car.

But I'm smiling.

I SPEND most of the day in meetings with the company that will be managing the bookstore, run home to feed Snowflake and check on my mom—who miraculously doesn't mention the fact that I slept elsewhere—then return to meet him outside the store. He wanted to pick me up, but I'd like to avoid my mother's input, if at all possible.

I know he spent most of the day helping Mac's family get him home, and I'm bad in situations like this—ones that require sensitivity and softness. I'm the worst possible person for him to be taking on a date tonight.

"Do you, uh, want to talk about it?" I ask haltingly as we head toward Santa Cruz.

He puts on his blinker to turn off the highway. "It's bad enough that I'm forcing you to go on a date. I'm not going to make you listen to what it's like to transport a body from overseas. And to be honest, I kind of compartmentalized everything just to get through it, and it's best if I can keep it compartmentalized for now. But do you mind if we make a detour?"

"What kind of detour?"

"It's time for you to meet my family," he replies, turning off the road.

"*What?*" My heart thunders in my ears. "Please tell me this is a joke, Liam."

He laughs. "It's not, but I promise it's not a big deal. My niece just got home, and I want to say hi to her and my sister. That's it."

"Who are you going to say I am?"

He rolls his eyes. "Em, it's flattering how disturbed you are by the idea someone might know we're dating."

"We're *not* dating," I insist, as he pulls into the driveway of a small split-level home. "We've never been on a single date."

"Yes, we have. You just didn't acknowledge it. Eventually you will, and in the meantime, I'll just say you're a friend."

I don't like that much either, but it looks like I'm not going to get much of a choice since he's already out of the truck and coming around to my side to help me down. "If this *is* a date, it's off to a roaring start," I mutter, and he laughs.

He leads me inside the home without knocking.

"Hello?" he calls, and seconds later, I see the woman from the other night along with a blonde bombshell—all curves, almond eyes, and full, pouty lips—who is in no way the "little niece" I was expecting. If Brigitte Bardot, Pamela Anderson, and Kate Upton had a baby, it might come out *half* as blonde and seductive as this girl.

"This is little Lazy Daisy," says Liam, ruffling her hair as if she's five.

"You know I fucking hate that nickname," the girl says with

a cheerful eye roll as she turns to me. "It's just Daisy. I *am* extremely lazy, but I'm trying not to advertise it."

I'm introduced to Bridget's best friend Jackie and handed a sweating Coke I definitely won't drink, and then Bridget announces they were just about to watch her wedding video.

"Mom," Daisy groans. "No one, and I repeat, no one, wants to watch your wedding video."

"Sure they do," Bridget says, turning to me. "You want to see this guy as an obnoxious twenty-something?"

"No, she doesn't," Liam says.

"Yes," I correct. "She *does*, actually."

That's all the persuading Bridget needs.

She loads the video. Her wedding begins on the TV and my gaze goes straight to Liam, one of the groomsmen.

He's lankier and has *player* written all over him—cocky, overconfident, ready to feed any girl he meets a line and get her quickly undressed. Liam a decade ago is the kind of guy who tries to get in your pants and then tries to get back out of them as fast as humanly possible. Liam now is the kind of guy who wants what he wants...but refuses to hurt anyone in the process.

I wouldn't trust the Liam of a decade ago, but I trust the one beside me more than I've trusted anyone in a very long time. The realization makes my breath come a little too fast. It's definitely going to end badly but I know I'm not willing to stop it yet either.

Liam starts to laugh as the camera turns to a kid with pitch-black hair, cut off at her ears. Daisy throws a pillow at him. "Fuck off, Liam."

"That's you?" I ask, only recognizing her as she turns to glare at the camera.

"It was a phase," Daisy says.

"A *long* phase," Liam suggests.

There's some bickering over whether or not to watch the

vows and it's forwarded to the sight of young Daisy, glaring once more as she stands against the wall with her arms folded.

"There she is," says a man's voice. "Goth Wedding Barbie." The camera turns toward a guy I saw with Liam a few weeks ago, looking much younger and happier than he does now.

"Mmmm. Wouldn't kick him out of bed for eating crackers," says Jackie.

"You missed your shot, my friend," Bridget replies. "Harrison's already seeing someone."

Daisy's head whips toward Liam. "*Already?* Who?"

Liam shrugs. "Some girl in LA. None of us have met her, but it must be serious."

And at that, Daisy—the lovely, non-Goth version currently across from me—looks absolutely crestfallen before she covers it up. I wonder if Liam even has a clue that his beloved little Lazy Daisy is head over heels for one of his best friends? If he does, I doubt he's taking it seriously, but if I had a niece who looked like her, I'd be taking it very seriously indeed.

This girl could have anyone she wanted...including her uncle's friend.

We don't stay long. Liam and Daisy make plans to get dinner together and then we get back in his truck and ride down to this casual place in Capitola, where an outdoor deck looks over the ocean and the crowded street below.

"I used to come down here with my dad," I say with a faint smile. "We'd jump in the water then bundle up and get donuts and hot chocolate. It was cold as hell, but I wanted to be just like him, so I pretended to love all the things he loved."

"Money laundering?"

I laugh. "Wow, I can't believe you went there. No. I did not pretend to enjoy money laundering, though it does seem like the kind of thing I'd enjoy *now*. But jumping in the ocean in the middle of winter without a wetsuit wasn't great. Nor was watching *Dr. Who*, which I thought was terrifying."

"What's terrifying about *Dr. Who*?"

"Don't you remember those weeping angel statues? They were so creepy. And if you smash them, they gain power. So we crafted very elaborate plans for how we'd smash them and bury the pieces all over the world so they couldn't come back together."

He grins at me. "So your violence toward Frank the rooster has some precedent."

"Frank is the only thing I hate more than those statues," I tell him, taking a sip of my wine.

"What about Bradley Grimm?"

"Oh, right. Okay, it's Bradley, then Frank, then those statues. But basically, I want all of them to die."

He laughs as if I don't mean a word of it when I'm pretty sure I do. I like the person he imagines I am: one who talks a good game but wouldn't hurt a fly. I like it so much that I want to become her, but I'm no longer the pathetic little kid so desperate for love that she'd become someone else entirely in pursuit of it. It's precisely the sort of weakness that makes you feel like an asshole when it's over.

After dinner, we walk along the beach under the stars, carrying our shoes in our hands. "I know it wasn't much of a date compared to what you're used to, but we don't have world-famous restaurants and carriage rides here."

My steps falter. "I already told you I don't date. You aren't being held to some lofty standard."

"But at some point, you've gone on dates in New York, and I'm guessing the guy didn't drive a truck you could barely climb into. I'm also guessing he was a lot more like Damien Ellis than I am."

I'm silent, weighing whether or not I should just let this go. I'd prefer to have him continue thinking I'm this glamorous NYC girl who's wined and dined all over the city. I'm scared that if he knows I'm not that girl at all, he'll like me less.

But if he isn't going to like who I actually am, it'd be easier just to end this right now anyway.

"I only go on dates when I want something," I reply.

His eyes narrow. "What does *that* mean?"

"It means that I'll go out with someone if I think it can get me ahead somehow, but I've never gone out with someone just...because. Because I wanted to."

He looks unnerved. I guess I would too. I'm about to change the subject but he speaks before I can get to it. "*Why?* Why are you only dating people if they can get you *ahead*?"

"Because then, if it turns out to be a trick on his end, well... it was a trick on mine, too, so that's fair."

He pulls me to a stop under a beam of light from the nearest lamppost, his brow furrowed. "I don't understand. Why would it ever be a trick on *anyone's* end?"

I love that Liam is worried on my behalf, that he wants to fight my battles, but he can't fight battles that took place a decade ago, and I'm at my limit for rehashing the past. "Can we please just leave it alone? I don't want to discuss this."

The wind whips my hair across my face, and he reaches out and pushes a lock behind my ear. He's frowning, but he doesn't push for more. "Thank you for trusting me enough to give this a shot tonight."

I dig a toe into the sand. "You didn't give me much of a choice."

He laughs. "Em, no one has ever made you do a goddamn thing you didn't want to do. You had a choice. You trust me."

I do, but I don't want to say it aloud. I've been proven wrong before, after all. It feels as if there's safety in refusing to admit it. "We'll see."

He sighs, running his free hand through his hair. "Why is it so hard for you to agree?"

"Because every guy who asks you out wants something.

Even if he himself thinks he has good intentions, what he's really after isn't good intentioned at all."

"And what is it you think I want? You've already slept with me, and you made it exceedingly clear that we didn't have to go out to do it again."

I hitch a shoulder. "I don't know. Maybe you've got an ulterior motive. Like you're hoping I'll abandon Lucas Hall or something."

He laughs. "I don't know you well, but I know you a hell of a lot better than that, Em."

Yeah, I guess he does.

We spend the ride home talking about the plans for Mac's funeral and what a bitch I was when I first met him. It's sad sometimes and it's funny sometimes, and the weird thing is how easily it all comes. That even as we approach Elliott Springs, it still feels like we have hours and hours more conversation we won't be getting to.

He delivers me to my car and walks me to my door.

I wait for him to suggest that we drive to his house, but instead, he leans forward and presses his lips to the top of my head. "Thanks for coming out tonight."

I stiffen, fighting this ache in the center of my chest. Liam said he wanted to know me, but I give him even a glimpse and suddenly we're ending this like colleagues, nothing more. "Why are you seeing me off like I'm your teenage daughter?"

His smile is slight and sad. "I'm not. I can't prove anything to you about my intentions. Maybe you'll believe me about Lucas Hall once you've won it, and it seems pretty clear you will, so all I can do now is this: I can take you out on a date and not try to get anything for myself at its end, because that's not what tonight was about. It would be the icing on the cake, but the cake is what I was after."

"That's wholly unnecessary. The part where we go to your house is the part *I* was after."

He pushes the hair back from my face. "Princess, I don't know if you're lying to me or if you're lying to yourself, but I assure you...that would only be the icing for you too."

His lips press gently to mine and he ushers me into my car. I'm still upset about the way tonight ended, but he's calling before I've even reached the bridge.

"What's up?" I ask coolly.

"Don't be like that," he replies. "You know you want to talk to me while you brush your teeth."

He's right. I do.

I'm okay with the way our night ended after all, I guess.

37

EMMY

"Want to go on a secret mission?" my father whispers.

It's dark out, and I'm groggy. He doesn't get me up this early unless we're doing sandbags.

"Is it raining?" I ask, struggling to open my eyes. I'm so tired that it feels as if I'm under water.

"Different kind of mission," my father says quietly, holding a finger to his lips. "A really big one."

I smile despite my sleepiness. It's been a bad week with my mother—she slapped me on the way home from the pediatrician's yesterday, hard enough to leave a mark, and when my father asked, she lied about it, daring me to counter her. But he knew. He always seems to know when it's a good day to swoop in and reset the balance.

He wraps my coat around my shoulders and hands me my shoes. We tiptoe out of the house, and he closes the door so quietly that even I don't hear the sound, though I'm standing right there. Jeff is sixteen now—old enough that he'd no longer want to come anyway, but I know my dad still worries.

I buckle my seat belt and wait for him to climb in before I speak.

"Where are we going?" Even as I ask, I'm nestling my face into the passenger seat, longing for bed.

"It's a surprise," he replies. "You can go back to sleep if you want."

"Are we getting Bradley?" She comes along with us most of the time now.

His smile fades. I've never seen my father cry, but for a moment I'm worried he's about to.

"No," he says. "Not this time."

We start to drive. He's listening to one of those news stations, and every voice sounds the same. I want to stay awake; I want to try to guess the surprise, but I cannot.

I blink my eyes open for only seconds at a time—clocking the lights of Santa Cruz, the farms to its south, the big signs for Monterey.

The sky is starting to lighten when the guy on the radio says interest rates are going down. "You should buy stock, Daddy," I mumble, rousing myself.

My father laughs. "Yeah? Why's that?"

I rub my eyes. "Because if it costs less to borrow money, people will buy more things and the stock prices will go up."

Once again, his smile fades. He's sadder than usual today. "That's probably true. What do you think I ought to buy?"

"I like Google and Apple," I tell him, rousing to the conversation. "But I also like Disney. Kids always want to go to Disney, whether their parents have money or not. But more parents will go if they've got money."

"Yeah," he says, his voice barely audible, "that's true."

The sky is just light enough that I can make out the ocean to my right, which means we've been driving south for a long time.

"Are we going to Disney?" I ask. "Is that the surprise?"

"Not this time," he says, swallowing. "It may be a while before I can take you to Disney."

"That's okay. I don't really care about Disney." That is kind of a lie. I would like to go to Disney, but I don't want him to think I'm disappointed.

"No?" he asks. "What would you choose for our adventure if you could choose anything?"

"Wall Street," I say, though if I thought about it more, I could probably come up with something better. My head is just stuck on the stock market. "Do you think if I get into Harvard, I'll be able to get a job on Wall Street when I'm grown up?"

It seems like a long time before he replies. "I'm sure you could, hon. But you don't have to go to Harvard. You can get any job you want if you set your mind to it, no matter where you go."

I shake my head. "Harvard has a really strong alumni network. I read about it."

"A lot of schools do," he says, but his mouth is tight.

"What's an alumni network anyway?" I ask.

"It's just people who already graduated from that school," he says, and then he turns up the radio, which is what my mother does when she wants me to shut up, when she's on the verge of snapping. He's never done it before, and it hurts my feelings. I don't understand why I'm messing up with him so much today, why I seem to be ruining this outing.

I tug my knees to my chest to make myself small, hoping that if I'm quiet long enough, he'll forget I made him mad. It helps, sometimes, with my mom. I stay like that, watching the ocean change from charcoal to blue under the rising sun until we finally arrive in a city I've never been to, bigger than Elliott Springs and fancier than Santa Cruz.

"Where are we?" I ask through a yawn. I don't know how long we've been driving, but I really need to pee.

He pulls into a parking lot. "Santa Barbara. Let's see if their donuts are better than the ones near us." His smile is forced, and he's not quite meeting my eyes.

We find a bakery. We usually buy a dozen and he eats half of them on the way home, but today he only buys two. He says he's not hungry and hands me both.

We walk toward the wharf. "How do you feel about trains?" he asks.

The only train I've ever been on is the old-timey steam train he and I sometimes take to the top of Bear Mountain. It doesn't even have a roof. I shrug. "They're okay."

"They have a special train here called the Surfliner," he says. "How would you like to take it home?"

I swallow the bite of donut in my mouth. "What about our car?"

"I have a few things to do here, so I'm going to stay a while. You take the train and tell me how it was. I'll make sure you get picked up."

My steps stutter. Is this because I upset him when I asked about Harvard? I want to apologize, to ask for another chance, but I'm still not even sure what I did. I follow him into the train station, worrying my lip the whole way. He buys me a ticket and stands with me while I wait to climb on the train. I must have done something wrong for him to be sending me home. Maybe I shouldn't have talked. Maybe I shouldn't have brought up Disney. It's the kind of thing I'm careful about with my mom, but I've never had to be careful with him.

"I'd rather wait with you," I plead.

He kneels on the ground and hugs me. "I messed some things up that I have to fix," he says. It's weird that he's hugging me. His affection usually comes in the form of a pat on the head, an arm around my shoulders. He's rising before I can ask what's wrong. His hands shake.

"Be good, Emmy," he says when it's my turn to climb aboard, his voice breaking. "I love you." When I glance out the window to watch him go, his shoulders are stooped as if he's an old man and suddenly it all feels very final.

I still don't know what I did wrong.

I arrive in San Jose many hours later. A nice man hands me a bag of snacks he says he's not planning to eat and I wait, hour after *hour, for my mother to show. The man sits across the way the entire time, watching me, and when a homeless guy comes over, the man tells him to move along.*

It's dark out when my mother finally arrives at the station, furious with me in her scariest sort of way—beady-eyed, silent, lips a tight line. She says nothing on the way home, but the minute we walk in the door, she slaps me so hard across the face that I fall backward and crack my head on the banister.

She doesn't care. She's already walking away, untroubled, pleased with herself. Please hurry home, Dad, *I whisper in my head as she goes.*

It's a steady chant in my head until the police arrive...and tell me my father won't be coming home at all. That he ran away and used me to do it.

It's as if he never cared any more than my mother did. He was just better at hiding it.

I WAKE with this sick heaviness in my chest and jump from the bed, pulling a sweatshirt over my pajamas as I head out to my car.

I don't even question the fact that I'm knocking on Liam's door until I hear his steps moving toward me. That's when it hits me how fucking *needy* it is that I'm here like this, in my pajamas, for God's sake. The porch light flips on, and the door opens.

"Hey," he says. A puzzled furrow forms between his brows. "What's up?"

It's the middle of the night. *Why the hell did I think this was okay?*

"I'm sorry," I breathe. "I shouldn't have come."

I step backward and he stops me with his hand wrapped around my arm before he pulls me inside and shuts the door.

It's darker in here, and I can only tell it's him by feel as he tugs me into him. "Are you okay?" he asks.

I nod, letting my hand slide down his chest and into the waistband of his boxers. I love how quickly he responds to me. Even if he doesn't want me here, one part of his anatomy does.

He stills my hand. "What are you doing?"

"I thought that was fairly obvious."

"You don't have to do that. I mean, it's okay for you to come here without that."

"I want to." I need him to drive every thought out of my head and put me somewhere where it's impossible to think of anything at all, even if it only lasts a moment. "Please."

He pulls me back to his bedroom. He's gentle as he removes the sweatshirt, the tank, the shorts, studying my face in the dim moonlight.

He scoops me up and sets me on the bed, pushing my knees out as he settles between them. I've come twice before he finishes himself, shuddering quietly above me.

He rolls to my side and pulls me onto his chest while he catches his breath. I don't try to leave when it's done, though part of me thinks I should.

"What happened?" he asks after a long moment.

"I just had a bad dream and wanted to get out of the house," I reply.

"What was your dream about?"

I flop onto my back. "Nothing."

His hand squeezes my hip. "You woke me up at two in the morning. The least you could do is tell me the truth."

Here we go again. Liam and his tedious need for honesty and earnestness all the time. I'm half-inclined to lie, to tell him my greatest nightmare is that Elliott Springs stays as lame as it currently is.

"It was about the last time I saw my dad in Santa Barbara. I just remembered a bunch of things I'd forgotten."

"Like what?"

"Has anyone ever told you that you pry a lot?"

He laughs, pressing his lips to my neck. "Em," he says against my ear, "when the guy you've been flirting with for months and sleeping with for weeks asks you about your bad dream, it's not *prying*."

"Fine. I just remembered how sad he was when he left. And how I felt like I'd finally ruined things with him too, like he saw the things my mother did and decided to go. Obviously, he'd already planned to leave. I've just had it in my head for so long that I was a disappointment to both of them. It was a surprise to remember I once didn't think so."

"Princess, you were ten," Liam says. "There was nothing you could have said to anyone that would make them hate you. *Or* leave. Whatever was going on with your dad and whatever is still going on with your mom...I don't think it has anything to do with you."

I force a smile. "I'm not so sure. I was asking him about the stock market. No one wants to discuss the stock market with a ten-year-old."

"I wouldn't mind hearing a ten-year-old Emmy talk about the stock market for hours on end," he says, running a hand over my hip.

"I'm a little uncomfortable with the fact that you're talking about me as a ten-year-old while you initiate sex."

He laughs and removes his hand. "I wasn't initiating sex, asshole. I was trying to *comfort* you. Do you think maybe he was trying to take you with him and changed his mind?"

I lift my shoulder. "He didn't pack any of my stuff. He didn't take my passport. Given how thoroughly he appeared to have planned, I don't think he'd have just *forgotten* that."

"You know he did the right thing by leaving you, yeah?" Liam asks. "What kind of life would you have had on the run like that? You had advantages here that he could never have provided."

I sigh. "I guess."

I have little reason to think that he made it out alive. I have little reason to think I'd have had a nice childhood on the run in South America. But I still wish he'd tried.

And I wish his final act as my dad didn't involve using me to get away.

He ruined every good memory I have of him with that last one.

WE'VE BARELY BEEN asleep for two hours when Frank wakes me up. I don't know how Liam stands it.

"I'm going to kill that fucking rooster."

There's a rumbly laugh into the pillow beside mine. "No, you're not."

"I am. Watch me."

He rolls to face me, his face dim in the early morning light. "Have you ever killed anything before?"

"I hit a squirrel once with my car."

He smiles. "You'd have a hard time hitting Frank with your car. The Willoughbys have a really tall fence."

"I don't need the car. Do you have a gun? You seem like the kind of guy who'd have a gun."

"And you seem like the kind of woman I wouldn't trust with my gun, if I had one."

I shrug. I wouldn't trust me with a gun either. "Fine. I won't shoot the rooster. I'll stab it to death."

"Just to be clear, your plan is to scale the Willoughbys' ten-foot fence with a knife in your hand—"

"Don't be an idiot...I can't scale a fence one-handed. I'd carry the knife in my teeth."

He grins wide. "Fine, you'd scale a ten-foot fence with a knife between your teeth, chase and somehow capture Frank, and stab him to death."

"That about sums it up."

He smooths my hair back from my face. "Ignoring the unbelievable amount of noise that would make, what would you do with the body if you got away with it? Bury it? Make it look like a suicide?"

"Of course not. I'd put its head on a spike as a warning like Henry the Eighth did to traitors. That way, they'd know not to buy a new rooster."

"It's truly astonishing that no man has tried to lock you down yet," he says, pulling me closer. But there's a smile in his voice, as if he doesn't actually mean it.

38

LIAM

I've been to a fair number of funerals in my life, but Mac's is sad in a way none of the others were. His parents and brothers are devastated, while Cassie is in shock still, pale, and absent.

"The doctor gave her something," Brenda says when we reach Mac's parents' house. "Her mom says she's been like this for days."

I blow out a breath. "It's got to be rough. I don't think she ever even dated anyone else."

Brenda looks around and leans in, her voice lowering. "You know, not now, obviously, but in a few months, you should ask her out. She's exactly what you always said you wanted—she's sweet, she's cute, she's dying to have kids."

I stare at Brenda for a long moment. First, because I can't believe she's brought this up an hour after Mac's funeral. Second, because...*did* I say that? I guess it's possible. But it was sort of like choosing a favorite country before I'd visited many of them. It's as if I'd said, "I want a tropical island" and continued visiting only tropical islands, though I was bored by the view and immediately sick of the heat every single time.

Now I know exactly what I'm looking for. And it's not at all what I'd thought. "I don't think so, Brenda."

She smiles. "Ah, JP mentioned you've got a crush."

I allow her to think it, though what I want to say is *it's so much more.*

I take the guys to Beck's after the wake and we have a somber beer in Mac's honor. It still hasn't really hit any of us that he won't be returning next week with his dopey grin and those fucking Steelers jerseys he wore every fall just to piss us off.

And I don't want to be here for even a minute of it. I tell them I'm calling it a night, and then I drive straight to Main Street because I have a feeling she's still at work.

I unlock the store. "Put the scissors down, Em," I call. "It's just me."

She walks out from the back, smiling but wary. "How was it?" she asks quietly.

"Hard."

She steps into me and lets her head rest against my chest. "You'd probably be better off with a girl who's pleasant and actually *good* in situations like this. Might I interest you in a sympathy blow job? I have no idea what to say to make it better."

I laugh and cradle her head in my hands.

I don't want a Cassie, and I've never wanted a Cassie. My favorite country, as it turns out, is one that goes from arctic to fiery without any warning. It threatens to kill the local rooster and babies the living hell out of a dog it purports to dislike and is awkward when it can't take charge of the situation. I doubt it's ever expressed love for another human being, but I suspect it could grow to love me if I just had more time.

And I don't, but I'm not going to think about that now.

"Let's go for a ride."

She glances up at me, her eyes uncertain once more. "You

mean just...riding? With no destination? Or is going for a *ride* some small-town euphemism for especially graphic sex acts?"

I kiss her forehead. "I just meant riding. Though given how open you sound to the idea of especially graphic sex acts, I'm probably going to suggest one on the way."

We walk out to my truck. I help her climb in and then I turn toward the mountains and crank up the radio. I roll down the windows and she smiles as her hair starts to whip in the breeze.

"I feel like I'm in a country music video," she says.

I reach out to twine her fingers with mine. "You love it," I reply, and when she doesn't argue, when I see her fighting a smile, I feel like a kid whose crush has finally looked his way.

That's when I realize something I should have figured out long ago—it's not a fucking crush at all. I'm head over heels in love for the first time in my life.

With a girl who's only here for another few weeks.

39

EMMY

"You're never going to believe who personally invited you to a gallery opening in LA on Friday," Stella says.

"Damien Ellis?"

"I guess you'll believe it after all," she replies, disappointed.

I should be ecstatic. I probably *am* ecstatic—it's just buried under an odd layer of unwillingness.

If I attend this opening, there's a strong possibility that Ellis is going to ask me back to his room to discuss Inspired Building again, and there's an *equally* strong possibility that I'll go. Just because Liam continues to insist we're dating doesn't mean I need to feel guilty about whatever occurs. But I think I might anyway.

I feed Snowflake and go to yoga, where I ignore Chloe's repeated request for details of a very graphic nature about Liam's dick. I wander down to the grocery store afterward and Liam's gaze brushes over me, head to foot, as he starts packing up.

"I'm not staying," I tell him. "I need to shower."

He rises and walks toward me, sticking his index finger in the waistband of my leggings to pull me his way. "I think you know better than to walk in here dressed like that and tell me you can't stay. I have a shower."

I smile despite myself. "Fine. I can't stay *long*. I have to pack. Damien Ellis just invited me to a gallery opening in LA. It's a good chance for me to push him into buying out Inspired Building."

He stills. "Inviting you to a gallery opening sounds like a date, not a business meeting."

I shrug. "These things tend to get a little blurry. It'll become a business meeting even if that's not what he initially intended."

He tips my chin up and I meet his eyes. "Em, don't even think about fucking him."

We aren't really a couple, so this isn't something he can demand. And the truth is that while I have no desire to sleep with Damien Ellis, I have a job to do, and I'm going to get it done one way or another. "You don't control me."

"I know I don't control you. That's why I'm *telling* you not to fuck him. Otherwise, I'd just use the remote to shut down your power every night."

I laugh. "My remote? You've given a lot of thought to this."

"I tried building a robot version of you first, but I've decided I'll just implant a chip in your shoulder, which will suddenly make you want to stay in Elliott Springs and do what I say."

"I imagine you'd program me to suck you off on demand first and get so excited you'd implant the chip before you got to anything else."

He exhales as if I've punched him, wincing as he adjusts himself. "You can't suggest something like that and expect me to wait 'til we get home. On your knees, robot."

I laugh against his ear. "Even a robotically controlled

version of me would have enough sense not to blow you in full view of Main Street." I tug on his hand. "Let's go."

He pulls me back. "Okay. But Em...tomorrow night?" He shakes his head instead of completing the words, and then he kisses me hard and thoroughly, with his hands on my face, as if I'm going off to war and he might never see me again.

I wish I could swear nothing's going to happen with Damien, but I can't. I live my whole life as if it's a war. If only one of us can win, me or Liam, it's going to be me.

I LAND in LA and spend a few hours shopping in Brentwood after I've checked into the hotel. The crowd there is minimal and everyone is smiling. There's a courtyard where people enjoy their lattes and croissants, and I picture being here with Liam. He'd tell me to get the croissant and latte when I was only going to get black coffee. I'd take him through the stores, and he'd be appalled by the kind of money the clothes cost, but if something made me happy, he'd push me to get it. If something made me happy and I couldn't afford it, I wouldn't even *mention* wanting it because I know he'd try to find a way to make it happen.

How did we end up where we are? He is loving and generous and kind, and anyone would adore him. I'm ruthless and amoral and self-centered, and only *he* could like me in spite of it.

I'm scared of what might change about my life if I believed this thing between us would last.

I walk into the gallery a half hour late, wearing a black halter dress that makes me look as leggy as a supermodel, my hair pulled back in a sleek ponytail, my red lips the only pop of color.

"There she is," says Damien, reaching out to pull me into

the circle of sycophants who surround him, his eyes sweeping over me from head to toe. "The exquisite Miss Hughes."

He introduces me to various people I will likely forget. The gallerist, his assistant, a couple whose names are familiar though I'm not sure why.

He hands me a glass of champagne and then says he wants to show me a piece around the corner. I smile, sipping from the flute, but the popping bubbles in my mouth sound like tiny alarm bells.

"So, Miss Hughes, tell me something," he says, grinning that same seductive half-smile I've seen on magazine covers, all sex and promise, "what is it you're after?"

He wants me to flirt. He wants me to say, "*Many things, but it's a Friday night and this champagne is delicious, so I'm open to suggestions.*"

"I'd like to talk to you about Inspired Building," I say instead. "I think they could be printing money with the right leadership."

He sizes me up, waiting for me to offer him something more, when what I'm offering him already is plenty: it's an investment that would pay off significantly.

"The right leadership meaning...you?" he asks.

"No," I reply. "The right leadership meaning *us*. I can show you numbers, but they're spending too much time and money on areas that are already sought after instead of looking ahead, finding the place nobody wants, and making it a destination."

There's a glint of interest in his eyes. "It's very selfless of you to bring me this proposal, Miss Hughes, but I get the feeling you're not here out of the goodness of your heart."

"There's some dead weight at the top that would need to go, and I'd like to fill the vacancy once it happens."

"What an interesting girl you are," he muses. "You look like a model but you sound like a cutthroat CEO, and I think I like the combination. I've got a room across the street. I'll order up a bottle of wine and we'll look at your numbers."

My heart is skittering in my throat. It's on the tip of my tongue to agree.

And then I think of Liam moving me to the inside of the sidewalk as we walk down the street, saving my stores when I'd never even been nice to him. I think of him laughing at my threats on Frank's life, beating up Paul Bellamy on my behalf and never even mentioning he did it. Saying if he could control me, he'd just shut me down at night with the remote.

It will all amount to nothing, and I'm sure I'll later curse myself for blowing this chance, but I just can't act as if it's all meaningless. It's not, even if it should be.

"I'm sorry," I tell Ellis. "I've got someone waiting on me at home. But I can email you the numbers if you're open to it."

That avid light in his eyes dims a little, and I can't even blame him. He wasn't initially interested in speaking to me because I look *smart*. I used the possibility of sex to get my foot in the door and now I'm removing it. "Sure," he says, pulling a card from his pocket. "But if you find you're free after all, my cell is on there. I'll send a car for you."

I thank him and walk away. I'm pretty sure I'm going to spend the rest of my life regretting that I didn't go for it. But right now nothing matters quite so much as hearing Liam's voice.

I call him the minute the car drops me off at the hotel. "I'm on my way back to my room," I tell him. "How goes work on the implant?"

"Just don't look in my garage. The robot prototypes are doing things to each other even *I* didn't know were possible."

I laugh as I unlock my door. "You wouldn't want a robot to suck you off anyway. Think how often self-driving cars make dangerous errors."

"Yeah, but you're not here," he says. "What option do I have?"

I've never had phone sex. It's another one of those trust things. I've always pictured my voice caught on tape, played in public, saying dirtier things than I'd ever say in person.

"Pull it out," I reply. "I'll talk you through it."

I trust him. I hope it's not a mistake.

40

EMMY

"Jeff and Jordan are coming over for dinner," my mother says. "This place needs to be cleaned up."

I went straight to Liam's yesterday and came home after she was already in bed. This is the first thing she's said to me since I got back. In fact, it's the first thing she's said since last week, when she told me to stay in the car during PT.

"I'm not the help, Mom, and I've got a full day of work ahead. If you want it cleaned, then clean it." She is perfectly capable of walking around to dust and pick up her coffee cups, though she hasn't been doing it. I wish I'd said it weeks ago.

"That's why you're here," she snarls. Her hand trembles slightly no doubt with the urge to hit me. I'm an adult and she's not all that mobile, but she's still clearly wondering if she can get away with it.

"No, I'm here to drive you to appointments and make sure you've got food, though you're well past the six-week point and should be driving yourself."

I open the door for Snowflake and keep walking, drawn like a magnet toward the sight of Liam in the yard, talking to one of his guys. The moment he spies Snowflake, he turns toward the house and the slow smile on his face is precisely the antidote I needed.

I meet him a couple feet from the bottom of the deck. He reaches out and presses a thumb to the space between my brows. "That little worry line is showing. What's wrong?"

I bite my lip. "It's stupid. My mother is having Jeff and Jordan over for dinner tonight. She seems to think I should spend my day cleaning."

His head tilts. "I've never seen you struggle to tell someone to fuck off."

"It's different with her," I say, my voice dropping though I know she can't hear me. "And she and Jeff tend to gang up on me, so tonight was already going to suck, but now—" I shrug. Now it's going to be unbearable.

He glances over his shoulder to make sure no one's looking, and then his hand reaches out to slide over my hip. "Invite me."

"To *dinner*?"

He laughs. "You don't have to look so horrified. I promise I'm not going to tell them I'm your boyfriend or something."

They'll want to know what he is, though, if he's not my boyfriend, and there's no answer that will suffice. She'll be livid that I've invited *him, the help*, to dinner.

"Invite me," he says again. "You want me there."

My mouth opens to make a polite excuse, but just the thought of him by my side makes me feel a little less alone. And his presence there will force her to at least be *civil*.

"Get ready for lots of stories about my weight." I try to laugh and it comes out shaky.

He steps close and leans down until his mouth is beside my ear. "Tell Sandra to bring out every one of them," he says. "I'm fucking ready."

It's going to be an absolute shitshow, but I'm smiling as I walk inside.

My mother's excitement about seeing the son who lives less than thirty minutes away is palpable. It would be easier to bear her hatred if she adored Jeff slightly less.

Was I always so unlovable? I don't know. My father didn't seem to hate me, but look at how he left. And he must not have been much of a judge of character anyway. He married *her* after all.

She hands me a shopping list. There's not a single item on here she wouldn't judge me for eating, but she's more than happy to serve them all up to her beloved son, which leaves me increasingly okay with the fact that I haven't told her I'm bringing a guest.

I drop off the groceries and spend the day in town simply to avoid her, arriving at the house just as Jeff and Jordan are walking in.

I take after my dad, but Jeff is an Atwell, through and through. He came out of the womb looking like a mid-level manager and that's still how he looks. "Hey," I say, nodding at him as I kneel to greet Snowflake.

Jordan enters the room a moment later.

"Hiiiiiiiiii!" she cries. "Oh my God it's so good to seeeee you!" She throws her arms around me and I respond tentatively —I'm really not much of one for hugs, obviously, but it's more that I now know she's the kind of girl who'd abandon her dog with my mother, a woman no one should even entrust with a plant.

My mother tells me to set the table while Jeff and Jordan take a seat on the couch, like fucking royalty.

"You've got to start dusting those figurines, Mom," Jeff says as I cross to the kitchen for the flatware. "They're disgusting."

It's the kind of comment that would leave her not speaking

to me for a week, but when Jeff says it, she just shrugs. "I ought to just throw them out."

"You collected them for so long, though," he argues.

She shakes her head. "That was your father's doing. I wanted one and he just kept buying them because he didn't know what else to get me."

I sort of doubt this, especially given the way she collects everything. "Then why'd you get us angels the Christmas after Dad left?" I ask.

Her lips purse. "I have never bought you angels."

"You did. I remember it."

Jeff frowns. "Em's right. I got one too. I didn't know what the hell you were thinking."

"They weren't from me. Someone left them for you at the front door—everyone was treating us like a charity case after your father took off." My mother turns from Jeff to glare at me. "Why are you setting five places?" she demands just as the doorbell rings.

I smile. Relief is whipping through me and he's not even in the room yet. "Oh, didn't I mention? I invited Liam."

"You did *what*?" she snaps, but I keep moving toward the door.

She will be awful to me all night, and she'll be awful to Liam, but once he's within hearing distance, she won't actively protest his presence.

I open the door and the hit of relief is instantaneous. *I don't ever want to look at anyone but him.* It's a ridiculous thought and I dismiss it fast, but I've never seen Liam in anything but sweats or shorts or jeans, and the sight of him in khakis and a button-down is making my brain short-circuit.

I'd like to maul him right here, in full view of my family.

"Do you own a suit?" I ask as he steps inside.

His mouth falls open. "Was I *supposed* to wear a suit?"

I go on my toes to press a kiss to his cheek, right beside his ear. "No. It just occurred to me how much I'd enjoy taking you out of one."

His hand lands on my ass, which he pinches hard. "Do not start with that shit right before you introduce me," he growls.

We walk around the corner. "Guys, this is Liam. Liam, you've met my mom, of course. And this is my brother Jeff and his fiancée, Jordan."

My mother lets the pan she's holding slam down on the counter. "Liam. What an unexpected surprise."

The words drip with what she really means, which is that it's an *unpleasant* surprise. I guess I warned him, though.

Jeff is reserved, taking his cue from my mother, while Jordan's hug is overly friendly and her smile is slightly too wide. Jeff better be careful or Snowflake's not going to be the only thing Jordan ditches at my mom's house.

I open the bottle of wine Liam brought and pour two glasses. I hand one to Liam and when I start to sip from the other instead of handing it to Jeff or Jordan, my brother rolls his eyes and gets off the couch to retrieve his own.

"So, you two are...dating?" Jordan asks.

Liam and I glance at each other and he grins. "Yeah, Emmy," he says with a low laugh, "we're dating. Don't try to walk it back."

"I *wasn't*," I argue, though that's precisely what I'd been hoping to do.

"Emmy's dating half the town, apparently," my mother says, turning to Liam. "She's also dating my doctor. Were you aware of that?"

I roll my eyes. Maybe this is why she was so awful last week, though I guess that still doesn't explain the preceding twenty-eight years. "I went out with your doctor once, and it was nearly a month ago, Mom."

"Well, back in my day, we had a name for a woman who's

dating multiple men and doesn't even come home 'til morning."

"*Popular?*" I ask.

"No," she replies with a mean smile as she takes her seat at the head of the table, "that wasn't the word I had in mind. My knee is starting to ache. Emmy, finish up in the kitchen."

Well played, Sandra.

"I'll help," says Liam, rising when I do.

"Don't trust me with the knives?" I ask. Behind us, my mother's voice drops to a whisper.

"Just want to make sure you poison the right person's food," he replies under his breath and I laugh.

My mother's head jerks toward the sound. She suspects we're laughing at her, and I guess we are, but for the first time in ages, it doesn't really matter that she's mad. It doesn't matter that she basically called me a whore a minute ago, that she's probably bitching to Jeff and Jordan about me right now.

It doesn't matter what she says. It doesn't matter what she thinks. With Liam here, I have an ally for the first time since my father left, and it's shifted the balance in some way I can't put my finger on.

Maybe it's just that, for the first time in ages, I don't feel so alone in my family home.

The food is mostly ready. I put it on platters, finish the potatoes, and make a quick salad while Liam starts carrying things out. We're in the kitchen getting the last two dishes when my mother starts serving the food.

"Should we wait for Liam and Emmy?" Jordan asks.

"I'm not waiting for someone who wasn't welcome in the first place," my mother replies.

Before I react, Liam's hand wraps over mine—his way of telling me it doesn't matter. And the fact that he's here, that he's in this with me, makes that almost seem true.

We go to the table, and Liam and I begin serving ourselves.

My mother is in the middle of a story about some supposed friend of hers who hasn't come by once in the weeks I've been here, but stops in the middle of it when Liam hands me the potatoes.

"That's going to go straight to your ass. Restraint has never been a strength of Emmy's," she adds for Liam's benefit.

Ah, excellent. A joke where I am the punchline.

Jeff laughs and Jordan, who's already taken a large helping, looks confused but *sort of* laughs. Only Liam remains silent, staring at my mother, then me, in turn.

Suddenly there's a lump in my throat that makes it hard to swallow around. What is it about him that makes me so soft?

"I'm confused," Liam says. "Emmy has plenty of restraint. So is all this commentary based solely on the fact that she weighed more in high school?"

My mother laughs again. "She simply weighed *more*—is that what you think, Liam? I should show you some photos. Remember how big she was, Jeff?"

Jeff nods like a good little boy, though he's apparently slightly uncomfortable doing it with witnesses.

"Well, I think Emmy looks great," Jordan says.

"Go get the photo album, Jeff," my mother says. "It's on the bookcase in the upstairs hall."

Jeff, dutiful son that he is, rises.

"Are you serious right now, Mom?" I demand. "You want to pass a photo album around the table during dinner just to show everyone how disgusting you found me?"

"No," she replies. "I want to pass the photo album around because two people here seem to think I'm lying."

Jordan looks from me to my mother. "Sandra, I wasn't trying to say you were lying. I just meant that Emmy looks good now."

"I know, dear. But Emmy wants to sell you all a story about how cruel I am, as if she just had a little baby fat, and it was far more than that. Even *she* seemed to think it was no big deal, marching around with her chin up like she was better than everyone."

I swallow hard over the lump in my throat.

I walked around with my chin up so no one would think they'd *gotten* to me. I walked around with my chin up as if I hadn't heard them, because I couldn't think of another way to survive. But my mother has always found a way to see the worst in me in every single thing I do.

"So you'd have preferred it if I slunk around apologizing to everyone for something that was none of their business?" I demand as Jeff re-enters the room. "You'd have preferred to have me *ashamed*?"

"I'd have preferred it if you weren't fat in the first place," she replies.

Jordan's eyes widen, but it's Liam who breaks the stunned silence after she speaks.

"Are you serious right now?" he finally asks, his voice hoarse.

"Jeff, hand the album to Liam," my mother insists.

"Hand me that album, Jeff, and I will shove it down your fucking throat." Liam reaches for my hand, his fingers tightening with mine. "Em, let's go." He rises, pulling me with him.

"*Go?*" I ask.

"Go."

He squeezes my hand. Everything he hasn't said is in his eyes: *You've given her enough. You've given her enough chances, enough of your time. Stop trying.*

There's a part of me that wants to argue—that same part of me that's spent twenty-eight years trying to convince her to *like* me, that's tried to convince her I'm worthy of her care. But I've jumped through every fucking hoop, and it never changes. Liam's right. It's time to go. She's had her last chance.

I rise and my mother gives an exasperated sigh. "This is ridiculous. Emerson, *sit down*."

But we're already past that. *I'm* already past that. In that moment when Liam told me it was time to go, a door shut, and it's going to stay closed.

"I need to get my stuff," I tell him, and he nods. Snowflake rouses from her nap and comes bounding to my side.

Shit. I can't leave her here, and I won't. "Snowflake's coming with me too," I announce, which is when they finally seem to believe I'm not coming back.

"You can't just leave," Jeff says. "Who's going to drive her to PT?"

Liam is already leading me away. "You seem eager to assist, Jeff," he says over his shoulder. "Consider it a promotion."

We go upstairs. Liam blinks in dismay when he sees the bedroom I had to cut a path through in order to reach the bed. "I can't believe you've been living like this."

I guess I'd stopped seeing it. I'd stopped seeing a lot of things. I'd grown so accustomed to my mother's disdain and her commentary about my weight that I became blind to it.

If I hadn't had to view my life through Liam's eyes just now, I'd *still* be sitting down there trying my hardest not to eat the potatoes.

I throw a suitcase on the bed and begin to pack. "I have a huge favor to ask. Do you mind taking Snowflake? I can't bring her to a hotel, but I'll look for an Airbnb in the morning."

Though God knows what I'm going to do with her in New York. I'm barely ever home.

He frowns. "I assumed you'd just stay with me."

I freeze halfway through rolling up a jacket. "You mean tonight?"

He laughs ruefully. "Em, we've spent every day together for weeks. Would it be so terrible just to stay at my place until you're done here?"

"I never said it would be terrible. I just didn't think—" I hitch a shoulder.

"You didn't think I'd want you there?" he asks, pulling me toward him with his hands on my waist. "Then you must not have noticed I can't stand having you anywhere else."

His lips brush against mine, then move to my forehead and hold there.

"She's right, you know," I say quietly. "My mom? You like me the way I am now. You wouldn't look at me twice if I gained all that weight back."

"Try me, Emmy. Regain every pound. Because there's a long list of things about you I adore, and your weight has never, ever been on there. I was crazy about you before I'd ever even seen your face."

I blink back tears as I stare at his chest. I don't want to be the weak girl who just admitted to an insecurity. I don't want to be the formerly chubby girl he's forced to reassure.

"What about my mean mouth?" I ask, the words a little hoarse. "Is my mean mouth on the list?"

He laughs and presses his lips to my neck. "When you run that mean mouth, I've got this almost irresistible urge to bend you in half and fuck you until you can't stand up straight, so yeah, weirdly, the mean mouth is on the list."

"I'm suddenly tempted to say something mean."

His smile is gentle. "Don't do it," he says, pulling me back to him. "That's not what I want right now. I just want to hold you for a sec, and then I'm gonna take you and Snowflake home."

I'd rather feel used and punished, but that's not who he is.

I've accidentally fallen for a guy who can't stand to see me hurt, who wants to ease every ache and pain.

"I guess I can live with that," I whisper, relaxing against him.

"**S**eriously, Liam," she announces in the dead of night, "if you cared about me at all, you'd have killed that fucking rooster by now."

I'm only half awake, but I'm already laughing. One of these days I'm going to call her bluff and tell her I'm doing it. She'll have stopped me before I've even climbed out of bed.

Today, though, I have something else in mind. I climb above her and slide down the mattress, spreading her open wide.

"You know, you don't have to pretend you want to kill the rooster every time you want me to go down on you."

"I'm not—" She gasps as my tongue glides over her.

I smirk as I glance up. "So should I stop?"

She runs her fingers through my hair, signaling that she wants me to stay where I am. "Since you're already there you may as well keep going."

When we wake next, we are both in a rush. There isn't time to do a quarter of the things I'd like to do, and that in and of itself is different: when was the last time I woke up with a woman and my first thought wasn't about how to extricate myself?

Emmy makes me wish it was a Saturday, not that she'd take Saturday off. She makes me wish we had time to eat a leisurely breakfast, not that she eats breakfast, and then go for a hike.

"Do you hike?" I ask as she emerges from the bathroom with her hair wrapped in a towel.

"You mean...on purpose?"

I laugh. "I guess that's a no."

She sits on the edge of the bed and starts to rub moisturizer into her long, bare legs. I glance at my watch, wondering if I can afford to be late to the first jobsite, though I know I can't. But there's something about the way that she runs her hands over her legs that makes me really wish I could.

"It's been a while. Not a lot of hiking in New York City."

"And by a while, we're talking..."

"Eighteen years."

"Let's hike before you leave."

"You're pushing it," she replies. But she's smiling as she walks into my closet.

Emmy thinks I'm doing her a favor by letting her stay here, but I'm the one who wants this. Even if I only get to experience a few weeks of what life with her would be like, even if it's going to really fucking hurt to let her go...I want those two weeks.

I'll take that handful of weeks with her and hold them inside me forever.

THAT NIGHT, her last one here for several days, we make dinner together. I think I'm crazy about every version of her, but this one is my favorite: Em, barefoot, hair in a ponytail, sitting on a counter laughing and doing very little to assist but freely providing direction.

"I smell something burning," she says, her lips still pressed to the rim of her wine glass.

"Maybe you should learn to cook since you're so good at noticing what I'm doing wrong."

She smiles. "I'll get right on that as soon as I stop making four times your salary. On second thought, I *will* learn to cook after I get back. How would you feel about a nice bowl of rooster soup? Or rooster parmigiana?"

I laugh, taking the wine glass from her hand as I push her legs apart and step between them. "I respect the fact that you're willing to take on a domestic skill only if it also involves murdering a living thing first."

She leans close. "You love it. But you're right. I don't need cooking as an excuse. I'm just gonna kill that fucking rooster."

She's right. I do love it. And I'm going to miss her so much when this is done.

After we've cleaned up dinner, she pulls out her laptop to start working again.

"Don't you ever relax?" I ask.

She frowns. "We just had dinner. That was my relaxation. And you could stand to relax a little less, if we're offering advice. I haven't seen you do a damn thing to get ready for the hearing on Lucas Hall."

"I'm not sure there's a point," I counter. "I could do nothing but work on getting ready for the hearing, but I can't buy the mayor a park. I can't bribe town council members."

Her shoulders sag. "You could run a grassroots campaign arguing your side. Explain to town residents what a massive apartment complex will do to traffic patterns and the environment and town values, and that a rise in property values will make it difficult, if not impossible, to ever buy a home or rent a storefront here again."

"I imagine it's too late for that." Though that's not the real reason I haven't done something along those lines.

"I'm sorry," she says, closing her laptop. "Might I interest you in an apology blow job?"

I laugh. "Eventually you might need to find something to offer as an apology other than sex acts."

"So that's a *no*?" she asks.

I tug her to her feet. "Of course not. I just want to make sure you come up with something else if you ever have to apologize to Damien Ellis."

42

EMMY

Liam and I talk on the phone for hours every night while I'm in Nashville.

I hear the jingle of Snowflake's collar near the phone and smile. "You've got her on the bed, don't you?" I ask.

"She's lonely," he says. "She keeps watching for you. It seemed like the least I could do."

Tears sting my eyes unexpectedly. I hate the idea of her watching for me, wondering when I'll get home every day. "I don't know what I'm going to do with her in New York," I say, my voice slightly hoarse. "There's a dog walker who comes to the building, but it seems like such a lonely day for her. I'm never home."

He's quiet for a moment. We haven't really discussed the fact that I'm leaving, that this is nearly done, and I'd rather not discuss it. I'll be checking on the progress of the construction once we've torn down Lucas Hall, but I won't be back often. These last few days with him are really the only ones I'm going to get.

"I can keep her," he says. "Depends on the job that's underway, but I'm spending more and more of my days just driving between jobsites and she can come with me for that."

I swallow. It's a kind offer. It's the best solution. I don't know why it makes me so fucking sad. "Thank you," I whisper. "Well, I need to get to bed."

"Are you crying, Em?" he asks.

I brush the tears off my cheeks. "I don't cry."

He laughs. "Of course you don't. But Em? We're going to miss you too."

⁓

I RETURN on Friday and head straight to the grocery store. Liam's guys are already done here—it's pristine and ready for business, aside from the empty shelves. It's no longer my problem—we've hired a manager and as long as she does her job well, my involvement is done.

I walk back to my office for the final time, and my throat is tight. It's a shitty office—not a single window, cinderblock walls. I should be thrilled that I'm finally clearing my shit out. But it was a little island in time, an awful space where I was strangely happy. Which I guess could be said of Elliott Springs as well, these past few months.

I've just finished packing the final box when Charles calls. I'm tempted not to answer, but he'll just keep calling if I don't.

"Has the diner agreed to sell?" he demands in lieu of a greeting.

I don't actually blame him for being so persistent. While most of Main Street consists of old rowhouses we can't get torn down, the diner sits on its own large parcel of land. There are a million things we could do with it once the apartment building is in.

"No," I reply. "It's been in their family for forty years. I think you'd need to make a really nice offer for them to even consider it."

"It's not worth *shit* at the moment," he argues. "I'm not clueing them in to what it's worth by offering them millions. Did you call the health department?"

"Yes," I lie. Paul is a dick, but I just don't have it in me to ruin Jeannie's business. It seems to me she's suffering enough just having him as a kid. "Elliott Springs is inconvenient. It might take them a while."

"Time there has made you fucking incompetent," he says as he hangs up. "I'll do it myself."

I sink into my chair. It's so...wrong. It's so incredibly wrong. He's going to destroy this woman's family business because he thinks it will make him money. But I've been helping him because I wanted revenge, half of it against people and places that never did anything to me, which probably isn't any better.

Being bullied probably should have taught me that bullying was wrong. Instead I decided to be the biggest bully of them all.

I throw the last box in my car and walk to the diner just as the lunch shift is dying down. It's probably not the best time to talk to Jeannie, but I'm not sure there's ever a great time. She's here all day long, and she's always working.

If Charles was just willing to make her a decent offer for the property, I'd think she should take it. As things stand, though, selling the diner will simply mean she's entering the job market for the first time at an age where most people are retiring.

Paul is wiping down the laminated menu with a cloth I can smell from four feet away. He has a bandaged nose and a black eye—I imagine I know who did it.

"What do *you* want?" he asks, as surly as ever.

"For you to fuck off and die," I answer with a tight smile. "If that's not an option, however, I'd like to talk to your mom."

"She doesn't need to talk to you," he replies. "If you're trying to buy us up like you've done with the rest of the town, the answer's *no*."

"Hmmm, if I wanted to have an important business conversation, it wouldn't be with the guy whose primary responsibility is wiping down the menus," I reply, walking past him toward the kitchen. I'm improving, but I'll never be a fucking saint.

I poke my head in. Jeannie's at the far end, talking to one of the line cooks, but comes over quickly. "Hi Emerson," she says, "is everything okay?"

"Not really," I reply. "Can we speak in private?"

She frowns and leads me back to a tiny office that's full of boxes and piles of paper and still is a marvel of cleanliness compared to my mother's house. She gestures to the chair across from her. "Sorry about the mess. What's up?"

I take a deep breath. "I'm going to tell you to do something, and I need you not to ask a single question. I also need you to never tell a single person what I'm about to say."

Her eyes widen. Her nod is barely perceptible.

"Get a commercial cleaning company in here. Today. You need to have them clean everything, top to bottom. You need to be able to eat off the floor when they're done."

"Are we getting inspected?" she whispers.

"I think so. I don't know how fast it'll happen, but I suspect it will be really fast. And for the next couple of days, don't have anyone working that could get you in trouble."

"Trouble?"

"I'm not asking about this, and I don't want to know, but if you've got anyone here who's undocumented, give them tomorrow off. If you have anyone who's violating parole, who's wanted for something...give them the day off too."

"We've been inspected before," she says faintly. "We always do okay."

I stare at the floor. "Jeannie, this isn't going to be that kind of inspection."

I want to tell her *they're gunning for you. They're going to make it so hard to operate your business that you just give up.* But as much as I like Jeannie, I know that anything I say could come back to bite me in the ass. If I admit how Inspired Building operates, she could appear at the final hearing about Lucas Hall and ruin everything.

"Did you make this happen?" she whispers.

I shake my head. "No."

Suddenly, I'm so fucking glad not to be a part of it.

"That was a nice thing you did," Liam says over dinner.

I look at our plates. "I barely helped you cook. You said, and I quote, that my assistance is 'mostly ornamental, and we're safer that way.'"

He grins. "I meant what you said to Jeannie. At the diner."

I exhale loudly. "For fuck's sake. She wasn't supposed to go running her mouth about that."

His tongue prods the inside of his cheek. "She wasn't running her mouth. She was telling your boyfriend—"

My mouth opens to correct him, and he stops me. "You fucking live with me. Don't argue about *that*. Anyway, she was telling your *boyfriend* about what a nice thing you did."

My arms fold. "She still shouldn't have said anything. I mean, she just gave information that could get me fired to my only competitor for Lucas Hall."

Any hint of a smile leaves his face. "Are you serious right now? Would you not have told me about that because you still think I'm trying to steal Lucas Hall? After everything we've been through, you still think I'd fuck you over?"

No, I don't. But that's the thing about having the rug pulled out from under you: it's *always* when you don't expect it.

"Crazier things have happened," I reply.

He pushes away from the table. "Jesus Christ, Em. I don't even know what to say." His hands press to the top of his head, tugging at his hair. And then he grabs his keys and walks out the door. Panic swells in my chest, but I've no clue how to back things up, how to fix them. A few seconds later, the truck roars as he tears off down the street. I swallow hard and press my face to my hands, trying not to cry.

I don't want to be like this. I don't want to be this cynical and untrusting. I was made this way by being put in the exact situation he's putting me in now: by being asked to trust someone, by having someone assure me he had my best interests at heart. How many times did I meet someone new and later learn he or she had only been nice to me because they were helping Bradley with one of her schemes? It didn't happen once, or even twice— it happened *multiple* times and I fell for it again and again.

I start cleaning up dinner, but when every last dish is in the washer and there's nothing left to be done, tears start to stream down my face. I hate that he left. I hate that I have no one in the world, other than him, and now he's gone too. I hate that nothing about destroying Elliott Springs feels the way I'd hoped it would.

The lights of his truck sweep the kitchen as he pulls into the driveway. I turn toward the sink and remain there, trying to pull my shit together. He crosses the room while I grab a sponge and start to scrub the already spotless stainless steel. I can't seem to stop crying.

"Em," he says quietly, pulling me toward him.

I resist, but eventually I've got no choice but to drop the sponge and turn.

"Oh, honey," he says, brushing the tears off my cheeks. "Is

this because I left? I was just trying to clear my head before I said the wrong thing. I was always going to come back."

I nod as if I already knew this, my tears soaking his shirt, but I didn't. "I trust you, Liam," I whisper, "but that's what's so terrifying."

He leads me to the couch and turns off the light so we are mostly sitting in darkness. He pulls my head to his chest and runs a hand over my hair. "I just don't understand, Em. I'm killing myself here to move at your pace, to show you how I feel. I just don't understand why nothing seems to work."

It's time, I guess. I don't want to tell him this story and it might ruin everything, but I need him to understand. "So what you need to understand is this," I begin, my voice barely a whisper. "I had no friends in high school. I probably would have, but everyone was too scared of Bradley for that. I skipped lunch because she made fun of me for eating. I skipped every school event because I had no one to attend with. I was alone at home, I was alone at school, I was alone everywhere. That's why I created the online book club."

His hand runs in circles over my back.

I continue. "It was on Facebook. Mostly women who like Jane Austen. And then this boy joined. James. He lived in San Francisco and we were the same age. He started messaging me and I was so fucking happy to have a friend."

I swallow. God, the whole thing sounds even more pathetic aloud than it did in my head.

"He liked me. He sent me photos of himself, and when I finally worked up the nerve to send him photos back, he told me I was perfect just as I was. This went on for about six months and messaging him was the highlight of my whole day. He convinced his mom to drive him down from San Francisco so he could take me to homecoming. He'd gotten a bright blue bow tie to match my dress..."

My voice trails off, remembering it all. Our discussions

about corsages and matching ties and how late he might be able to stay. He was a virgin too. He was nice about not pushing me too hard, but I knew he was hopeful, and I was too. I was so fucking hopeful. I worried seeing me in person would change something, but I knew it also might *confirm* something.

"They got stuck in traffic, so he asked me to meet him at Lucas Hall instead of picking me up. He kept texting with updates, saying they were closer. I looked like an idiot standing out there, and I knew it, but I kept on waiting. It was a full hour before he finally texted to say he was on Main Street. I said something like, 'I can't wait to see you!' and he said, 'I can't believe you thought I'd date a fat pig.'"

Liam's arm stiffens. "Wait. *What?*"

My voice is rough. I can't believe I'm still upset well over a decade later. "There was no James. Bradley fabricated the whole thing. And right after she sent that final text, she and her posse came outside and threw copies of all the messages I'd sent 'James' from the top of the stairs. It was all the pictures, everything, blowing down the steps. And it wasn't until they started laughing that I realized he'd never existed in the first place."

"God."

How many decades will it be before I stop feeling ashamed of it? Before I don't cringe at the memory of those photos of me blowing all over the stairs? I never sent him nudes, the way he requested, but the pictures I did send were bad enough. And those ridiculous, impassioned emails: *James, I love you more every day. I can't wait until we are at the same college.*

Of course, he'd said those things to me too. He'd said *more*, so much more, all calculated to get me to say it back. But all that mattered after that night were *my* words, repeated back to me as I walked through the hall.

The pictures of me in a bra would pop up at random for the next two years—papering the lockers when we got back into school Monday, raining down from the sky when we threw our caps at graduation. Bradley and her little followers would quote my most heartfelt, pathetic missives to me as I walked through the halls.

I wanted to die, and the only thing that got me through it was by telling myself I was going to make them pay.

His lips press to my head. "I'm so sorry, Em. So, so sorry."

"It isn't that I don't trust you," I whisper, and my voice cracks again. "The problem is that I do. So don't fuck up, okay?"

He pulls me tighter. "I won't. As God is my witness, I won't."

I believe him. But that doesn't mean I'm not still scared, too.

43

LIAM

I know Bradley. Not *well*, but well enough to notice how icy she's been to me since I started working on the grocery store. And well enough to have said with some certainty, before last night, that she isn't a sociopath.

So am I just a terrible judge of character, or is there some element of all this that I'm missing?

The next day, Em leaves for meetings in San Francisco, and I remain behind to fume about the way she was treated. Can someone ever move past the kind of shit she endured as a kid? I really don't know, but when I see Bradley exiting the convenience store just as I'm climbing out of my truck, I don't even think—I charge toward her, only slightly less furious than I was that night at the bar with Paul Bellamy.

Her eyes narrow as I cross the street. "If you're here to apologize for trying to run us out of business, save your breath."

I laugh. "Apologize? You must be out of your fucking mind. Why would I apologize?"

"Because you're siding with the enemy, asshole." She flips her long blond hair behind her shoulders. "You think Emerson Hughes really cares about this town?"

"Who would blame her after the shit you put her through?" I counter.

Her laugh is sharp and bitter. "Oh, right. Poor Emmy had it so rough compared to the rest of us—is that it? Poor Emmy, with her perfect grades and her money, was the innocent little victim."

I stare at her. "Do you really think the fact that Emmy did well in school and wasn't *broke* justified what you did to her at homecoming?"

There's the tiniest flicker of guilt in her eyes before she blinks it away. "No, but the shit she did to me personally sure did. Before you start rushing to that bitch's defense, ask her what she *took* from me first."

"This has been going on since you were both ten. What the hell could Em have ever taken from you?"

She climbs into her car. "My father, for starters," she says as she slams the door.

IT MAKES NO SENSE. For hours, it makes no sense. And when I finally do come around to an explanation, it seems too crazy to be true.

It *seems* too crazy, and yet, is it? The more I think about it, the more it also seems...obvious.

Em gets in late, grinning at Snowflake and then me, but the smile fades fast when she sees my face.

"What's the matter?" she asks. Already I can see her battening the hatches, preparing for a storm.

"Why don't you sit down?"

She swallows. "Either someone is dead or you're ending this, and I don't care which one it is, but I do care about the way you're wasting time spitting it out."

"No one has died, and I'm not ending things. Now sit the

fuck down." Irritation prickles my skin. "And if I was ending things, you'd care."

She perches on the edge of the couch, rigid, ready to spring away and run. "Whatever. Tell me what's going on."

"I ran into Bradley today. Walking to her car." It's sort of true.

"Did you slam her face into a bar?"

I didn't know she was aware of the Paul incident. "I certainly wanted to at a few points," I reply. "But anyway, she said something about you having taken things away from her."

Her sigh is heavy, fatigued. "Right. As if Bradley Grimm had anything I'd have wanted. What could I have stolen from her? One of those sexy Grimm's Convenience T-shirts she wears? That piece-of-shit Honda she drives?"

Here we go. I already know she's going to hate my answer. "Her father."

She laughs. "*What?*"

"She said you stole her father. And then she slammed her door and drove away."

"Her *father*?" Em jumps to her feet. Her arms fly out to either side for emphasis. "Did you remind her that she didn't have a father? The dude left when her mom was pregnant."

I reach out for her hand and pull her back to the couch. She comes, unwillingly, and I say nothing, waiting for her mind to follow the same path mine did earlier.

She laughs again. "Oh my God, Liam. You don't believe Bradley and I are actually related, do you? How would that even be possible?"

"I don't know, Em. It seemed crazy at first but the more I think about it, the more I see similarities."

She glares at me. "*My* bitchiness was created, not inherited. I was a pretty nice kid before she and her friends decided to take a dump on me."

I wrap an arm around her. "Think about it, babe. I know it

seems crazy, but think about it. Didn't you say you used to tell people you were twins?"

She rolls her eyes. "We were just stupid kids, Liam. And we're not twins. We don't even have the same birthday."

"I'm not trying to say you are. I'm trying to say that it's a little strange that you look a bit similar and that she didn't have a father but yours started taking her on all your outings."

"Because she was my best friend!" she cries, but already... I'm seeing the wheels spin. She's beginning to consider the similarities between them, things they'd assumed were coincidence: their eye color, something about the way they smile, their height.

Maybe even the extremes they'll go to in seeking revenge.

"You don't really believe this, right?" she asks. "Someone would have told me. *She* would have told me. She'd have told someone, and eventually it would have made its way to me."

I squeeze her hand. "I don't know. It's nuts, but the more I think about it...the more I can't imagine it's *not* true. And if she believed you'd known and hidden it from her all this time, it wouldn't justify what she did, but it might help it make a little sense."

She leans back and closes her eyes. "This is ridiculous. It's impossible. Someone would have told me. And who the hell would I even ask? It's not like my mom's going to admit it even if she *does* know."

"Right," I conclude. "Which is why your best bet is Bradley and her mother."

44

EMMY

Beverly and Bradley Grimm no longer own the small house they had back when she and I were friends. They moved into an apartment above the store shortly after my dad left, and suddenly, the timing of that seems suspicious.

Suddenly *everything* seems suspicious: The fact that Bradley wasn't allowed in my home, that we had to keep Bradley's attendance on those weekend outings secret.

Or the way my father would sometimes wrap an arm around us both and refer to us as "his" girls. All that time I'd assumed he was just being nice to Bradley because he pitied her, but maybe he wasn't being nice at all. Maybe he was doing the absolute bare minimum he could as a father.

My finger is poised over the intercom buzzer for their apartment. Liam—who's with me for moral support—nods, and I push it. A few moments later, a woman's voice comes on, irritated and fatigued. "Yes?" she asks with a deep sigh.

"This is Emerson Hughes. Can I speak to you for a moment?"

There is a long moment of silence. "I don't have anything to say to you."

"It's about my father."

There's another moment of silence. "Fine, but make it snappy. I don't want Bradley seeing you if she gets home."

Bradley, the ultimate bully of my childhood, wouldn't want to see me. That's rich. I narrowly refrain from saying it aloud.

Beverly buzzes us in and we climb a dank, narrow staircase. The smell of fried food hangs heavily in the hall, accompanied by the sour stink of a very old, very dirty building. I'd never have guessed that Bradley, with all her judgment and condescension, was living *here*.

We knock on the door, and Beverly answers. I'd always thought Bradley looked exactly like her pretty mom, and now I see all the ways she *doesn't*...Bradley's eyes are a paler blue, like mine, and her full lips didn't come from Beverly either. Aside from the pale hair, they really don't look much alike at all.

Beverly begrudgingly ushers us inside. The apartment consists of a tiny studio kitchen and a combined living and dining area that is smaller than my mother's family room. The walls are stacked high with boxes from food distributors—she's using her tiny apartment as a storage area too. There's a pillow and blankets folded on the floor beside the couch as if someone has been sleeping out here.

Jesus. Is it Bradley? Has she been sleeping on a pull-out bed in the family room for the last seventeen years?

My first impulse, of course, is to be angry. She talked so much shit about my weight and my hair and my clothes and my shoes while she was living like *this*?

Sympathy comes a moment later. Maybe part of the reason she talked so much shit was *because* she lived like this. If Liam's right, and we had the same dad, but only one of us benefitted from it...I can see why she'd be a little ticked off.

"I'm not sure what you think I'd have to tell you about your father," Beverly says, lips pressed tight as we take a seat on the couch. She waves to the room around her. "He left us high and dry decades ago, clearly."

I inhale in surprise. She's already answered my question before I could even pose it, I think. "So he's Bradley's father too?"

She rolls her eyes. "Do you really expect me to believe you didn't know that?"

I sink into the couch, shocked. Yes, I'd been...coming around to it. But the confirmation is something else. Something far worse.

Liam's hand squeezes mine. "She didn't have a clue, Bev," he tells her quietly. "When I suggested it to her after I saw Bradley yesterday, she laughed in my face."

God. I'm twenty-eight. How could I possibly be learning this now? Did my father know all along? My mother? Bradley? The whole goddamned town?

I just don't understand how information of this magnitude never made its way to me.

My eyes close as I try to gather my thoughts. The temptation to blame Beverly is strong, but it won't get me anywhere. "So," I begin, my voice clipped, "you had an affair with my father and decided the best way to handle it was never to tell me or, I presume, Bradley?"

She waves a dismissive hand. "Bradley had put it together on her own by the time he left, whereas you're so smart, in theory, that you've only worked it out now. Guess that shows which one of you really deserved to go to Princeton."

"If *my* mother ran around sleeping with married men all the time, I might have put it together sooner."

"Em," Liam says quietly, placing a hand on my knee—a silent way of saying, *"Don't piss her off until you've gotten what you came here for."*

"*I'm* the one he cheated on. He'd already told Sandra he was leaving, but they were waiting for the end of the school year so Jeff would have some time to process it. Your manipulative shrew of a mother seduced him and got herself knocked up. And she was so fucking awful that he didn't trust her to raise you alone, so he stayed."

I have no idea if anything she's saying is true, but it's clear that there are *only* villains in this story: Beverly was sleeping with a married man, my father was cheating on someone, and my mother...well, I already knew she was terrible. Nothing surprises me there. And between the group of them they created two of the worst people to ever come out of this town: me and Bradley.

"Even if Bradley knew," Liam says, "and even if she *thought* Emmy knew, that doesn't explain why she was so awful to her for so long. I mean, she discovered she had a sister, for Christ's sake. You'd think she'd be excited."

"*Excited?*" Beverly cries. "Are you fucking kidding me? Our whole lives were uprooted when Doug left. We had to move into this dump, and I had to cut back on staff at the store, which meant Bradley had to spend every afternoon and evening with me while *you* were living in that big house and strolling into school in fancy shoes. Did you ever notice that suddenly, only one of you was in all the honors classes? You had endless time to study. You had tutors. Bradley had to start working in a goddamn store when she was *ten* because your father put all his assets in Sandra's name. I couldn't even sue for child support because he was gone, and it was *her* money."

I had one tutor, ever, and I wore Nikes, not Louboutins, but I perhaps can almost see her point. My life superficially remained the same after my dad left while Bradley's was decimated. I guess I'd have been pretty bitter about it too. "So my father was supporting you?"

Her eyes narrow. "Don't make me sound like some kind of trophy mistress. I was doing okay when I was single, running the store. I just didn't want that life for Bradley, and Doug didn't either. He took extra work to make ends meet over here. It's clear how *that* turned out." She shoots another angry look my way. I'm not sure if I'm annoyed or amused by the amount of blame she's placing on someone who was a baby when all this unfolded. "He'd never have gotten involved with those guys otherwise."

A logical part of me has understood why my father ran away, even if I hated the way he did it. But I never understood, until now, why he started doing all that shady stuff in the first place when he'd spent so much time talking to me about *integrity* and *doing the right thing*. I guess supporting two households might drive you to do a whole lot of shit you normally wouldn't.

"It seems to me that your anger, and Bradley's, should have been directed at my parents, not an innocent ten-year-old who didn't know it was going on."

Beverly's mouth pinches. "He chose you over her. How was she supposed to feel?"

I throw out my hands. "Your reframing of this situation is incredibly bizarre. He didn't *choose* me. He *remained* with his wife and two children."

"He made it pretty clear for years that you were his favorite," she argues, "and when he ran, he only took you. He didn't even ask me if we wanted to come."

"Did it somehow escape your attention that I remained in Elliott Springs for the next eight years? I didn't run away with him. He *used* me to get away and threw me on a train back home when he'd made it far south enough."

"Of course he was taking you!" she shouts. "Why else would they have found all that stuff in his car—the fake passports, the clothes?"

"They found his car?" My voice is barely audible. My breath stills.

Liam's arm goes around me, pulling me close, and for the first time, Beverly looks uncertain.

"Jesus. Sandra really didn't tell you anything, did she?" Her shoulders drop. "They found his car about a year after he left with all his stuff inside. And your stuff too. He had fake passports made for both of you. John and Jenny Smith. He was a creative guy. I'm not sure why the names were so boring."

My arms prickle with goose bumps. I do. *I* know why he chose those names.

John Smith was one of Dr. Who's aliases. Jenny was his daughter.

And if you go to the trouble of buying a fake passport for someone, you're not using her to get away. I think of our conversation on the way down to Santa Barbara, my blathering about going to Harvard, about working on Wall Street, about the strength of an alumni network.

My dad wasn't ever planning to leave me behind.

I talked him into it.

45

EMMY

Liam makes dinner, and I offer minimal help. I can be trusted with chopping and not much else.

"I worry when you're this quiet," he says, looking over his shoulder at me from the stove. "Especially when you've got a knife in your hands."

"I'm not really in the mood to kill Frank right now if that's your concern," I reply. "Check back just before five in the morning, however."

"I'm more worried about your mom. Or Beverly."

I release a quiet, sad laugh. "Yeah, that makes more sense."

Liam's asked me no fewer than ten times how I'm doing since we left Beverly's apartment, and I keep telling him I'm fine. The truth is both better and worse than I could have hoped: my dad did some terrible things, but it's also pretty clear he loved me, and that matters most. He's probably dead, but I'd mostly assumed that already. My mother did many terrible things to me—keeping me in the dark the least of them—but at least now there's a slight reason for the way she hated me. She had a baby to save a marriage that wasn't especially good in the first place, and that baby ended up looking very much like the daughter his mistress had had two weeks prior. And then those girls met in kindergarten and became best friends, running all over town telling everyone they were twins.

I wonder how many goddamn people in Elliott Springs suspected the truth.

"Are you going to talk to your mom about it?" he asks.

My jaw grinds. My mother knew a great deal of the shit that was happening at school and she never said a word to me. She allowed me to believe I was the problem when she should have told me why it was happening and placed me somewhere away from Bradley at the very least. I mean, it probably had almost nothing to do with my weight at all. I'll never forgive her for letting me believe it was, but I was already never going to forgive her before all this came to light. "I'm not sure there's much of a point. She'll just spend the whole conversation finding a way to blame me for how things went down and defending her bad decisions."

"What about Bradley?"

Ugh. That's more complicated. Looking back, I can see how every one of my successes must have needled her. My grades, my placement test scores, the schools I got into. Academically, I did better and better while she started to slide precipitously from age ten onward. I was winning awards; I was valedictorian. I'm guessing she blamed it entirely on the fact that we were living off money that should have been partly hers.

But could any of that make up for the way she tortured me?

"Between the shit she *did* and the shit my mother *said*, they pretty much broke me," I finally reply. "No matter what her life was like after my dad left, I don't see myself letting it go."

"Did you know that lead becomes two hundred times stronger under pressure?" he asks out of nowhere.

I frown. "You're incredibly bad at changing the subject."

He pulls the knife from my hands and turns me toward the mirror. "I'm not changing the subject. I'm telling you to look at yourself and realize that no one broke you. You're one of the strongest people I know, and a lot of that is *because* of what you went through. How much of yourself would you give away to have *not* gone through it all?"

I sigh. "A lot. I'd give away a lot."

"I know. I'm working on that." He presses a kiss to the top of my head and wraps his arms around me, still holding my gaze in the mirror. "Because I wouldn't want you to give away a single goddamn thing."

~

I DON'T TALK to Bradley. I don't talk to my mom. I'm finishing up the last few contracts on Main Street and finalizing my presentation for the Lucas Hall hearing next week, and I'm busy.

When Liam points out that I'm not too busy to take Snowflake on long walks, cook dinner with him, and have sex... I tell him I'm thinking I'll cut back on all those things too.

That shuts him right up.

"Come on, Em," he groans, two nights before the hearing on Lucas Hall. "You've done enough."

"No, I haven't. And neither have you. Don't you want to work on it a *little*?"

"Nope," he says, kicking back on the couch, "and yours is fine too. Come watch something with me."

"Mine isn't fine and neither is yours. Liam...you've got to do something. At least show them the history of the building. Remind them what they're giving up."

He hitches a shoulder. "There's no point. Face it, Em. You've won."

I slap a hand to my forehead. "Since when are you such a quitter? I haven't *won*. There are a million things you could do. You're just not doing them."

His smile is gentle. "Em, I'm not a quitter. I'm a realist. And what I want most right now is to enjoy these last nights with you because I don't know how many more of them I'm going to get."

Something flips over in my stomach—a grief so intense I feel sick from it. What will I have left when this is done? I'll have everything I thought I wanted, and nothing I actually want.

I close my laptop and sit by his side.

"You could stop me, you know." I stare straight ahead at the television, seeing nothing. "Easily. All you have to do is get it designated as a historic landmark."

"I doubt there's time for that at this point." He reaches for the remote. "Okay, so there's this movie about a female vigilante who—"

"You could get an injunction." I swallow. I can't believe I'm doing this. "It would keep the council from deciding anything while it was under consideration. Inspired Building fudged some of the reports to keep it from going before the historic preservation committee. You could argue that the reports were wrong."

He presses his lips to the top of my head. "I'm still not going to, Em. This is what you want, and if you take anything from your time here, I want it to be that one person in Elliott Springs loved you enough to put you first."

I freeze. He's just said, more or less, that he loves me. He's just said that he's not stopping me, though he could. He worked on this for two years and now, on behalf of a girl he still doesn't know all that well, he's giving up his dreams.

When she's the one who sabotaged those dreams in the first place.

My throat is clogged. It's bullshit that he's not going to fight me on this. It's bullshit that he's giving up what he wanted so damn badly just because he wants my happiness more than his own.

Only one of us can win, so it's going to be me. Isn't that what I told myself? And I said it assuming that Liam was thinking the same thing. But he wasn't. Liam was thinking, *"Only one of us can win, so I want it to be her."*

And it hurts.

"I have to go," I whisper, rising.

"Now?" he asks.

I nod quickly. "I'll be back."

I grab my keys and phone and walk out while he's still asking questions. And then I march toward the town while tears run down my face.

It hurts that he cares this much. It hurts that he's not getting what he wants, that a building he loves is going to be destroyed because I want revenge—revenge on a bunch of former teenage idiots who had issues of their own, who probably don't even care all that much about Lucas Hall. Not the way Liam does.

I find myself on Main Street. I don't know why I've walked here—nothing but the diner's even open this late, and it's not as if I'd want someone to see me crying anyway.

The street is quiet and empty and I wish it were otherwise. Being in New York City was lonelier in a way—I could go through an entire day without ever speaking to another person —but I've never felt alone there the way I do now.

There is nowhere I deserve to go and no one I deserve to speak to, and that breaks my heart. *Liam* breaks my heart. Doesn't he realize he could do so much better than me? How could he possibly care so much when I've done nothing but show him I'm unworthy of it?

"Emmy? Are you all right?"

Jeannie is standing in the alley next to the diner, smoking a cigarette.

Instead of the forced smile I'd planned to offer her, a sob emerges instead. "No," I reply. "Not really."

She throws the cigarette on the ground and stamps it out with her foot. "Oh, hon," she says, throwing her arms around me. "What happened?"

"I sort of had a fight," I reply, "with Liam."

Her eyes widen. "With Liam? Didn't know he had it in him."

I choke on a weeping laugh. "You didn't know he had it in him to *fight*? After what he did to Paul?"

"I didn't know he had it in him to fight with *you*," she amends.

My eyes close, and two large tears slide down my face. "He doesn't," I reply. "That's what we fought about. He isn't going to present his plan to save Lucas Hall on Friday. At all. He said it matters more to him that I get what I want."

I press my hands to my face and cry, large, gasping sobs. I'm humiliated to be seen like this, but I can't seem to help it.

"I don't understand," she says. "I think it's sort of sweet."

"I don't want him to give up his dream," I reply. "I don't want to win by default. I wanted to win because I had the best plan. I think maybe beating him felt more impartial. If he's not even going to try though…"

If he's not even going to try, then he's made a sacrifice on my behalf. Liam, who's done nothing but give and wait for me, is just going to keep on giving, and I'm going to keep on taking.

"You're tired, Emmy," she says gently. "I have a spare room if you need a place to stay."

I shake my head, *no,* but the question just makes me cry harder. I've never done anything to deserve her kindness or her care, yet she's offering it to me anyway. Liam did, too, and I repaid him by stealing his dream away from him.

"Eventually he'll hate me for it," I whisper. "He'll come to his senses, and then he won't forgive me."

She tips my chin up with her index finger, forcing me to

meet her eye. "Emmy, that boy's been crazy about you, as far as I can tell, for months now. There will never be a time when he doesn't find a way to forgive you. You've just got to figure out how you'll forgive yourself."

I swallow. Could she be right? Is this a me problem—not a Liam one? I'm not sure, but I know I won't find the answer crying here. "Thanks, Jeannie. I guess maybe I'll head home."

She smiles. "I think that would be wise."

As I walk up the hill to Liam's house, Jeannie's words play over and over again in my head until I finally hear the truth in them.

She was right. The issue was never with Liam. He's forgiven every shitty thing I've ever done, and he'll forgive this one too.

This issue is me. And I won't be able to forgive myself if I'm the reason he gave up his dream.

Only one of us can win, and if that's the case...it needs to be him.

Even if it means blowing up everything I'd planned.

46

LIAM

On the morning of the Lucas Hall hearing, Em is sleeping so hard that even Frank's crowing doesn't wake her.

I have no idea what's going on, but ever since I said I wasn't going to fight her, she's been off. She got up at the crack of dawn yesterday and didn't return until long after I'd gone to bed.

And it all happened right after I told her I loved her.

Maybe it was too much, but it sure doesn't bode well for us when she leaves for good.

She's groggy, half-asleep, as I start to get dressed. She seems to have to force herself to sit up in bed. "Will you come today?" she asks. "To the hearing?"

I hesitate. I look like a quitter, with the way I dropped my plan. It was obvious, even during the initial hearing, that I wasn't going to get my way, but I'd still have gone in there with guns blazing if it wasn't for Emmy. Everyone who sees me watching her will think I'm a lovesick sap, and why shouldn't they? That's exactly what I am.

"Do you want me there?" I ask, hoping the question will prompt her to let me off the hook.

She nods. "I really do. I need you. It matters."

She's never once told me *outright* she needs me for anything. I have a full day planned, but there's no way I'm failing her now. "Then I'll be there."

To watch you put the final nail in the town's coffin.

And mine. Because this means you're leaving.

I run around to check on my projects and pull up on Main Street just before noon.

THE PRINCESS

I'm waiting on the steps.

Pulling onto Main Street.

I've heard those words before. You're not about to send Bradley out here to tell me she made you up, right?

Even Bradley's fervent imagination couldn't make up anyone as good in bed as me.

You're okay.

I walk down the street and smile when I see her there, waiting.

She's so beautiful in the afternoon light. Simply looking at her is enough to make me really understand what it means to want something. To want it desperately.

Some people would say she's too much work. But what I see is her strength. She's been through some shit, but she still stands proud. And she's beautiful, sure, but it's her strength that makes her so much more than that.

I climb the stairs and tug her against me, letting my mouth find hers.

"You're ruining my street cred," she says, but she's smiling.

"I love you," I tell her because I want to make sure she's heard it. And then I slide my fingers through hers and pull her toward the door so she isn't pressured into saying it back or explaining why she can't yet. "Let's do this."

The ballroom is full by the time we get inside. We find seats near the front and she reaches for my hand again. I can feel her anxiety echoing through my fingers.

I laugh quietly. "Why are you nervous, babe? I've never seen anyone cover their bases as thoroughly as you have. It would take a fucking earthquake to make this fall through, and actually...an earthquake would help your case, because this building would definitely cave in."

Her smile is tired and strained. "I think you'd be surprised by how fast things like this can go off the rails."

The minutes are read. Em's proposal and mine are mentioned, and the secretary clears her throat. "Actually, the offer made by Long Point Construction has been rescinded. Therefore, the only offer on the table is the one made by Inspired Building. If there are no objections, we can take it to a vote now. Miss Hughes, would you like to say anything before we begin?"

I glance at Emmy, expecting another presentation, this time with fireworks or cash shooting out of a cannon. But instead, she's looking toward the door where Harrison, of all people, is striding in. Her face relaxes at last. That hand clenching mine still holds on but less tightly.

He walks to the front of the room. "My name is Harrison Reid," he says. I suddenly remember why we called him *Hollywood* as a teen—because he's got old-time movie-star looks and commands a room like guys on TV do, all square-jawed and self-assured. "I'm an attorney with Baker Karlsson, here on behalf of a client who wishes to remain anonymous at the present time. Before I begin, however, I should mention that there were some flaws in the inspection report, and I have an injunction from the California Department of Planning which states that, due to the building's potential historic significance, it can't be torn down until the matter has been adjudicated—a decision that could take some time. I also have in hand a competing offer made by my client, which involves no destruction of the building whatsoever. If I may?" he asks the council members, pulling out his laptop.

The mayor's brow furrows in irritation as he glances at the rest of the council. He sighs in exasperation. "I suppose. Go ahead."

On the screen, a photo of Lucas Hall appears in black and white from another century. "There were a number of flaws in the initial report about Lucas Hall's structural integrity. It is my very strong belief that once those flaws have been addressed, any plans that involve the building's removal will prove impossible due to the historic nature of the building." Harrison pauses, looking from the council to the audience with a brow raised. "My client is proposing that Lucas Hall become a resort instead, which would meet the state's preservation requirements while bringing a new tourist base to Elliott Springs. My client has proposed devoting the halls and lobby to the history of the town—a strategy that has been implemented with great success in other hotels around the world." Pictures begin to flash up on the screen of other hotels. It has all the slickness of one of Emmy's presentations but is diametrically opposed to what she wants. And then there's an image I recognize. It's the goddamn plans *I* had drawn up for the hotel.

"What the fuck," I hiss under my breath to Emmy. "That's *my* fucking plan."

"It's you," she says quietly. My head jerks toward her. "You're the anonymous buyer if you want to be, with the backing of two investors."

For a moment, I'm too astonished to speak. "I can't buy

Lucas Hall, Em," I say at last. "I don't have the money, and the bank turned me down."

She swallows. "I took care of it, I believe." She checks her phone and then glances over her shoulder as a girl I've never laid eyes on before rushes forward and hands a file to Harrison.

He flips it open, nods, and then walks forward to the town council. "Here's what we're willing to offer."

What the hell is happening right now? Is the council actually looking over a financial offer made on my behalf without me even knowing what it is?

"There's no way this is legal," I tell her.

She laughs low, under her breath. "It's...mostly legal. Don't worry. I'm the only one breaking some laws."

"Miss Hughes," says the mayor, "I assume you'll be fighting these motions?"

She smooths her skirt as she stands. "This is all a shock to me, Mr. Mayor. If there actually is an injunction, as Mr. Reid *claims*, Inspired Building will need to reassess the situation, as court battles of this sort tend to drag on far longer than is financially viable."

If the mayor cared about Elliott Springs a fraction of the way I do, he'd see a resort is the best solution for the town—a middle ground that reenergizes our commercial base without destroying our history. It says everything about him that he's absolutely crestfallen instead. He just wanted his fucking park and the clout that comes with leading a mid-size city.

He accepts the package from Harrison with a scowl and announces the meeting will need to be postponed. Harrison turns toward the door, giving Emmy a wink as he goes.

"What the hell is happening here? Why is my friend, who you don't even know, winking at you, and how the hell could you have gotten me a loan without involving me?"

"I called Harrison yesterday," she says, "and got him to help secure the injunction. And then I flew to LA to talk to a potential investor, and he agreed."

"*Who* agreed?"

Her gaze grows a trifle wary. "Damien Ellis. I can lend you or get you enough cash upfront so that you'll own more than fifty percent. Ellis has agreed to put up the rest."

My shock gives way to something that feels a lot like...jealousy. Last night, when I thought she was off at work, she was in LA with a guy who definitely was hoping to fuck her. "What exactly did you have to offer Damien Ellis to make that happen?"

"Me," she says, and my stomach drops. "No, not in the way you're thinking, though it's flattering that despite my intellect, you still think my primary value rests between my legs. I agreed to come to work for him rather than trying to get him to buy Inspired Building. It's not entirely what I wanted, but the executive board will realize how useless Charles is without me and fire him anyway, and that's the part that mattered most."

"And the illegal part?"

She sighs. "There are potentially some conflict-of-interest issues here. It looks pretty bad that Charles' project now belongs to my new employer, but Damien thinks he can finesse it."

"I don't love that you're now calling him Damien," I growl.

She laughs as she climbs to her feet. "Seriously, Liam? I just gave up all my plans and put myself in a legally questionable situation, and all you can focus on is the fact I'm calling my boss by his first name?"

I stand and pull her toward me with my hands on her hips, letting my forehead press to hers.

She gave up everything for me. She gave up every plan for her future and the town's future, all so I could have this thing I wanted. "Why'd you do it?"

She shrugs a shoulder. "It was the thing you wanted most."

"Em," I say quietly, pressing my lips to her head, "it hasn't been the thing I wanted most for quite a while now."

I can't see her face, but her fingers tighten on my shirt, and I get the feeling she's smiling.

We walk toward Harrison, waiting in the building's lobby with the redhead who brought him the offer from the back of the room.

"Now you've done it," the woman says to Em. She holds up her phone, where a series of all-caps texts litter the screen. "Charles is going fucking nuts."

"How would you feel about working for Damien Ellis's company instead?" Em asks her, which is when I finally realize this must be her assistant, Stella. "I'm still going to need someone to fire people for me."

"I do have a lot of experience at that now," she replies. She nods toward me. "Is this the hot contractor?"

Em sighs as she turns my way. "Just for the record, *I* didn't call you that. *Julie* called you that."

Stella yawns and rolls her eyes. "It was lovely to meet you both," she says to Harrison before locking eyes with Emmy. "I'm going to my hotel to sleep. And you've been making it clear for months that you thought he was hot. Stop lying."

She walks away, and I glance at Harrison. "I still don't understand how this happened. How are *you* involved in all this? Do you work for Ellis too?"

He fights a smile. "I'm involved because your girlfriend here burst into my office yesterday morning when she couldn't get a call through and demanded I drop everything to help get the injunction. And then I'm pretty sure she flew down to LA and did the same thing to Damien Ellis."

"He has bodyguards," Em counters with a roll of her eyes. "You can't just *burst into* his office."

I laugh. "So what exactly *did* you do?"

She raises a shoulder. "I don't love the way you're assuming it was something obnoxious. I snuck through a restaurant and interrupted him during a meeting."

"You've got a live one, Liam," Harrison says, glancing from Em to me. "But since I, too, have been awake all night, I'm going back to bed. Let's catch up soon."

"We want to meet this mystery girlfriend of yours at some point!" I call after him, and his smile is slightly troubled as he nods and waves goodbye.

"So does this mean you'll be based out of LA?" I ask Emmy as we walk outside after him.

She shakes her head. "Damien said I could stay in New York and fly out a few times a month. I was thinking I'd stay here a few more weeks just to help you get the money taken care of, though."

"Or," I counter, stopping in place to face her, pulling her hands into mine, "you could just stay with me. For good."

"But I hate Elliott Springs."

"Maybe," I reply, "but you love me."

"Whatever." Her smile is wide. "Maybe. I guess you're okay."

47

EMMY

T he next three weeks are a flurry of meetings and paperwork and contracts. There's still no guarantee this will work out—Charles could always hire lawyers to fight the historic designation, and Ellis doesn't have enough money on the line to make it worth his while to fight back, though I suspect he would anyway. He actually seems like a pretty good guy, and every meeting we've had has been respectful and entirely free of sexual innuendo. Ultimately, what he cares most about is making money. And that's something I do rather well.

In my spare time, I've been helping a few of the businesses in town—Jeannie's in particular—prepare for the changes to come. They need better marketing, a small overhaul in what they offer, and some renovations, but I think they'll be just fine once they've finished those improvements. And in between all those meetings, I do the one thing I'd have sworn on my life would never happen: I meet with Bradley.

It's she who texts me, asking if we can talk. Based on our history, I'm understandably nervous, but she's my half-sister, after all. And if nothing else, if I'm going to stick around Elliott Springs for a while, we need to clear the air.

She arrives at Liam's wearing the same sneakers and outdated jeans I saw her in when we saw each other in town. The last time, I gloried in the differences between us, in the fact that I looked wealthy, and she looked downtrodden, but it's a little harder now. If my mother hadn't kept every penny of my dad's money, would the difference between us be lessened? Of course it would.

She takes the seat beside mine on Liam's porch. "So," she says.

"So."

"My mom said you didn't know. About your mom keeping all the money."

I sigh. "I didn't even know we were *related*, Bradley. The bit about my mom keeping the money was a relatively small revelation by contrast."

"Small for you maybe," she says snippily.

This is going about as well as I'd expected it would.

"Jesus, are you still bitter about this? Don't you think the endless shit you did to me for eight years straight more than made up for the fact that a person I had no control over withheld funds?"

"Do you think so?" she snaps. "I mean, look at the two of us. You've got a fucking graduate degree from an Ivy League school, and that car you've been renting since you got here probably costs more per month than I earn in a year. I have to live with the fact that our father only chose to take *you*. Do you really think a little high school bullying *made up* for all that? Do you want to fucking trade places with me? Because I'd sure as shit trade places with you."

I roll my eyes. "Our father only chose to take me because *my* mother, not yours, is a sociopath who has hated me since I was born. Did it ever occur to you that maybe my life was already hard enough, being stuck with her?"

She swallows, and for a half second I almost think I see remorse in her eyes before her gaze turns steely again. "And," I add, "you were punishing *the wrong goddamn person* the entire time. I *personally* took nothing from you."

She folds her arms, glaring at me. "No, but you were the *beneficiary* of it, weren't you?"

I don't think I've ever met anyone in my life so unable to accept responsibility for their own bullshit—aside from my mother.

"And did it help your situation in some way, plastering photos of my texts all over the halls?" I demand. "Did that improve your SATs a little? Did it give you the extra edge you needed in a science fair?"

Her eyes narrow. "No, but it made me feel a little better about the fact that none of those things were coming together for me."

Her expression is truculent; her arms are folded while she glares at me. She reminds me of someone. When I realize who it is, I start laughing despite myself.

"What's so funny?" she demands.

"I just realized who you remind me of," I tell her. "You're pissy and vengeful and completely blinded by rage, and I'm exactly the same way."

She stares at me, and then her glare gives way just a little. Her mouth twitches. "I don't remember much about our dad, but I can't say I love the parts of him I see in the two of us."

I sigh. "He was a good man. Aside from, you know, the money laundering and abandoning us and cheating."

She frowns. "Now I'm pissed again. Because you have a thousand memories with him, and what do I have? Some donuts on the pier in Santa Cruz and those fucking angels he sent."

A chill slides up my spine. "Angels?" I ask quietly. "What angels?"

"He sent one to me and one to my mom the Christmas after he left. Someone must have dropped them off for him. No idea who."

"What makes you think they were from him?" My voice is weak.

She shrugs. "My mom told me they were. She said he always used to buy them for your mom. She was pretty pissed about it. For all I know, they were just from someone who came into the store and felt sorry for us."

"No," I whisper. "They were from him."

She frowns at me. "How are you so sure?"

God. *God*. All this time, and the answer was right under my nose.

"Because I got one too," I reply. "And I think I know what we're supposed to do with them."

~

BRADLEY WAS dubious when she left—I hope I didn't mislead her. Any small progress we've made toward a truce is probably ruined if I just told her to go smash up the only memory she has of her dad for no reason.

"You really think you're supposed to break it open?" Liam asks as he drives me to my mother's house.

"It would be pretty fucked up to talk about smashing angels into a million pieces with your daughter and then send her an angel with nothing inside it," I counter.

His worried gaze flickers to me and back to the road. I know exactly what he's thinking: *your dad did a whole lot of fucked up stuff. Why assume now that he's reasonable or thoughtful?* And he certainly has a point. My father definitely cheated on *someone*, and then he started working for a crime syndicate to support his second family. It's pretty easy to imagine a guy like that wouldn't be the most sensitive of parents.

"You don't think your mom got rid of them?" he asks.

I shake my head—my mom doesn't seem to get rid of much. But wouldn't it just figure if *this* was the one exception?

He pulls into the driveway, and we walk to the shelves on the front porch together. We've just turned on a flashlight when my mother emerges from the front door. "What the hell do you think you're doing?" she demands. "You've got no business on my property."

I stare at her and feel...nothing. I feel no desire for her approval, and therefore, no fear. She made a choice to keep me in the dark about Bradley and then she allowed me to believe my father had simply been using me to get away. She also refused to use any of the funds my father left behind to help Bradley and her mom, and with the way this town gossips, she must have known how they were living and that Bradley worked all hours as a young kid too.

Maybe if I were a better person, I'd feel some sympathy for her; her husband cheated on her, after all, and when he ran away, he only took me.

But there's none inside me. She bled every emotion out of me with her carelessness. "I'm just getting what's mine."

I find the angel and grab it. If she'd even been civil tonight, I'd have told her to look inside hers too. But no—she can remain in this junky old house alone, without any final bits of truth from my dad. She doesn't seem to care about the truth much anyway.

"Next time I'll call the police," my mother warns as Liam and I head to the truck.

"There won't be a next time," I reply.

I'm mostly silent on the way home, the angel clutched in my sweaty fist. I'll feel like an idiot if there's nothing inside it.

Liam helps me out of the truck and hands me a hammer from his toolbox. "Do the honors," he says.

With one last look at this final gift from my dad, I swing. The angel snaps open into three distinct pieces.

And there's something inside. It's an old key with foam taped around it, and a small note, which Liam unwraps and hands to me.

> Emmy,
> I'm so sorry. I should never have tried to take you with me and then put you on that train alone. I hate that your last memory might be of me running off like a coward. God, I hope it's not. I've got someone keeping an eye on you, making sure you've got what you need until I can get back. The key is to the lockbox in the shed, which now belongs to you. Maybe it won't seem all that special. Just know it contains my entire heart. I miss you so much.
> Love,
> Dad
> P.S. I imagine you know by now that Bradley is your sister. Please make sure she knows to break her angel open too.

My eyes jerk to Liam's. "Shit."

Why did I tell him to throw it out? Why was I so scared of what it would reveal about my dad, so angry about his abandonment, that I never even looked?

He bites down on a smile. "Hang on," he says.

He walks into the garage and returns with the lockbox.

"I told you to throw it out!" I gasp.

He grins. "Sometimes your ideas are bad. And I ignore them."

I reach for the key and then hesitate. "He was working for some kind of gang. What if there's a human hand in there? Or fingers? What if it's something they were after?"

Liam's smile is gentle. "I'm a little troubled by the way your mind always goes to severed limbs."

He unwraps the key from its packaging, fits it into the lock, and slides the box to me. "Open it, Em. It's pretty clear your dad loved you. I'm guessing it's not a hand."

Gingerly, I unlock the box. It's full of papers, with a small note on top.

> Emmy,
> If you're opening this, it means my plan to get us out of here safely didn't work, and for that I'm so sorry. I've saved every drawing and card you ever made me. I'm taking a few on the trip and leaving the rest behind in case things don't work out. I just want you to know that being your father was my greatest joy and my greatest accomplishment. And I'm so sorry I got us into this mess.
>
> Love,
> Dad

Beneath it are drawings I made of the two of us. Lifting sandbags, eating donuts. Stick figures shivering after doing the polar bear plunge on New Year's Day, stick figures riding the redwood train. There are cards I made him for every occasion, and stupid little kid certificates I won. The second-grade math championship. A newspaper clip of me holding a winning science project aloft.

None of these things mattered to my mother. She was annoyed by the cards I brought home from school. *More of this glitter crap*, she'd say. I'd see them at the top of the trash can later.

But they all mattered to my dad.

I swallow hard, fighting tears as I look at Liam. My father's final gift to me was simply letting me know he cared.

And it's enough.

48

EMMY

One week later, we leave Snowflake in Chloe's care and fly into Newark to get my condo ready for the movers. While I haven't agreed to stay in Elliott Springs *forever*, I can see myself being in California for the next year, so I'm going to rent my condo out for a while and see how it goes.

I'm starting to not mind my old hometown quite as much as I once did. Jeannie has proven incapable of keeping her mouth shut, so an increasing number of residents know I helped both her and Liam—which means business owners are asking me for advice, and strangers smile at me as I walk down the street. The last bit seems like overkill, but I guess it's all right. I once loved my anonymity in New York City, but I might actually enjoy my *lack* of anonymity even more.

Even Bradley smiles, in a half-assed Bradley sort of way. The angel she received from my dad only held a note of apology and a promise that he was going to try to make things right. She groused about it, but it also seemed to settle some anger she held toward him and me. I'm slowly getting over the anger I felt toward her too. If I had to choose one outcome, her life or mine, I'd definitely take mine.

Liam is the bright spot that makes everything else worthwhile—although he's become progressively less chipper since the New York City skyline came into view.

"What's up?" I ask. "It's too late to decide helping people move sucks, you know."

His returning smile is small. *Forced.* "I'm worried you're going to miss it."

"The majestic beauty of the New Jersey Turnpike makes you wonder if I'm going to miss the city?"

"I've been to New York City before, Em. There's slightly more to it."

What really worries him, I think, is that I've left this openended. I'll still own the condo. I can always change my mind. And he's right—there *is* more to it. I know that there will be quiet mornings when I walk the streets of Elliott Springs and long for slightly more chaos. There will be nights when I long for more opportunity—I never ate Thai food at three a.m., but I liked knowing I *could*.

But those joys are nothing compared to the joy of my life as it is now—of waking up next to Liam and describing how I'll kill the rooster, mostly to make him laugh and in part because I want to kill the rooster. Or being home at night when he arrives and pulls me close, as if he's missed me too.

For every single thing I liked about my life up here, there's a counterpoint in Elliott Springs—Liam—and it's always better. It's one I don't just like but love.

"I bet you missed home when you left for college, right?" I ask. I didn't, but most people do. "But you were also so happy at school that you didn't think about it much. Well, that's New York for me. What I have in its place is so much better that there's almost no space inside me to miss it. I had something I liked. Now I've got someone I *love*. And that's entirely different."

"It's about fucking time you said it," he grumbles, squeezing my hand tight.

I laugh, resting my head on his shoulder. "I sort of figured you already knew."

"I did," he says, his voice softening. "I just wasn't sure *you* knew."

We get to 76th Street. The driver double parks while cars honk at us because someone is *already* illegally parked in front of the building. I add honking to the list of things I won't miss.

Giorgio does a double take—he's never seen me in jeans and a ponytail. "Miss Hughes?" he asks, eyes wide. "You're finally back?"

"Not for long," I reply. "I'm moving to California. This is Liam, my..." I trail off because *boyfriend* sounds so dumb, so childlike.

"Boyfriend," he supplies. It clearly doesn't bother Liam. He turns to me and shakes his head, as if he's trying to hold in a smile. "That shouldn't have been such a hard one for you."

"Well, we're sure gonna miss you, Miss Hughes," Giorgio says as he follows us inside.

I try to remember why I hated him so much back in the day and I don't have much of an excuse. He's a nice guy who enjoys small talk. I've really changed during the past few months, I guess.

He follows us all the way back to the elevator. "But I bet you won't miss this weather up here, eh? I'm sweating the minute I walk outside in this suit, let me tell ya."

Yes, I've really changed. Too bad Giorgio won't be around to benefit from it.

The elevator door opens. Giorgio holds it, still talking, while Liam and I walk in. And then we're both inside and he... continues to hold the door so he can finish his dumb story and then begin a new one.

"I was just telling my wife the other day..." he says, and

something inside me starts to die. "I said, 'Stacy, we need to get ourselves somewhere where it never gets above eighty.' And she says, 'Where's that, Giorgio? Iceland?'"

He releases the door at last. Liam starts to laugh as we hit the second floor. "I bet that guy annoyed the living *shit* out of you."

"He did. He still does, apparently. And I was starting to think I'd changed."

He pulls me against him, nuzzling my neck. "You know what? We never talk about the weather. We should do that more. Every single day. At length."

"I'll kill you in your sleep. The rooster for practice, then you."

He laughs. I've found the one man alive who will laugh when I threaten to kill him. How have I gotten so lucky?

We get to my apartment, and when the door opens, I try to see it through his eyes. For what I paid for this place, we could buy an entire block of houses in Elliott Springs. And yet...it's empty. The gray travertine floors are cold, the light filtering through the floor-to-ceiling windows is dim, and inside there is not a single personal item—not even my degrees. No pictures or throw blankets or pillows. I've stayed in hotels that felt more personal.

I stripped my world bare so it would feel as if I were a new person, one without my past. But I remained who I was anyway, floating around in an empty life.

I wasn't happy in this condo. I wasn't happy when I was at work. The closest thing I ever felt to happiness was *triumph*, and it took being around Liam to realize they're not the same thing.

Happiness is quieter, warmer. It spreads through your blood like water rising toward the banks of a river but never overflowing it. It's more stable than triumph ever was and doesn't have its sharp bite—the tang of blood that accompanies it.

I want to keep feeling happiness, but triumph—at least the way I've experienced it in the past—is something I'm done with.

"I'm going to sell," I tell him.

His eyes widen. "You are? I thought you said it was a good investment."

I shrug. "It is. But other things are good investments too. And...I like knowing this part of my life is over. Everything I want, I've already got."

There's not a bone in my body worried that I'll end up regretting this decision. The world remains an uncertain place, but Liam...he's the one thing I know I can count on.

I left here to destroy everything he loves.

Thank God I was so bad at it.

EPILOGUE

EMMY

Liam strolls into our shared office inside Lucas Hall just as the sun is starting to set. "Do you have a minute?" he asks.

It's on the tip of my tongue to say *no*. He's got his first code inspection coming up in two days, and though the opening is still months away, the suppliers for his linens have suddenly decided they want to price gouge him—there is shit to be dealt with, new enemies to vanquish. Not to mention, I have my *own* job to handle. But he's got that grin on his face and his eyes are bright, and he's impossible to turn down when he looks like that.

"What's up?" I ask, looking up from my laptop as he perches on the edge of my desk.

"I commend you for not saying *no* outright," he says, "because I know you were tempted. I want you to come see the lawn. I just finished getting it all marked out."

I sigh. "I still don't understand why you insisted on that. We could have put a tennis court there."

But I rise and let his fingers twine with mine. I've learned to cede control on occasion, and even if I rarely hand over the reins, I've at least stopped holding them so tightly. I have eggs benedict at least once a week now. I don't force myself to run five miles if I've had a burger. Of course, it's not without consequence—I've put on ten pounds. Liam says he likes me a little curvier, and while I suspect there will never be a time when I don't hear my mother's judgment in my head, I'm happy despite it. And it's a relief to know that the world isn't going to explode if I have a little cake, if I gain ten pounds, if I run into my mother and she makes a comment. On the rare occasion I do see her, however, she doesn't say a word, and I'm not sure it would matter if she did. She holds no power over me anymore.

We wind our way through the offices with Snowflake at our feet and head out to the large veranda off the back. He leads me down to his much-loved green space, where the sod is so new that it still looks like quilt pieces poorly sewn together.

"So through here, we can have outdoor games—like croquet and lawn darts," he says. I open my mouth to speak, and he cuts me off. "No, we have not time traveled back to 1920, if that was your question."

My mouth closes, but I'm fighting a smile.

"People like having a place where they can be outdoors and away from the chaos of the pool."

I disagree but fine. No chaos, *blah, blah blah*. He points out where the benches will go and the fountain, and finally, at the very end of the lawn, the gazebo.

I groan. "Seriously? What the hell does anyone do with a *gazebo*?"

"Think about it," he says, taking my hand again. "We can hold outdoor concerts here, weddings…"

I force myself to see his point. I guess it *would* draw the wedding crowd.

He kneels in the grass and fiddles with an errant sprinkler head.

"Liam, you have guys to do that now, and you pay them a *lot* of money. If they're not doing their job, I'm more than happy to have Stella fire them." A tiger can't change its stripes.

"I wanted to show you one more use for the gazebo," he says, and there in his palm rests a black velvet box.

I'm so shocked I don't know what to say. We haven't really discussed this. I'm not even sure if he's serious right now. That age-old fear creeps up. *Is this a joke? Am I about to look like an asshole?*

I fold my arms across my chest. "You're taking this marketing pitch for the gazebo really far."

But he's not laughing. He's not even smiling. In his face, there's something I've never seen before. Is he...*nervous?* Liam Doherty, who's never had a nervous moment in the year I've known him, is totally freaking out.

"Emerson, in spite of the fact that you think marriage is, and I quote, 'a prison conceived of by men who are tired of doing their own laundry and cooking their own meals,' we both know you can't do laundry for shit and I'm the better cook."

My laughter is quietly stunned. I take the box, my hand shaking as I do.

"So you decided to propose," I say hoarsely, "by listing my flaws and not actually asking a question?"

He laughs, his shoulders settling a bit as he rises to his feet and picks me up in one fluid move. "I want you to marry me. Because I don't care about your lack of domestic skills. I care about the fact that you're the smartest girl I've ever met, and sweeter than you'll ever admit."

"I also give really good head."

"You do," he says. "I was getting to that."

I laugh again. It diffuses some of the awkwardness from the moment, but not all of it.

I'm terrified because I think I want this.

I'm terrified because I could easily fuck it up.

I'm terrified because I know, without a shadow of a doubt, that I'm going to say yes.

"I realize you hate taking advice," he says, "but I really think you ought to marry me."

I press my face to his chest and my tears soak his shirt.

"Okay," I whisper, my throat tight. "But not because you said I should."

He laughs. He laughs so that his chest shakes under my head, and then his arms tighten around me. "That's my girl."

ACKNOWLEDGMENTS

Thanks , first and foremost, to my beta readers: Samantha Brentmoor, Maren Channer, Michelle Chen, Katie Friend, Katie Meyer, Nikita Navalknar, Jen Owens and Tawanna Williams.

Endless gratitude and hugs to my amazing editing team: Sali Benbow-Powers, Lauren McKellar and Christine Estevez.

Much love to everyone at Valentine PR, and thanks so much to my agent, Kimberly Brower, and the gang at Piatkus.

Laura Pavlov, I adore you. Thanks for listening to me rant.

Can't get enough of the Summer Series?

Go back to the beginning and meet Luke and Juliet.

Turn the page for the first chapter of *The Summer We Fell*.

He might not be the devil, but working
under him for six weeks is my idea of hell.

Meet the temp assistant and the
British boss she loves to hate . . .

Available now.

PIATKUS

A sexy blend of spice, romance and grumpy men.

Prepare to laugh, swoon
and cry ... perfect for fans
of Christina Lauren.

Available now

Do you love contemporary romance?

Want the chance to hear news about your favourite
authors (and the chance to win free books)?

Kristen Ashley
Ashley Herring Blake
Meg Cabot
Olivia Dade
Rosie Danan
J. Daniels
Farah Heron
Talia Hibbert
Sarah Hogle
Helena Hunting
Abby Jimenez
Elle Kennedy
Christina Lauren
Alisha Rai
Sally Thorne
Lacie Waldon
Denise Williams
Meryl Wilsner
Samantha Young

Then visit the Piatkus website
www.yourswithlove.co.uk

And follow us on Facebook and Instagram
www.facebook.com/yourswithlovex | @yourswithlovex

PIATKUS